D0380298

The Neverland Wars

By:

Audrey Greathouse

The Neverland Wars

ISBN: 978-1-63422-171-9
Cover Design by: Marya Heiman
Typography by: Courtney Nuckels
Editing by: Cynthia Shepp

To my love, my Zaq—
The boy I will never grow old with

For more information about our content disclosure, please utilize the QR code above with your smart phone or visit us at

www.CleanTeenPublishing.com.

THE EVENING WAS STILL BRIGHT AND YOUNG WHEN THE MUSIC started. Gwen had played all day in the backyard, and her dolls' plastic faces were smudged with dirt to prove it. They had gluttonously devoured all of Gwen's mud pies, and she was intently plucking daisy petals, one at a time, to determine if some unimagined boy was somewhere out there, madly in love with her. She had to start over with several daisies. Her eight-year-old hand did not have the requisite coordination for the task.

When she found a purple-edged daisy, she was too engrossed with its size and color to notice the music. Instead, she promptly plucked the flower and ran, barefoot, into the kitchen where her mother was still cleaning up from dinner. Mrs. Hoffman took the flower and got down a tiny vase. Gwen stood on tiptoe to kiss her swollen stomach. "It's for my little sister."

Her mother gave her an adult smile, putting the vase back into the cupboard. "I'm not sure it will keep until she gets here, Gwen. Maybe we should press it."

On the living room couch, her mother helped her press the daisy between the pages of a book, and when the doorbell rang, her father answered it. Gwen wandered back outside to play more, unconcerned with the two harried men at the door.

It was only then that she heard the enchanting music pushing its way through the evening air. She could tell it was far away, yet she could clearly hear it. Picking up her stuffed lion, she clutched him to share her excitement and his courage. The melody felt familiar but new. She wanted to follow it.

Her mother emerged at the back door in a very different mood. "Gwen, it's bedtime! Time to come in!"

The peculiar music was so much more interesting though, and she was reluctant to give up her playtime. Her mother walked out and took Gwen's hand, leading her in despite her objections. With only her lion in hand, she asked, "What about my dolls?"

"I'll bring them in later," her mother promised, but she locked the door as they headed inside.

There were two men, dressed like grown-ups, standing in the entryway with her father. One had a map, and he was muttering about the perimeter they'd established. Her father was pulling on his overcoat. "I've got to go," he said, walking over to give his wife a worried peck on the cheek. "He's close. Watch Gwen."

"Where's Daddy going?"

"To do business with his work friends," her mother answered as Mr. Hoffman's brisk pace led him out the door with the two men. "Now let's get you upstairs to bed."

Gwen brushed her teeth and was ushered into her nightgown. It seemed awfully early for bed, and horribly unfair. She wanted to know where her father was going, or at least stay up until he returned. Her mother was adamantly against it. Soon, Gwen was left snuggly in bed, alone in her room, and wide awake.

She wanted to stay up though. It was still light out, and Gwen remained curious about the music. Slipping out of bed, she tiptoed over the carpeted floor to draw the blinds and open her window.

It was hard for her little hands to lift the heavy window pane, but she opened it enough to let the music in. There were pipes somewhere; it sounded closer than it had before. Her first thought was that it was an ice-cream truck, but this was not a trite melody broadcasted over a crude speaker. It was soft like a lullaby, yet energetic. Its complicated rhythm and endearing melody made it sound like the soundtrack to a wonderful dream.

Her mother came in, having heard the sound of the window opening. The girl assumed she was in trouble and explained, “I want to stay up and listen to the music.”

Gwen was too young to understand what panic looked like on her mother’s face. “Oh Gwen, no, close the window. There’s no music out there. Let me wind your music box.” Her mother shut the window, locking the top so that Gwen could not open it again. She wound the music box, and Gwen trudged back to her bed as mechanical tones replaced the beautiful sound of the fluting.

“I want to stay up!” Gwen insisted. “Like you and Dad. I want to stay up until he gets back.”

Her mother tucked her in, again. “No, not tonight.”

“When can I stay up?"

“When you’re older. When you grow up, you’ll be able to stay up as late as Mommy and Daddy.”

She nestled in her covers, listening to the tinny sound of the music box. As her mother kissed her forehead, Gwen thought about all the wonderful things she would do, when she was older and could stay up late. As she began to think of the future, the piping faded from her mind.

"You'll be able to stay up as late as you want, someday," her mother promised, and Gwen nuzzled her stuffed lion in eager anticipation of that magical, late-night someday.

1

"AND THEN WHAT HAPPENED?" ROSEMARY ASKED, CLUTCHING Tootles in her arms until he mewed with discomfort.

"Shush!" Gwen warned, whispering. "If Mom hears, we'll both be in trouble."

Rosemary let go of poor Tootles, and the tabby cat immediately scampered off the bed and away from the enthralled eight-year-old. Gwen sat cross-legged on her bed, trying to imagine how she could conclude her story. It was already past her little sister's bedtime, and Gwen still needed to finish writing a paper. Regardless, she was as happy as her sister to be sitting on her downy purple comforter under the glow of the twinkling white Christmas lights strung up over her bed. "And then," Gwen continued, knowing that Rosemary preferred all of her plot points to be prefaced with those two words, "Margaret May ran through the woods. Even though the mysterious old woman had given her the beautiful music box, she was still lost and afraid she would never make it home in time for Prince Jay's coronation. It was starting to get dark in the woods and, seeing no other option,

Margaret May gave up and sat down under a willow tree."

Rosemary's eyes went wide with disbelief. She clutched a limp teddy bear close to her, one of the many old stuffed animals that still resided on her big sister's bed. "Margaret May can't *give up*!"

"Shush. But she did." Gwen chucked a handful of popcorn into her mouth and let Rosemary wallow in surprise a moment more before continuing. She ignored the chime of a new text on her phone—she held her own stuffed lion and stayed wrapped in the story she was spinning. "Under the willow tree, Margaret May did not cry, because she was still very brave. She was also very clever, so she decided to wind the music box and listen to its song. This caused something very strange to happen. Although the music box didn't make any noise, Margaret May heard a mysterious music in the distance. She got up and followed the magical music until it stopped, at which point she wound her music box and the music started again somewhere far away."

"Where was the music coming from?"

"Quiet, Rosemary. Mom will be mad if she finds out I'm keeping you up."

"Okay," Rosemary whispered. Taking a tiny handful of popcorn, she put it up to her face to nibble at it like a squirrel. She'd been chewing everything with only her front teeth for the past week.

"And then," Gwen watched Rosemary's eyes twinkle at those words, "Margaret May followed the music until she found where it was coming from… the raven tree."

Rosemary gasped. "She found it!" When she laughed, she bounced on the bed, her poofy hair bobbing ridiculously with her. The missing tooth in her broad smile only made her look happier. Gwen couldn't help but laugh too. Even at sixteen, she felt totally in her element sharing the joy of a fairy tale with her little sister. Rosemary's whimsy was catching.

The young girl felt totally at home in her big sister's room, still surrounded by stuffed animals, art projects, and relics from Gwen's childhood that had nowhere else to go. The biggest difference between the girls' rooms was the size of the furniture.

"After all her searching, she had finally found the raven tree, full of its feather-leafs and egg fruit. The bark was covered in little snapping beaks, but Margaret May did not need to get close in order to pluck one of the sparkling, black eggs from a low branch. Its shell looked like the night sky, and Margaret May tucked it into the pocket of her plaid dress before—"

The bedroom door opened. "What's going on in here?"

Mrs. Hoffman found her daughters huddled on the bed, staring at her with guilty eyes. Her hand still on the doorknob, an unamused look took an immediate hold of her features. She was a wiry woman, and her fashionable slacks and blouse hung on her the same way they hung on mannequins in the store. Her hair was much redder than either of her daughters, mostly due to the fact that she'd started dyeing it. "Gwendolyn, what are you doing? Rosemary, why aren't you in bed?"

"Gwen was telling a story! She was just getting to the good part."

"I was almost done. We were just going to be another two minutes."

Their mother's eyebrows rose at this response. "It's a school night. Rosemary should have been in bed an hour ago."

"Really?" Gwen's mind froze momentarily as she wondered what time it was. Evenings had a way of getting away from her when she started storytelling. Checking her phone, she saw that it was minutes to nine, and that the message she'd heard buzz was from Claire. Drawn away from her story, she checked the text.

When r u picking me up Saturday?

"Are you listening to me, Gwendolyn?"

"Yeah, just checking the time, Mom." She flung her phone aside on the bed. "I'm sorry. I didn't mean to keep Rose up so late."

"How did you know we were up?" Rosemary asked, astounded that anyone could have uncovered their covert story time.

"A mother knows," Mrs. Hoffman replied, having heard Rosemary's unrestrained gasps and laughter from downstairs. Seeing the bag between the girls, Mrs. Hoffman asked, "Are you eating in bed?"

"Gwen had popcorn!" Rosemary seemed surprised when her mother failed to share her enthusiasm.

"Oh goodness… Rosemary, go brush your teeth again. Gwen, you know you are not allowed to eat in your room."

"It's my room, Mom."

"Rosemary, go. I don't want to have to fight you about this."

"But Gwen's not done with her story! We just found the raven tree!"

This had no effect on their mother. "She can finish it tomorrow. She needs to sleep, too."

"I need to finish my paper for speech and debate." Gwen unfolded her legs and stood up to get her laptop off her desk. When she woke it up from the screen saver, she tried to minimize Facebook before her mother could see it. Downstairs, Gwen heard the front door and knew that her father was home from his networking dinner or whatever event he had gone to with his fellow financial advisors.

Her arms crossed, Mrs. Hoffman announced, "You should know better than to keep your little sister up and to be eating in your room."

"I said I was sorry. Time got away from me, and Rosemary really wanted a story."

"You need to be her big sister, not some compatriot in mischief."

"Why I am the only one who gets chewed out? She was the one who interrupted my homework for a story."

"I'm sorry—are you actually surprised I'm holding you to a higher standard than your eight-year-old sister?"

"I want to hear the end of the story!"

Their mother was getting exasperated, and she was visibly relieved when Mr. Hoffman came upstairs and poked his head in the door. "What's all the commotion up here?"

"Gwen's telling a story and is almost finished and I have to hear the end." The whole of Rosemary's persuasive skills consisted of stating her position as quick and loud as possible, hoping it would be taken as fact.

"Robert, help me get Rosemary to bed. She needs to brush her teeth again."

"What are you still doing up, Rosie?" he asked, coming over and playfully sweeping her off the bed and into his arms. He stood, comfortable and calm, even in his suit after a long day. "It's bedtime, girly."

"But—"

"No buts about it," he answered, firm but not frustrated as he set her down. "Let's go get those teeth brushed." Rosemary trudged slowly as her father steered her to the bathroom. The Jack-and-Jill bathroom that conjoined the girls' bedrooms was convenient at times, but it mostly served as a means for her to sneak into her sister's room after bedtime.

"Goodnight, Rosemary. We'll finish our story tomorrow," Gwen told her.

Rosemary pouted in response, marching at a turtle's pace in her fluffy, pink nightgown.

"This is totally inappropriate," her mother told her. "You need to stop this, Gwen. I've half a mind to ground you for the week."

"You can't ground me! Claire and I are going shopping for homecoming dresses on Saturday!"

"I can ground you for homecoming if I have to. I don't want to punish you, Gwendolyn; I just want you to start acting like a big sister."

"How am I in trouble for this?" Gwen looked around the room and felt that everyone was against her—except for Rosemary, who was too busy drawing out the process of going back to her room. She made a noise like a tired cow. "You're always talking about how you want us to get along, but when we do bond, I get in trouble for it."

"You can get along with your sister while still exercising more judgment than an eight-year-old."

"We don't have to have this conversation now, Helen," Mr. Hoffman announced, now pushing Rosemary to the bathroom. "It's late. The girls are tired."

Gwen felt under attack though, and she was not going to drop the conversation just to have it at length later. "What do you mean? Why do we have to have a conversation?"

Trying to keep the peace, her father simply explained, "It's just not appropriate for you to indulge Rosemary like that. We can talk about it later."

"Make sure her window's still closed tonight," Mrs. Hoffman reminded her husband.

He finally got Rosemary into the bathroom, shutting the door behind him to isolate the little girl from any further distraction. Gwen was left on her bed to face the judgment of her more reactionary mother. "You should get some sleep. Your father's right. We can talk about this tomorrow."

"Yeah, well, whatever," Gwen sputtered, lacking a

response. "If you don't mind though, I've still got a lot of work to do on my debate paper before I can go to bed."

"Goodnight, Gwen," her mother sighed, "try not to stay up too late."

Her mother left, closing the door behind her. Alone in her room, she could hear the hum of Rosemary's toothbrush and, later, her affectionate giggles as their parents tucked her into bed. Gwen burned with an irrational envy, listening to her parents lavish their love on Rosemary and usher her to fantastical dreams. Meanwhile, Gwen was stuck in a teenage world that was supposed to revolve around shopping, homecoming, and other celebrations of independence that could be revoked at a moment's notice by her mother.

Surely, everyone bemoaned the inbetweeness of being a teenager, yet for Gwen, it was something else entirely. There was the inescapable sense that she was being forced in a direction she did not want to go. It was not that the transition into adulthood was hard because it was a transition, but rather because it was hurtling her toward something unpleasant and irreversible. At least her peers were assuaged by a sense of impending freedom. They carried a sense of conviction that adulthood held some liberating significance to it, but Gwen was blind to the glamour they saw in adult life.

Admittedly, she finally got to stay up late, but what for?

She plugged away at her paper for a few minutes, but was checking Facebook and scrolling through someone's summer vacation pictures when she heard a noise at the bathroom door. Rosemary peeked out to look at Gwen.

"Rose, go to bed. I'm in enough trouble with Mom already."

"That's okay. I just wanted to say goodnight," she explained. "Are you okay?"

"Yeah, I'm fine. Why? Did Mom and Dad tell you I'm not?"

"No," Rosemary answered. She was quiet for a minute, staring up at the vast collection of books and stuffed animals on the bright blue bookshelf Gwen had painted years ago. It seemed most of the things that came into Gwen's room never left. Finally, trying not to arouse suspicion, Rosemary asked, "Gwen, what are hormones?"

Gwen set her laptop aside on the nightstand. She smirked, but she resented the implication that all of her behavior and feelings had been dismissed as an inevitable, impersonal product of her adolescence. "They're little things that get inside of you once you start growing up. They're like tiny bugs that start changing how you feel about everything. They bite at every part of your insides, infecting you with grownupness before you even know you've caught them."

Rosemary stared at her, almost as horror-stricken as she was curious. "How do they do that?"

"Very slowly," Gwen told her. "They change everything inside of you, filling you up with seriousness, replacing all the parts of you that remember how to play with your toys and how to dress up. They make it so you hate when things don't make sense. Then they make you so incredibly silly and irrational that you hate it when you realize nothing inside of you makes any sense. Finally, when you hate it enough, things start making sense again, and that's when you're an adult."

Rosemary stoically took in her explanation. "So they're like cooties?"

"Pretty much," Gwen admitted. "Only you don't realize you've caught them until it's already too late."

Tootles mewed, and then bounded onto the bed. Gwen welcomed him into her lap, and the orange cat purred as she petted him. The more she thought about it in Rosemary's logical framework, the more her own life made sense. Nothing was fundamentally wrong with her—she was just trying to stave off a terrible case of cooties that left her nostalgia-prone and quick to fight with her mother. It made so much sense.

Rosemary pensively stared out the dark window. Finally, she asked, "Should I be scared?"

Tootles sashayed to Rosemary, but the younger girl was too engrossed in her concerns to pay attention to him. "No," Gwen assured her. "It happens whether you're scared or not… and everybody goes through it, so it can't be that bad, right? And grown-up things are fun… right?"

Rosemary didn't have an answer.

Gwen sighed and repositioned herself on her bed. "You should go to bed, Rose."

"But you get to stay up! It's not fair!"

Gwen smiled, remembering when that had been her view of the world as well. She wished she could break the vicious cycle for Rosemary, but the inevitability of adulthood hung before both of them. "I've got to stay up and write this paper."

"But you have to wake up before I do! When do you sleep?"

"After the hormones, I think." Gwen rubbed her eyes. "I've got to get back to work, and you've got to sleep."

Reluctantly, Rosemary wandered back into the bathroom and toward her room, taking Tootles to her room as a consolation.

"Goodnight, Gwen."

"Goodnight, Rosemary."

The little girl hung back in the bathroom doorway, swaying as she held onto their tabby cat. Gwen pulled her computer back onto her lap, but looked up when she noticed Rosemary still at the door.

"Gwen?" she finally asked. "Is it worth it? To grow up, I mean?"

Gwen took a deep breath, remembering how often she had wondered the same thing when she was Rosemary's age. She had reached all the wrong conclusions about it on her own. Everyone she knew had lied to her about it, and now halfway to adulthood herself, she knew why everyone always lied to children. She knew what she was supposed to tell Rosemary, but Gwen couldn't bring herself to fill her little sister with all the same delusions she had grown into—that staying up late would be glamorous, and that dress shopping and homecoming were somehow better than raven trees.

"No," she answered. "I don't think it is."

CHAPTER 2

THE FOLLOWING MORNING, GWEN WOKE UP THREE TIMES IN snooze-button intervals. Half an hour after the initial alarm, she drudged out of bed, the covers hopelessly mangled and slipping off the bed altogether. She did not remember her dream, but a deep sense of ennui clung to her, proving that she was still a teenager. Sloughing her pajamas onto the floor where they would not be lonely among so many other wrinkled clothes, she pulled on a blue sundress from her closet.

When she crept into the bathroom to comb her ash-brown hair and brush her teeth, Gwen was surprised to see Rosemary's door shut. The bathroom light was on as always, but usually, Rosemary slept with her door open so the light could shine into her room. It was more dignified than a night-light, and the only disadvantage was that Gwen needed to be a little quieter getting up in the morning. Gwen had thought she heard a door slam sometime in the night, but had dismissed it groggily as part of some frustrating dream.

Over the hum of her electric toothbrush, she heard a

scratching noise at the door. She would have ignored it, but Tootles yowled so miserably that Gwen quietly opened the door to Rosemary's bedroom, allowing a frantic Tootles to leap into the bathroom.

A distinct chill struck Gwen when she opened the door, and she caught the door before it blew shut again. Rosemary's bedroom window was open, and an autumn wind was barreling in from outside. The sudden breeze blew in a crisp smell—like cinnamon and clover. The girls weren't supposed to leave their windows open; it caused the doors to slam shut during the night and raised the heating bill. She didn't want Rosemary to get in trouble for the open window though, so Gwen snuck quietly past the heap of blankets Rosemary was somewhere buried under. Very slowly, very silently, she shut the window. There was no stir or sigh from under the blankets as Gwen left.

Pulling her hair into a sloppy French braid, Gwen went quickly through her morning routine. She never bothered with makeup, or worried about straightening her hair. She knew better than to try to appease the self-consciousness that perpetually plagued her teenage mind. She tromped downstairs moments after she heard her father leave for the office. He was so much more mechanical in his routine, and always out the door on time. Gwen was equal parts in awe and disgusted by the meticulous punctuality expected of financial advisors. When she whirlwinded out of the house three minutes behind schedule, she still had toast in her hand, which she devoured as she got into her car. Gwen had inherited the old Honda Civic when her mother bought a new car last winter. The red paint was chipping off the car door, and there were spots of gluey residue on the windows where Gwen and Rosemary had long ago plastered stickers, but Gwen had happily accepted the hand-me-down vehicle and took a vicious satisfaction in not worrying about toast crumbs on the seat.

She turned on the radio as she backed out of the driveway. Driving with the radio on was the only time she familiarized herself with popular music, and she was generally unimpressed. It was important though, if only so she would know what she was dancing to at homecoming. She was looking forward to going dress shopping this weekend, even though she knew it would be a disappointing experience. Sorting through Vanna White costumes at the mall would get old quickly, and Gwen knew the Cinderella-esque gown she still secretly dreamed of would be nowhere in the racks.

She bobbed her head along with the synthesized instrumentation of a Katy Perry song she had heard everywhere and nowhere before. Gwen did not begrudge the world its catchy pop hits, but the more she listened to the song, the more alienated she felt. "Teenage Dream" played on, but Gwen found herself wondering if skin-tight jeans and sex on the beach really were supposed to be the height of teenage ambition. If that was what teenage dreams were, then what kind of dreams did Gwen have? Before she even made it to school, she turned off the music, tired of listening to a woman ten years older than her sing about what it was to be young forever.

CHAPTER 3

GWEN WAS USUALLY ATTENTIVE DURING MATH, BUT THERE WAS something about this particular Wednesday morning, in conjunction with her sleep-deprivation, that kept her mind far off and away from algebra. As was so often the case, she felt trapped without purpose in a room of twenty other teenagers with whom she shared nothing in common but her age.

Gwen's tired apathy would have been bearable, if only she'd had more practice in not caring. The futility of sitting through an unnecessary math lesson sat poorly with her. So much of the fulfillment she derived from life was predicated on the idea that school was somehow worth the time she committed to it.

Her eraser had lost almost all of its flavor. Gwen would have rather chewed gum, but that was strictly prohibited in Ms. Whitman's class. She had settled, unconsciously, for the end of her pencil instead. She was finally getting used to the taste of the nebulous pink rubber when Wesley made an almost inaudible snoring noise beside her. He slouched in his seat, his arms folded over his chest. With his hoodie pulled tight over his head, he made a half-hearted attempt to hide that he had only shown up to this class to sleep through it. Gwen had been chemistry partners with Wesley Green last year. The banality of alphabetical seating meant Hoffman was never far from sleep-deprived Green. Of course, alphabetical seating did have its perks.

Gwen was certain that Jay would not have elected to sit next to her. If the students were given free rein over their seating assignments, Gwen would no doubt be up front where she could easily see the board and escape the slight snores and disgruntled sighs of her bored classmates. It didn't help that she was the only junior in the class. Pushed academically by her economist father, Gwen didn't have any friends to sit by among these seniors. Jay, on the other hand, would have his pick of friends. He'd be surrounded by gamer geeks, art students, and football players. He could slink away with cool posture, lounge in the back of the classroom, and follow the course loosely while effortlessly comprehending it. But Jay was tethered to his name, so Gwen happily knew that Hoek and Hoffman belonged together, if only alphabetically.

There had been rumors circulating in the halls earlier this morning that Jay would be on the homecoming ballot at lunch. It might have only been locker gossip though. While Jay was on the football team, he was not the glistening gem of popularity that their quarterback was, and Troy was certain to be on the ballot. Gwen was pretty sure that Polk High's entire athletic department, save for one or two heartbroken cheerleaders, would help elect Troy to the status of homecoming royalty. Still, she couldn't help but imagine Jay in a golden crown and herself in her Cinderella ball gown…

Staring at the whiteboard and blue equations, Gwen gave the impression that she was focusing on the lesson as she propped her head up and uninterestedly boxed in her answers a little darker in her composition book. She tried to think of something else, something less foolish. Before she could though, Jay caught her eye as he leaned over and began writing on the left page of her composition book. Gwen watched the chicken-scratch scribblings of his charcoal-smudged hands, but she could not read his message until he reclined back into his chair.

HAIKUS ARE AWESOME,
BUT THEY DON'T ALWAYS MAKE SENSE;
HIPPOPOTAMUS.

A stunning cartoon of a hippo accompanied his poor penmanship. She looked over at him and smiled. Gwen had long ago given up trying to determine whether Jay's jokes were funny. She was too biased to judge. Gwen couldn't have cared less what he wrote in her composition book; he had written in her book. He had put his charcoal-covered hands on her pages, leaving a dusty reminder of his ashy, arty smell.

While Jay smirked, Gwen was seized by a tremendous pressure to seem funny. Her little brain suddenly alert, she struggled to think of an amusing response. It occurred to her after just a moment, and she jotted it down beneath Jay's poem.

THERE ONCE WAS A MAN FROM PERU,
WHO DREAMED HE WAS EATING HIS SHOE.
HE AWOKE WITH A FRIGHT
IN THE MIDDLE OF THE NIGHT
TO FIND HIS DREAM HAD COME TRUE.

Jay, still smiling, leaned forward to read it. As his eyes panned over the words, his nonchalant smile turned into a teeth-baring grin. He laughed silently and responded with another line and illustration:

YOU GOT THAT FROM SPONGEBOB.

Gwen nodded, acknowledging her source, and she and Jay continued to smile. Reliving a cartoon episode together, they secured themselves against the dullness of the classroom around them. His eyes—bright and blue—gleamed with pervasive playfulness, and his short hair stood on end. Troy had convinced the entire football team to shave their heads at the start of the school year, and Jay's dark hair had finally grown out enough to be cute again.

Gwen was distracted by a vibration in her sweater pocket. Her cell phone buzzed silently, alerting her to a new text message. It surprised her; she couldn't think of anyone who would text her in the middle of third period.

Against her better judgment, Gwen reached into her pocket and drew out her smartphone. It couldn't be important. No matter what it was, it would have to wait another thirty-five minutes until school got out. Still, Gwen had cultured a bad habit of always indulging her curiosity. Clicking the phone on, she unlocked the screen and opened her messages app. If she had attempted to articulate her excitement, it would have sounded irrational, yet Gwen clung to a half-formed and unrealized hope that, someday, a less-than-140-character SMS message would bring her an adventure.

In reality, it was only a buzz to notify her of a new voice mail. Somehow, she'd missed two calls from her mother already. Baffled by this and trying to figure out why her mother would call her during school hours, Gwen didn't notice Ms. Whitman until she asked, "Miss Hoffman, have you received a communication you want to share with the class?"

A pang of embarrassment grabbed her; she hated to be called out in front of her peers. Ms. Whitman approached, her matronly skirt rustling as she walked. "No, Ms. Whitman." Even still, Gwen was forced to hand over her phone for the rest of the period. Ms. Whitman set the phone on her desk and returned to lecturing. Gwen resolved to pay attention and copy down the example problems in her composition book, but when she looked back down, a caricature of a girl behind jail bars was scribbled with the caption BUSTED.

She laughed with an unflattering snort. When Ms. Whitman shot her a look of academic disdain, Gwen tried to pass it off as a coughing fit. Gwen was acutely aware of how much more subtle Jay was as he silently laughed alongside her.

Class continued at a snail's pace once Jay had returned to his work. She distracted herself making notes in her margins about how to end the story of Margaret May and the raven tree. That kept her moderately entertained for the rest of class, imagining Rosemary's animated reaction to various plot twists. Class still dragged on though, and not just for Gwen. Five minutes before class was out, the students unanimously slipped away from their assignments and into sociable conversation. By the time Ms. Whitman noticed the class had abandoned their math entirely, it was too late to bully them back to work.

"I take it you have all finished your assignments, or are otherwise eager to do them on your own time," she announced. "Consequently, I'm assigning problems fifteen and seventeen as additional homework."

A unified groan gurgled up from the tired students. Gwen watched as Jay rolled his eyes. "Oh, come on, Ms. W."

"Since everyone is already packed up, you are dismissed so you can hurry to lunch and get started on that additional work."

"Okay, this is cool," Jay said, slinging his backpack onto one shoulder as he stood up, his massive sketch pad poking out of the bag. Gwen didn't even bother packing, throwing her backpack on and carrying her books instead. "It's such a bitch getting through the cafeteria lines. A head start is almost worth the extra homework."

"Funny how much difference a minute or two can make."

"Yeah. It helps to be one step ahead of the masses. That's why I'm heading to Montana at the first sign of a zombie outbreak."

Gwen laughed, stalling as she tried to think of something to add. Before she had a chance, Jay called out, "Hey, Jenny, wait up!" and dashed to catch up to the captain of the girls' swim team. They walked out together, and Gwen trudged to the front of the classroom to see Ms. Whitman.

She got her phone back, leaving right as the bell rang and released everyone else for lunch. She didn't bother checking the voice mail—she'd forgotten all about it. Her thoughts were lost in the commotion and clatter of slamming lockers and swarming students. Gwen pushed through the crowds, weaving gracefully with and against the conflicting flows of human traffic. Still holding her books tight to her chest, she made her way down the hall feeling very alone now that she was surrounded by people.

CHAPTER 4

GWEN BRAVED THE CAFETERIA AS SHE DID EVERY DAY, AND FOR the same underwhelming food she always encountered. With a rubbery pizza slice and a lackluster salad, she beelined for her friends and trusted their conversation would numb her to the reality of cafeteria food.

Claire and Katie were jittery with excitement, having just returned from the homecoming voting table.

"It's Troy, Jay, Marcus," Claire announced, using her celery stick as a gesticulation prop. "Jenny Malloy and Rebecca Harrison are the only real contenders for queen."

"Rebecca's got it, for sure. And Jay and Marcus don't stand a chance against the quarterback." Katie was furiously devouring her salad, as if that was an acceptable outlet for her manic social energy.

"I don't know about that." Claire seemed to take a superficial offense to the statement. "I voted for Jay. Everybody likes Jay… not just the football team. You know how he is."

"You just say that because *Michael* likes him," Katie accused. "You would vote a rock homecoming king if Michael

Kooseman thought it was a cool rock."

"Wouldn't you?"

"Tall, dork, and freckly isn't my type," Katie announced, even though it was well-established she'd had a crush on Michael Kooseman herself in the eighth grade. "Have either of them asked anyone to homecoming yet?"

"No," Gwen answered, popping the tab on her soda. "I overheard him talking to Troy before math last period. He hasn't asked anyone yet."

"He had that conversation in front of you?" Claire and Katie exchanged delighted looks.

"Did he pass you any more notes today?" Katie pried.

Gwen looked down at her rubbery pizza, desperately trying not to catch their foolish optimism. "Aren't he and Jenny turning into a thing?"

"Jenny Malloy?" Claire asked skeptically. "The bottle blonde with the hydrodynamic body of a fourteen-year-old boy? Gwen, you are so much prettier than her, even if you do refuse to wear makeup." Claire would know. She and Gwen had become best friends in the sixth grade, and since Gwen hadn't changed much since then, Claire considered herself an expert in all things Gwen.

"We'll go get fabulous dresses this weekend and do hair and makeup at my house before the dance," Katie announced. "I promise not to let you show up to the dance looking like a tomboy."

Something about that bothered Gwen. It sat wrong with her, not because she disliked the idea of being a tomboy, but because she fundamentally knew she wasn't one. She kept her hair long and she had even worn a dress today, taking advantage of one of the last warm days of October. Admittedly, it was just a sundress, more childish than feminine, but certainly, this did not warrant the title of tomboy. Gwen had never even gotten rid of her dolls and dress-up hat collection. "I'm not a tomboy," she defended.

"Well, you're something," Claire retorted, slurping her soda. "The point is that we're all going to look like beauty queens at the dance. Katie's mom is an *actual* hairdresser."

The conversation moved forward, dragging Gwen with it. She wasn't invested in the finer details of makeup and hair plans. Still, she didn't interrupt the teenage dream that her friends were building out of homecoming.

CHAPTER 5

After lunch, Gwen trudged to fifth period biology, and then hurried across campus for her final and favorite class. She liked Mr. Starkey's classroom. Her speech and debate teacher had turned the boxy room into a place that he felt comfortable in, and it showed. The walls were plastered with posters and quotations of great speakers, all of whom had lived and breathed the inspirational spirit of the sixties. John Kennedy and Martin Luther King Jr. hung beside Bob Dylan and John Lennon. When Mr. Starkey sat at his desk, he typed by the glow of an antique stained-glass lamp, the origins of which had never been explained.

Mr. Starkey tended to dress in a manner that made him look like a much older university professor, or a much younger actor from New York. He seemed to be under the delusion that he was teaching a college course, not a high school elective, but the students never minded the slight pretensions that accompanied this. Mr. Starkey acted like a college professor and treated his students like adults, something that won him instant favor with all of his classes.

Gwen certainly appreciated it, and was fond of the way he always smelled like old books.

Everyone turned in their papers at the start of class, and then settled into their seats for an animated lecture on logical fallacies. Gwen took ample, happy notes, finding it impossible not to share in Mr. Starkey's enthusiasm when he spoke so candidly and gesticulated with so much energy. There was a childlike passion in his personality, and that made him one of her favorite adults. If there was anything unpleasant about Starkey's class, it was only the apprehension that Gwen's speech in defense of the literary significance of fairy tales next week would pale in comparison to Starkey's daily lectures.

Sixth period flew by in a way that her third period math class with Ms. Whitman never had and never would. When Mr. Starkey dismissed the class a few minutes early, Gwen was forced to hurry through the process of packing up her notes while her peers fled by her desk. She chucked all her things into her backpack right as Mr. Starkey finished filing the yet-to-be-graded papers into an ancient, leathery briefcase.

"Would you do me a favor and make sure the computers in the back are powered off?" he requested.

"Sure, Mr. Starkey." Gwen clicked the mice of each of the four computers in the back of the classroom to confirm they were shut down. Mr. Starkey turned off his computer as she did so, and clicked off his colorful, stained glass lamp.

"Thank you, Gwen. I'm not usually in such a hurry to leave, but I've got to get down to the grade school and pick up my son today." As they left the classroom, Mr. Starkey turned off the florescent lights, leaving the posters of activists and artists in the dark as he locked the classroom door. No one else was in the halls yet. Mr. Starkey's class had vanished to the parking lot already, and the bell had not yet sounded to let the rest of the student body free for the afternoon.

"I'm looking forward to reading your paper," he announced, tapping his briefcase. "I really enjoyed seeing the outline. It's exciting to have a student broaching such an unusual topic."

"Oh, thanks," Gwen replied. The bell sounded, its harsh ring filling the locker-lined hall for a brief moment before students began swarming out of the classrooms.

"Fairy tales are fascinating, and they can be surprisingly hard to defend from a literary perspective. My son just turned seven and can hardly get his fill of them though, so I'm learning to appreciate them again myself."

Gwen nodded. She raised her voice to be heard over the clamor of students. "My little sister is the same way."

Starkey gave her an amused smile. "It's fun to watch how their imaginations run away with them… and how they sometimes end up running away with their imaginations."

"Hey, Gwen!"

Gwen would have looked behind her to see who was interrupting, but she already recognized Jay's voice. Starkey peeled away from her, continuing out to the staff parking lot before Gwen had a chance to respond to his odd remark, or even say goodbye. She turned to see Jay striding through the crowd, stopping to wait for him.

"Hi, Jay!" Gwen responded, trying not to betray her joy in its entirety. Still, she smiled as he approached.

"Hey," he responded. Jay held his books under one arm and dug his other hand into his pant pocket. "I've been trying to catch you all day."

"Yeah?" Gwen asked, feeling curious, fluttery, and other emotions she would sort through later.

"Yeah, I meant to talk to you after math, but I had to get my history book back from Jenny. Anyway, I just wanted to let you know…I'm having a party. Not this Saturday, but next."

"Columbus Day weekend?"

"Right. My parents are going to be out of town, but my brother Roger's coming down and going to buy us a whole bunch of booze. It's not going to be a huge thing, so keep it on the DL, but if you want to come, you're definitely invited."

Gwen processed this as coherently as she could. "I'm not much of a drinker." She'd never touched a drop in her life. "But I'd love to come to your party."

"Hey, that's cool," Jay answered, smiling with just half of his mouth, his vibrant blue eyes still fixed on Gwen. "Do you know where I live?" he asked.

"Oh, no, I don't… why don't I give you my number so you can text me the address? Then I'll have it in my phone."

"Sure." Jay pulled out his phone and typed on its touch screen with one hand as Gwen recited her phone number.

As he finished adding her to his contacts, Gwen thought to tell him, "Oh, hey, I heard you were on the homecoming ballot today. Congratulations."

Jay smirked and rolled his eyes. "Ah, who cares?"

"Hey, it's pretty cool," Gwen told him. "You've got a lot of friends around campus. That's neat. People like you."

Jay put his phone back into his pocket and looked up. "And you?"

Gwen laughed as she considered what sort of reputation she must have among her peers. "Claire and Katie like me, I don't know about the rest of them." She looked at the crowd of students herding themselves by. It was true she didn't really fit in, but who did? She wasn't concerned about her status, and neither was Jay.

Jay nodded, still smiling. "Cool. I guess I'll see you tomorrow then."

"See you in class," Gwen responded, watching as he

walked down the corridor to the senior parking lot. She waited until she was certain he would not look back before she did a prancing pirouette, happily taking off. Dashing past the few straggling students, Gwen hurried to the junior parking lot. Within a minute's time, her phone gave a quick vibration in her pocket. Knowing what it was, but unable to resist the temptation of confirming it, Gwen found a text from an unknown number with the address 1068 Park Street NE. She also noticed three missed calls from her mother, but that was irrelevant.

She was almost out the door when her heart stopped and her feet stuck.

"People like you."

"And you?"

What had Jay been asking? He was asking about whether people liked her, too, right? Gwen felt electrified as she considered the possibility that Jay's question concerned whether *she* liked *him*. She'd screwed up and misread him—maybe, sort of. What did the words 'and' and 'you' fundamentally mean, anyway? Swimming in an emotional brew of delight and self-consciousness, Gwen burst out of the school halls and down the steps to the junior parking lot. She began to panic in the most euphoric way possible.

CHAPTER 6

On the drive home, Gwen rolled down the windows and blasted her radio. Something was clicking. For a brief and glittering moment, she felt like a teenager. Pop music blared, and the October air blew wildly through the car. Her scalp ached from her braid, but Gwen pulled her hairband out and let the tired hair dance with the breeze. She felt fantastic.

When Gwen saw the police car, she immediately took her foot off the gas and slowed down, well aware she was driving a few miles over the residential speed limit. It took her a moment to process that it was parked in front of her house. The officer was not in his car. Gwen pulled into the driveway; her father's car was parked in her usual spot. What was he doing home from work?

Gwen's heart began beating faster as her mind shuffled through the possibilities. Both of her parents' cars were here, so there couldn't have been a car crash. If her father was home, something must have gone wrong with Mom. Could a burglary have happened while Mom was running errands?

Gwen knew that there was no positive outcome for this

situation. Something had gone wrong, and the police were here now. She was… excited.

She knew it was irrational, but something inside of her held its breath, hoping that if some disaster was unfolding inside, at least it would be poetic or adventurous. In a moment, she would curse herself, but for an apprehensive second, Gwen felt an innocent curiosity and longed for a spectacle.

She parked and anxiously dashed to the front door. It was unlocked, and Gwen barged right in.

Her mother was on the couch, sitting on the edge of the cushion and holding her head in her hands. Her father looked more distressed than she had seen him in a long time. His arms folded in front of him, he stared at his shoes. His blazer was resting on the couch, but it looked as though he had been pacing as the officer spoke to him.

The police officer's black slacks were crisply starched, as was his dark shirt. He had patches on it that identified him as an officer of the law, but Gwen's eyes went immediately to the walkie-talkie and gun on his belt. He stopped talking the second Gwen stepped into the door.

Her parents stared at her, and she had the sudden sense that she was interrupting something. They were giving her a look that told her she did not belong, and whatever was happening was a very grown-up thing she was not a part of. This faded though, as if her parents realized that Gwen was grown-up, or if not, she was going to have to be now.

"What's wrong?" Gwen asked, her heart trembling as she clutched the straps of her backpack at her chest.

"Gwen… Gwen, come sit down," her mother requested, patting the couch cushion beside her. Her voice broke as she spoke; she had been crying.

"Why? What's happening?" Gwen looked at the officer, but he shied away from the question, deferring it to her parents.

When it became obvious that Gwen was not going to budge until she got an answer, her father walked over to her and in a calm voice explained, “It’s Rosemary. She’s missing.”

“Since when?” Gwen demanded. “Missing?” What did that even mean? She had seen her little sister just last night. How could Rosemary have gotten lost since then? The grade school wasn’t even out yet.

Gwen gingerly lowered her backpack to the ground. Her mother didn’t even object to her setting the bag down in the way of walking. Gwen saw Rosemary’s bright blue pack hung up in the entryway. Rosemary hadn’t gone to school this morning.

“Your mother called me when she woke up and found Rosemary missing,” her father soberly informed her. “We couldn’t reach you, and the officers advised us not to contact the school.”

“Oh my God,” Gwen cried. Not knowing how else to respond, she threw herself into her dad’s arms, panicking within the confines of the hug. She felt her dad’s hand in her hair, but there was only so much comfort that he could impart. Gwen could feel his fear, and that shattered the support she desperately needed from him.

The officer continued with the line of questioning that Gwen had interrupted. “Are you sure nothing was missing from the room… no toys or stuffed animals? In kidnappings, the perpetrators often take things from the child’s room, familiar things to keep them calm.”

Gwen stared at the officer, feeling that he was an alien, unwanted presence in her home. He didn’t belong here, and she wanted to push him back out the doorway. Her thoughts were distracted when she saw the patch on the arm of his shirt. It dawned on Gwen how odd it was that there wasn’t any lettering on his uniform, no initials or numbers to denote his precinct or department. The patch on his arm was unlike any Gwen had seen on police officers. The symbol looked like an atom, but instead of a clustered nucleus, there was a golden star in the middle.

"I—I didn't notice anything missing," Mrs. Hoffman announced.

"When my partner comes back down, we'll have a clearer idea of what happened, Mrs. Hoffman… We'll see if the perpetrator left prints or if he left dust."

"I didn't see any dust," she insisted, panicking.

"It isn't always obvious, that's why Kubowski's inspecting the room. There's still a chance this isn't a kidnapping. It may very well be an abduction."

"What's that supposed to mean?" Gwen asked.

"That's not possible," her mother said, fighting back a sob. "Her window was closed this morning."

"It's possible he closed it on his way out, Mrs. Hoffman."

"No," her mother insisted. "The girls never sleep with their windows open. We make sure of it."

A stiffening chill crept down Gwen's spine. She pushed away from her father and addressed the officer. "Her window was open last night." Heart trembling in her chest, Gwen watched them lock their eyes on her. "I heard her bathroom door slam last night, and when I woke up this morning and Tootles wanted out of her room, I went in. I closed the window for her so she wouldn't get in trouble."

The adults looked at her, horror-struck. Gwen didn't understand the significance of this detail. She turned to the officer in the hopes that it would be easier to communicate with him. "We're not supposed to sleep with the windows open… the breeze slams doors and screws with the heating bill. I closed the window in the morning so she wouldn't get in trouble for it."

The officer, who still had not introduced himself to Gwen, ignored her and asked her parents, "I take it you haven't had this conversation with your daughter."

"She's only sixteen," Mr. Hoffman responded.

In a moment of crisis, the worst thing is to feel deprived of information. While no one was certain what had happened to Rosemary, Gwen felt a distinct gap between what her parents knew and what they were telling her. The gap between their understanding and Gwen's was painfully obvious, and it burned at her nerves. "What conversation!" she yelled. "What happened to Rosemary?"

The police officer did not answer her. "Was Rosemary in bed when you closed her window?"

"I thought so." Gwen didn't realize how loud she was yelling. "I mean, why wouldn't she be? I didn't check. I just assumed." All at once, Gwen burst into tears. There was no gradual progression. One moment, she was not crying, and the next, she was weeping. Was this somehow her fault? Was there something she should have done differently? She felt the eyes of the adults drilling guilt into her.

"It's okay, Gwen," her father told her, reflexively using the words without considering whether they were true. Gwen was not a little girl who could unthinkingly take her father's words at face value, and his lie sat bitterly with her.

"This changes things," the officer admitted. "This aligns with an abduction, not a kidnapping."

"What's the difference?" Gwen sobbed. As far as she knew, the terms were interchangeable. The technical legal distinction didn't matter to Gwen; a stranger had taken her sister.

It gave her a start when she heard someone tromping down the stairs. Gwen felt vulnerable and endangered, even in the light of day. Nothing was safe when Rosemary had vanished in the darkness of the previous night.

The noise was only the policeman's partner, Officer Kubowski. She came down the stairs, her dark hair pulled tight and her mannish eyebrows furrowed over her hard eyes. "We've got dust," she announced. She was wearing disposable gloves and held up a small, plastic evidence bag.

"Well, that settles that," he announced. "We'll send it to forensics for examination to be sure, but there's only one offender who fits this modus operandi. I want you to know there is a tremendous success rate for recovering the children he's taken. Eventually, they make their way home. Most of them come back totally unharmed. It's just a question of how long it takes them to break away from their captor."

Barely containing her tears, Mrs. Hoffman asked, "And how long is that, usually?"

He solemnly answered. "It's usually a matter of years, ma'am."

Gwen's mother burst into tears, and her father went to sit down beside her on the couch. He wrapped his arms around her for her sake as much as his own. "Helen, Helen," he coaxed, rocking his wife gently as she continued to cry.

Gwen was still coping with the shock of this news, and the full tragedy of it had not yet sank in. Looking for answers that her parents would not give her, she focused on Kubowski, and the strange bag she clutched in her hand. It didn't look like there was anything in it. When the light caught it, however, Gwen could see something gold and glittering within it. "What is that?" she asked, incredulous and distrusting.

"This is the sister, Berchem?" Officer Kubowski didn't even look her. Gwen felt invisible, overlooked in the middle of this disaster. Kubowski had the same strange star-atom patch on her uniform. She pulled the bag away, holding it where it would be harder for Gwen to see it.

"What is it?" Gwen demanded.

"She doesn't know," Officer Berchem responded, speaking over Gwen's growing hysteria.

Gwen had always imagined that disaster would be more glamorous. Time was supposed to rush by or suspend itself, or something. This conversation was not happening all at once, nor were these events unfolding as if in slow motion, and time was certainly not stopping.

Because of this though, Gwen was having a hard time comprehending everything that was being said as it was being said. The words loitered in her mind, hitting her whenever dark, momentary silences lapsed over the adults.

This was more than a momentary silence, however. Gwen slowly realized that everyone was staring at her. They looked to each other, but their eyes always fell with the same guilty heaviness on her.

...the children he's taken.

As all expression drained from her face, her father was the only one coherent enough to ask, "Gwen?"

"You know who took her!" Gwen accused, screaming and crying. "You know who did this!" She had no idea how they knew, but she was certain they did. They were behaving just the way adults always did when they were in the process of being caught with an ugly secret.

They were such adults, to treat her like such a child.

Officer Berchem shirked away from culpability. "We can't confirm that it's Pan's work until forensics returns the evidence."

Gwen was suddenly compromised by a wave of dizziness. She felt her body fighting to deny what she had just heard; it seemed like the only way to survive the shock of it was to deny it. No one was offering an explanation, and she didn't want one anymore. Bursting into a rush of new tears, she bolted for the staircase and fled to her room. She didn't heed her parents' calls, and they let her go. Gwen left them alone. They didn't want her there anyway.

When she got to her bedroom, she slammed the door shut and slumped down against it, as if that would keep reality from catching up to her. She sank down to the floor with the irrefutable feeling that she had just tumbled down a rabbit hole she would not be able to climb back out of.

She gasped for breath between sobs. Never before had she feared that she would stop breathing as she cried. The silence and loneliness of her room gave her space to breathe, and she quieted down as she clutched herself.

The tears did not slow down, but her breakdown became increasingly less dramatic. As she gained control of herself, she began to wish she could go back down and listen to the conversation without being ignored. She had nothing to say, but she didn't want to be treated as a nonentity. She didn't want to face those mysterious officers, but she did want to know what they knew.

To satisfy this desire, Gwen willed herself up and went to the other side of the room where a closed heater vent was embedded in the floor beside her bookshelf. She grabbed her fluffy lion off her bed and took him with her as she opened the vent and lay down beside it to listen through the shaft.

"But why us?" her mother cried. "Why Rosemary?"

Apologetically, Berchem informed her, "She was most likely targeted because of your husband's work."

"My work?" her father asked. "That's impossible. How would they know?"

"We're not sure they do know, but there's a growing trend for children who disappear to have parents who work in magical fields. Our department is getting better at systematically monitoring and following the chemical signature of magic. We think that Pan might have a more rudimentary means of this as well. Despite all precautions, magic is not done entirely in isolation. It follows you home, Mr. Hoffman, and it draws attention to your family."

"Oh God," he replied. Her father's voice sounded muffled, as if he were speaking into his hands.

Kubowski spoke up. "Your older daughter, she would have been here for the invasion of '08, yes?"

"Gwen was eight at the time," her mother answered. "Robert was escorted away from the house, but I sent Gwen to bed early… She said she could hear pipes."

"Your family was definitely targeted," Berchem insisted. "You took all the right precautions and did everything you could, but you can't anticipate everything."

The adults were all quiet until Gwen's mother began crying again.

"What line of work are you in, Mr. Hoffman?" Kubowski asked.

"Is this on the record?"

"It might help with the investigation."

Gwen clutched her stuffed lion a little harder and pressed her ear to the cold metal vent to hear better. What were they talking about? Her father was a financial advisor who worked at an office downtown. They talked softer now.

She heard her father sigh. "Economics. National debt department. My team works with the resources they ship in from Ireland to try to keep inflation from spiking."

"Ireland?" Berchem echoed.

"Yeah. You'd be surprised how much naturally occurring anomalous resources there are at the ends of the rainbows over there."

"Magic," her mother muttered.

"Yes... It's amazing people believe we can be eighteen trillion dollars in debt and prospering without it."

There was another moment of silence before Berchem announced, "I'm glad we can be honest with you about your daughter, Mr. Hoffman. So many parents can't know what's really happened; so many wouldn't believe it if we told them where their children are going."

"Officer, I've spent twenty years processing magic for the economy," her father announced, "and I still don't believe Rosemary's gone."

CHAPTER 7

"GWEN? GWEN?"

Her father knocked gently on the door again. He wasn't expecting permission to enter, only waiting to see if she would object.

Gwen couldn't muster an objection though. Her drive to wallow in shock and misery overpowered her ability to do anything, including defend her isolation. Curled up on her bed, she didn't budge as her father entered the room. She hadn't even turned on the little Christmas lights over her bed. Gwen had simply collapsed on top of her covers and made a sobbing mess of her pillow.

The police had already left. Gwen had heard the front door close behind them. She knew when they left that her parents would inevitably come up and deal with her. Once the adults were done talking about the technical and legal, then they would worry about talking to their daughter.

She clutched her lion close, but as she squeezed him against her chest, she realized he was far flatter than he used to be. His cotton had compressed after years of being squished against her for comfort. She wanted to hold him until he dissolved into her, but he was farther away than ever from her heart. There had been a time when the stuffed tiger toy could be crushed flat against her chest, closer to her heartbeat than anything else would ever come. Now, there was a layer of boobs between her lion and her heartbeat.

Maybe she could pretend to be asleep and her father—her lying, stupid father—would go away. Unfortunately, Mr. Hoffman knew his daughter too well to be convinced that she was sleeping now. He picked up the tissue box from her big, blue bookshelf and brought it over to her bedside table. Pulling her spinning office chair away from her desk as well, he sat in it beside her bed. After a moment, he announced, "I'm sorry you had to find out this way, Gwen."

"How did you want me to find out?" she demanded through her film of tears. "What was the best-case scenario for this?" Gwen was disgusted and confused. It was an unpleasant combination that left her afraid and combative. She was still struggling with the basic facts of what was happening. "Peter Pan took my little sister."

The words felt bizarre leaving her mouth. She waited for her father to correct her, to tell her that was every bit as nonsensical as raven trees and egg fruit. When her father nodded and told her, "Yep," Gwen had never been more devastated to find out she was right.

"Why did you lie to me?" Gwen asked, too upset to be as angry as she wanted to be. "Why did you tell me, all of those years, that magic wasn't real? Why bother to spend years convincing me that all of this fairy-tale stuff was just make-believe?"

"Think about the consequences of that," her father suggested. "What would happen if all parents knew and told their children magic was out there—that it was an option?

Think about how many more children would run off. Magic isn't like money, status, weapons, or any other kind of power. Everyone has access to it. But you can't just tell children they are capable of fantastic things that their parents can't control. You have to wait until they're old enough to appreciate how magic should be used."

Gwen finally sat up. She clutched her knees close to her chest, looking at her father with bloodshot eyes. "What do you mean—how it 'should be used?'"

"There's only so much magic in this world, Gwen," her father told her. "There wouldn't be a problem if it was an unlimited resource, but scarcity drives conflict. We can't have children consuming magic at the reckless, indulgent rates they are inclined to. We can't afford to waste magic on fairies and wonderlands. There are too many more pertinent issues we need to channel it into."

"Like what?"

"Well, think about your smartphone."

"What about it?"

"Those things have transformed communication. Social media has been an invaluable tool to the revolutions that have been happening in the Middle East, and the advent of cell phones gives rural Africa a means to modernize."

"But that's not magic," Gwen insisted. "That's technology."

"Any sufficiently advanced magic is indistinguishable from technology," her father told her. "It usually takes about ten or twenty years for science to catch up to magic. Scientists are just starting to understand how cell phones are constructed. Until now, they've been relying on magic to carry the signals and power the devices. Think of magic as an assembler, something that takes all the necessary components and arranges them in the manner they need to be arranged. Once it has, people work to reverse engineer that technology, and eventually stop depending on magic to do the heavy lifting."

"No, Dad, my phone has a SIM card. It wirelessly communicates with—"

"With satellites in space?" her father asked. "Gwen, does that sound reasonable in any way whatsoever?"

Her father was the one who had initially explained the concept to her, and though his explanation had been logically self-congruent, Gwen had taken it, in part, on faith. She didn't really understand much of what happened around her, but others seemed to, so she had gotten comfortable in the cursory understanding they'd given her. Now, her father seemed to be mocking her for ever having believed what he'd told her was true. "So that's it? Nobody's allowed to believe in fairies because our iPhones need to work?" She uncurled herself and crossed her legs. Gwen buried herself in this issue, distracting herself from its disastrous consequences by tying her attention up in the mechanics of it. For as angry and upset as she was, Gwen was curious too.

"It's more than that, Gwen. Think about the economy."

"What about it?"

"We're more than eighteen trillion dollars in debt. Don't you think it's a little odd that a country so beyond bankruptcy continues to function and prosper as well as the United States?"

"Well, yeah, but that's because China's bought most of our debt, and uh, two thirds of it is public debt, so..." Gwen felt incredibly uncomfortable, attempting to explain to her economist father that the economy wasn't magic.

"Gwen, there is no reason that we should be such a wealthy country, aside from the fact that we have some of the most inventive and entrepreneurial minds capturing magic and channeling it into the bureaucracy of our government.

There are countless aspects of life that we depend on magic for, and it's unreasonable to think that, given all the problems in the world, any of it should be spent fueling Santa Claus."

"Wait," Gwen objected. "Santa Claus is real?" She had already had this conversation years ago, but now she and her father were on opposite sides of it. Her parents had already lied to her once about his existence; she didn't know if she could trust anything they said on the matter. The stomach-turning shock felt no different. Once again, her parents were destroying her every notion of what life was.

"No," her father quickly answered. "Yours is the first generation to be completely without him. It's part of the reason we've been able to push the information age forward as quickly as we have. Rather than shelling out magic to let one man monopolize that season, parents united in order to accomplish the same thing in a manner that wouldn't drain any magic from out of the system."

"This doesn't make any sense," Gwen whispered, picking up her stuffed tiger lion again after flicking the switch for her lights..

"No one ever said life was going to."

Gwen wanted to fight that assertion too. Adults had left her with the distinct impression that life would make sense. If not now, then when she grew up. Now, her father was explaining that life wasn't any more sensible than it was fair.

How could he be so calm now? He wanted to be strong for his daughter, but he just seemed cold to Gwen. "You have to understand." He sighed. "We just wanted to protect you and Rosemary. That's all any parent wants, to keep their children safe."

"Safe from what? What is there to be afraid of? Wouldn't a Just-Say-No campaign have worked?"

"It isn't that easy, Gwen. When you're a kid, some things

have to be simplified for you. Your mother and I taught you not to get in cars with strangers because we couldn't explain pedophiles to you when you were six. We told you to keep your windows closed because you didn't need to know that Peter Pan was really out there."

"You didn't trust me not to run away?" Gwen looked at him through wet eyes, feeling smaller than ever and in all the wrong ways.

"You were in Rosemary's shoes once, too, Gwen."

"Well, maybe if you had talked to her and given her a reason to stay here, she wouldn't have left!" Gwen instantly regretted moving the blame onto her father, who was certainly wrestling that guilt already. What made it worse was that he did not let it show how her words affected him.

"What could I have said that wouldn't have inspired wanderlust in her? How could I brainwash her so well that her little heart would have the self-restraint to say 'no' to a world of fairies and flying? If she had to find out, she should have found out when she was old enough to understand that there are more important things in life than make-believe." With that remark, her father leaned down and kissed Gwen's head, making her feel even more treasured and even more guilty.

"So that's it?" Gwen asked, trying to piece together the larger picture and draw some sort of comfort out of it. "This is just one more thing grown-ups are all in on, like Santa Claus?" Gwen thought about her teachers, mall employees, her parents, and the newscasters who wrote, "Dear Virginia" letters and reported live-time updates for where Santa was last seen on Christmas Eve. She'd been fooled before, and it seemed she had not learned anything from the experience. Santa was just a distraction to keep their attention diverted from where magic was really happening.

"Not all parents. This isn't a massive conspiracy." Gwen

gave him a frustrated look, and he amended his words. "Okay, it's a pretty big conspiracy. But not everybody is in on it. Just the people who need to be. There are plenty of people in this world who go through their whole lives without ever realizing the impact or reality of magic." Mr. Hoffman ran his hand through his daughter's hair. She was trying now, and trying desperately, to understand where her father was coming from.

"How come you know? Who were those officers?" Gwen asked, sitting upright and scooting against the wall. She still clutched her lion, but with a little less desperation.

"My career went deep into a strange science that demands an understanding of magic," he answered. "Those officers were from an Anomalous Activity Unit. They're the ones who track lost children and try to bring them home."

The ensuing silence choked a question out of Gwen. "Is Rosemary going to come back?"

He didn't look into her eyes. "Maybe not for a very long time." He rested his hand on her foot, and Gwen felt she should have given him more of herself. She should have hugged him, but she felt as though she risked falling apart with every little motion.

"I love you, Dad," she said.

"I love you, too, sweetheart." He smiled at her, and Gwen felt awful, as if the words said more about their fear than their love in this moment. "Your mother does, too, and we're all going to get through this together. Whatever happens, we all love each other. And that's more important than magic."

Before he left his daughter's room, Mr. Hoffman ruffled her hair once more and gave her forehead a parting kiss. He had good timing. Gwen always liked how her father innately knew when to leave her alone, even if she still wasn't feeling well.

The room darkened as the last of the evening gave way

to night. Gwen felt that all her energy for the next three or three-hundred days had been drained out of her. Crawling under her covers, she reached down to unplug her little lights. She watched the quick spark from the metal plug as it lost its connection, wondering how long it had taken little lights to stop being magic and start being electricity. She clutched her pillow, hugging it to her as she cried into it. Her stuffed lion sat beside her.

CHAPTER 8

GWEN DID NOT SET HER ALARM FOR THE NEXT MORNING. SHE slept in, enduring fitful dreams she would not remember. Her parents didn't disturb her. Mrs. Hoffman only called the schools and told the administrators that her daughters would be absent. It wasn't until eleven thirty that Gwen's phone finally woke her up. She could not find the ringing phone until the call had already gone to voice mail. When she groggily dug it out of her purse, Gwen saw that she had missed what was the last in a long line of communications from Claire. Six new messages were waiting for her.

Running late?

Where are you?

GWEN.

Mom's driving me.

Are you cutting class?

Srsly girl, you OK?

She hadn't bothered to leave a voice mail, but Gwen knew she needed to say something. She'd forgotten that she was supposed to drive to school with Claire today. She could call back now that she was at lunch, but Gwen didn't know if she was even capable of speaking. Her throat was sore and her head cloudy from all her crying last night. She tried to imagine an appropriate text message.

Should she tell Claire there was a family emergency? That would raise too many questions. She could say she was sick, but she didn't want to lie to her best friend.

Not feeling well. Sorry. We'll talk later.

With that minimal text, Gwen lay back down and pulled her sheets tight around her. She had been so excited to be a teenager yesterday. She had been dying to gush to Claire and Katie about Jay's party. That all seemed so remote and insignificant now. She escaped her grief in sleep.

Even when Gwen could sleep no more, she stayed in bed. When she could no longer stand the aching futility of bed, she stayed in her room. A few times during the day, she could hear her mother crying in her own room. Both her parents came up to check on her intermittently through the day. Gwen couldn't tell what was frustration and what was sadness. She swelled with painful emotion, too terrible to decipher. She didn't want to talk.

At one point, her mother brought dinner up to her. Tomato soup and grilled cheese told Gwen that her mother was too distraught to cook, so her father had taken the initiative to make sure no one starved today. Gwen ignored the food out of a twisted martyrdom, but eventually realized she wasn't punishing anyone but herself. She ate it once the sandwich and soup were already cold.

Her dad took emergency leave from work, and Gwen knew they were going to spend some painful time together as a family. While her parents were concerned about their youngest daughter being off in an impossible world far out of reach, Gwen struggled more with the manner in which her sister had vanished.

The fact that she was gone became almost trivial. If Rosemary was with Peter Pan, how bad could it be? Gwen's initial impression of the situation was that some pedophile had stolen her away. Anything was better than that, and the idea that Rosemary had willingly gone off with a familiar boy and not a strange man, well, that didn't trouble her nearly as much.

Gwen went to bed early that night, but couldn't sleep a wink. Turning her string of lights on around two in the morning, she resigned herself to sleeplessness. She didn't have to get up for school in the morning; it didn't matter if she slept at all. Gwen only wanted to fall asleep to escape the tyranny of consciousness.

She didn't want to think about magic; she just wanted to sleep, but she was scared. In a dull, tired way, she was terrified. If she fell asleep, she might dream, and she couldn't stomach the thought of dipping into fantasy. Fairies, Santa Claus, werewolves… God only knew what was real anymore. She hadn't had the heart to grill her father and find out exactly what was fiction in this world. Gwen just wanted to find a little pocket of reality that was real and sane, if she was confined to it.

She couldn't help it, however. Her mind danced with unwanted fascinations as she considered what a real-life Neverland would look like. Images from her childhood imagination sprung back into her mind as if they had never left. Gwen thought of pink, cotton-candy clouds and adorable piglets that talked in Pig Latin. Were these things possible? Were they real?

She went to her blue bookshelf and searched the bottom row of picture books and chapter books. *Peter Pan* was nestled snuggly between two others, and Gwen hesitantly pulled it out. Scurrying back to bed as if she'd stolen the fairy tale, she found it challenging to work up the nerve to read from the book. She opened to random pages and read passages with critical, skeptical awe. Neverbirds, pirates, hollow trees, mermaids… it felt like a crime scene report. Was this really where Rosemary was? As she paged through it, a browning daisy fell out from between the pages. Gwen put the book aside and tried to quiet her mind again. She didn't want to think about magic.

Midway through the night, it occurred to her again, as if for the first time, that her little sister was gone. All else aside, Rosemary had disappeared and was not coming back.

Restless and looking for any solution, effective or otherwise, Gwen humored the downhearted impulse to get out of her room. Creeping through the bedroom, Gwen approached the bathroom.

Blind in the darkness, Gwen felt her way through the tiny room she had memorized. Tootles stayed firmly asleep at the foot of her bed, not following her as Gwen slipped into Rosemary's room.

Her sister's pale, lavender room was slightly smaller than Gwen's and full of stuffed animals and dolls. Rosemary had half a dozen plastic dolls and a tiny tea table with plastic chairs that Gwen had mastered the art of sitting on without breaking. Picture books were stacked and strewn everywhere, along with plastic food. Gwen highly suspected that Rosemary had more pretend food in her room than the rest of the family had real food in the kitchen.

A mobile of plastic fish spun over the bed, and Gwen collapsed on top of Rosemary's bed, hardly aware that she was crying again. Her sister's quilt was so much more colorful than her own trendy bedspread, and the tinier mattress had so much more give. Gwen looked out the window; Officer

Kubowski had left it open after inspecting it. The stars outside were dimly shining.

Gwen didn't think it would help to be in Rosemary's bed. If anything, she assumed it would keep her awake to wallow in her sadness. It didn't occur to her to get up and close the window. The cool breeze that fluttered the drapes gave her an excuse to tuck herself under the quilt.

CHAPTER 9

"GWEN? GWEN?" ROSEMARY'S VOICE WAS SO FAMILIAR. SHE HAD expected to find melancholy dreams, but as she listened to the voice, Gwen found herself waking up. The more she stirred herself awake, the clearer the whispering voice became. Although her dream faded, her sister whispered, "Gwen, wake up!"

She did so with startled curiosity. Rosemary's bright eyes were hovering inches away from her, her full waves of hair framing her round face. Her tiny hand shook Gwen's shoulder, but Rosemary was perched over Gwen, kneeling on her own bed beside her. Gwen's eyes took a moment to adapt to the darkness, but once she recognized her little sister, she sprung up. "Rosemary!" Gwen hissed, flinging her arms around the little girl. "Oh my God, we thought you ran away!" She didn't know why she was whispering. Part of her realized she would have to run and wake up her parents in a minute to let them know Rosemary was home, but another part of her wanted to savor this moment where she and her sister were alone together.

Gwen did not yet realize that she and Rosemary were not alone.

"I did," Rosemary quietly exclaimed. "We came back for you. I missed your stories." As Rosemary pushed out of her big sister's hug, she turned around and looked into the darkness at her escort.

A chill crept down Gwen's spine, and her eyes could not refocus fast enough. She clutched fistfuls of Rosemary's quilt, instinctively preparing to throw herself under it if there was a monster lurking in the dark. Gwen wasn't afraid in the normal sense of the term, but her heart raced as she noticed the boy sitting on the rocking chair in the corner of the room.

The chair rocked with a squeak as he stood up from it. Walking slowly toward the window, he came into view as he entered the moonlight. He stared at Gwen, and she stared back.

His eyes were steady in their intensity, but impish in all other manners. They impulsively surveyed the room, never lingering on any particular aspect of it, but always coming back to Gwen. A vine of ivy was wrapped around his waist and strewn across his shoulder like a belt and sash, just barely holding his tattered shirt and shorts to him. His clothes seemed held together with bits of twine and magic. He moved fluidly in his own skin. Gwen wasn't even conscious of how much she envied his playful motion. Even with his gangly, broad shoulders, he stood tall with a childish sense of confidence.

Gwen wasn't sure, but he looked like a freshman. He couldn't have been younger than fourteen.

He wore hemp bracelets and braided jewelry around his wrists; pine-cone chips and wooden beads were woven into his necklace. They jangled as he walked.

"This is your sister?" he asked. His question seemed

rudely incredulous. "Hollyhock, let me see her."

Before Gwen could make sense of this remark, an exploding light burst from an inexplicable place in the darkness. Gwen was disoriented when the light came so quickly at her. Circling around her, the golden light left a trail of fast dissolving glitter that rained down on her. What little of it touched her glowed faintly on her skin before disappearing. It felt like a pins-and-needles numbness in the best possible way.

The bright light that radiated from Hollyhock's little body half-blinded Gwen in the otherwise dark room, but Hollyhock flitted in front of her, and Gwen caught a glimpse of the creature. Her eyes were unusually wide, and her massive irises were an otherworldly color for which Gwen had no name. Her itty-bitty lips and nose were hardly there at all, but her sunny hair was pulled back in two long, dangling braids. Her limbs were like twigs, and she wore a leaf draped over her like a tunic. Gwen didn't need to be told that she was looking at a fairy.

"Huh," he responded, sitting down on the hardwood floor of Rosemary's room. "You said your sister was a kid."

"She is, Peter!" Rosemary defended. "I told you—she's a big kid."

Finally addressing her properly, Peter spoke to Gwen in a condescending tone. "I expected you to be younger."

"As did I of you," Gwen curtly returned.

Peter, the young man, shrugged with his eyebrows and looked away, indicating that he was not going to bother engaging a hostile girl.

Gwen didn't care. She couldn't have cared. While Hollyhock played in the fish mobile above the bed like an aquatic merry-go-round, Gwen clutched Rosemary close to her. "Rosemary, we were so worried! Thank God you came back."

"I had to come back, Gwenny," Rosemary told her. "I had to come back for you." Hollyhock, tiring of the mobile, zipped back down and buried herself in Rosemary's hair, poking her head out of it and trying to part it like curtains. Rosemary giggled, taking Gwen's hand. "Let's go."

"Whoa, wait, no." Gwen grabbed hold of Rosemary's arm. "We're not going anywhere. Mom and Dad are worried about you. The cops were here… You can't go—where?"

Hollyhock, on Rosemary's shoulder, said something that sounded like a sneeze and a hum. Rosemary translated the one word she had already learned in the fairy tongue. "Neverland."

"No," Gwen flatly denied.

"This was a mistake," Peter announced, standing up and striding toward the window. Moonlight washed over him as he stood before the open window, and Gwen's heart raced with the surrealness of the situation. "Come on, Rose," he said.

"No," Gwen again announced. She clutched her sister close. "Rosemary, we have to get Mom and Dad."

Peter perked up then, springing into the air and flying over to the edge of the bed in a quick panic. "You can't do that," he told her. "You can't."

Gwen looked up at the boy who was hovering beside her, childishly daring him. "Do you want to bet?"

"No, Gwen, don't!" Rosemary was just as agitated by the prospect.

Gwen threw off her covers and darted to the door, standing there with her hand on the doorknob. "I'll wake them up right now."

Rosemary had flown—her little sister had *flown*—to Peter's side. "We'll be gone before you can call them," Peter threatened.

Gwen knew it was true. She couldn't force Rosemary to stay, not when she had all the magic she needed to slip away to any far reach of this world or another. In a second's time, Rosemary would be gone, and Gwen would have to finish growing up without a little sister to remind her of why she was still irrevocably in love with childhood.

Rosemary was distraught by this turn of events. She had thought for sure that her sister would leap at the opportunity to escape the combative, hormonal world she purported to hate. "I came back for you," Rosemary pleaded. "Come with us. Neverland is amazing; you wouldn't believe it! Gwen, please!" She pouted and stomped silently on the air, clutching her skirt and begging Gwen.

Hollyhock circled around Gwen once more and bobbed in front of her, trying to egg Gwen forward. Peter and Rosemary were both silhouetted against the window. In a moment, they would dive back out and into the night, regardless of what Gwen did. There was nothing she could do to circumvent that.

"Alright," she finally announced. "I'll go with you, but once we've had your fun, we'll both come home, okay, Rosemary?" She felt the need to rationalize. "I'm only going to go because someone needs to keep an eye on you."

Rosemary jumped for joy and never landed. She hung happily in the air. "Oh Gwen, you'll never get tired of Neverland!"

Skeptical of the older girl, Peter remarked, "With an attitude like that, I don't know if she'll even be able to fly."

"Of course I'll be able to fly," Gwen indignantly responded.

Rosemary caught Hollyhock and held her in her hands. Zipping over to Gwen, she shook the fairy and covered her sister in a layer of the tickling, numbing fairy dust, all the while explaining, "Oh, she absolutely will! Gwen is the best at so many things, not just storytelling. She's better than me at everything—except for connect-the-dots and jump rope—and I'm such a good flier that she'll be even better."

When Rosemary finished shaking Hollyhock and let her go, the dizzy fairy stumbled through the air. Gwen felt tingly, as if her feet had fallen asleep and taken her whole body with them. She hardly realized she was doing it, but Gwen slowly lifted up into the air. When she was a few inches above the ground, Gwen looked down and squeaked in delighted shock when she saw that she was no longer standing on the ground. Painfully aware of how impossible this was, Gwen immediately fell back down to the ground, landing heavy on her feet.

"Try like you're swimming," Rosemary suggested, paddling through the air as though she were moving through water.

Peter said nothing, remaining quiet and cynical as he sat on the window's edge.

Gwen tried again, rising off her feet. The motion of swimming helped her. It made the sensation of gliding more familiar… Of course, she was lifting off and moving through the air! It was no different than swimming, and it felt perfectly natural. As Gwen took off, soaring around her little sister's bedroom, she lost all notion of reality for a minute. It made perfect sense in that moment. Of course a heart as light and buoyant as hers could carry her whole body like a balloon.

When she looked back at Peter, she caught him smiling. His eyes looked, at all times, as if he were just a second away from winking. "Let's go," he announced.

"Wait," Gwen pleaded, realizing how woefully unprepared she was to embark on this trip. "Give me just a second to put a dress on."

As eager and excited as she now was to takeoff for an

impossible paradise, Gwen did not feel as though it was in good taste to fly to Neverland in a tank top and polka-dotted pajama bottoms. Landing gracefully back on her feet, she ran through the Jack-and-Jill to her own room. Fumbling through the darkness, she found her blue sundress from yesterday and snatched it off the floor so that she could throw it on over her pajamas. She grabbed her satchel purse, but she didn't bother to put her wallet in it. She couldn't remember what was in the bag, but she didn't want to leave reality unprepared. That would have been childish. She stuffed a white cardigan into the purse and hoped for the best.

Tootles mewed, baring his pointy, white teeth from on top of Gwen's bed. His collar jangled as he shook himself, dropping cat hair all over her sheets. Thinking of her poor parents, Gwen knew it would be cruel to vanish with as little notice or reason as Rosemary had. Gwen grabbed a sharpie and a stack of post-it notes on her desk. Jotting the words down quickly in thick, black letters, she wrote:

Keeping Rose safe until I can bring her home.

They wouldn't notice it immediately, but Gwen hoped her parents' fears would be assuaged by this little note of explanation when they eventually found it. Gwen was trying to be responsible. As she turned, she knocked her school books off her desk. She grabbed her math composition book and saw it had fallen open to an elephant cartoon captioned: *This is irrelephant.*

Gwen had a moment of doubt, contemplating Jay's doodle.

Closing up her book, she set it gingerly on her desk. She would come back home and return to all of this later. Homecoming was still weeks away, and Ms. Whitman's math class wasn't going anywhere.

Hollyhock had flitted into the room after her. A

particularly curious fairy, she had wanted to investigate Gwen's bedroom. She was delightedly going through all the book titles she could neither read nor recognize. Hollyhock was about to inspect the stuffed animals and tiny Christmas lights over Gwen's bed, but Tootles hissed, so she scurried away from the feline.

Tootles was mewing up a storm now, as if screeching at Gwen not to leave. The tabby cat was running all around the room, constantly underfoot as Gwen made her way back to the bathroom. "Sorry, Tootles," she whispered. "Take care of Mom and Dad."

She closed the bathroom door behind her to keep Tootles from following after her. Hollyhock just barely made it back with her before the door shut, leaving a fast dissolving trail of fairy dust raining down on Tootles.

Peter and Rosemary were hanging right outside of the window. The window screen had fallen down into Mrs. Hoffman's rosebushes a story below. Gwen stepped up to the cold window, clutching her satchel bag at her side and holding a fistful of her blue dress with her other hand. Gwen was a wild mess, her bed-head entirely uncombed and her pajamas visible even under the blue dress. For a brief moment, she questioned whether she was prepared for the consequences of her decision, but she banished those thoughts. As soon as she did, she found that she was floating once again.

Rosemary pirouetted in the air and giggled as her sister flew out the window to join them. The October night air felt warmer as soon as Gwen gave herself over to it, and the chill vanished as she hovered magically through the air. As she floated, it never occurred to her that the fairy dust might give out and cause her to crash down. Gwen had given herself over to the promise and power of Peter's magic, and there was no doubt left in her mind as the young man smiled and announced, "To Neverland."

CHAPTER 10

THE NIGHT BECAME WARMER THE FARTHER INTO IT THEY FLEW. Gwen's dress fluttered at her legs and her polka-dotted pajama bottoms blew in the breeze she created. Zipping alongside her sister, following after Peter, she began laughing with hysterical joy. She could have pulled hair ties from out of her purse, but the feel of her hair flying around her was too much fun. She grabbed Rosemary's hand, not to keep track of her little sister as she had so many times before, but to communicate her joy. The experience of flying was too beautifully strange for Gwen to endure on her own. She had to hold onto someone, to feel another warm hand telling her that this moment was as real as it felt.

They flew over rooftops and housetops, already estranged from suburbia as they blew past its yellow streetlights and manicured lawns. The dark shingles and sleeping cars had been part of her world yesterday, but not tonight. As soon as she felt herself flying, Gwen's heart abandoned any qualms it might have had about disowning the world. It had been kind to her, but it had never made her feel as though she belonged in it.

She followed after Peter, amazed that he never looked back, until she realized she wasn't looking back either. Hollyhock danced through the air, going twice as fast as any of them, but zigzagging all around. She bounced on the air, full of glee.

"Where are we going?" Gwen asked. "Or, I mean, which way are we going to get there?" As far as she could tell, they were just aimlessly flying.

"Round the moon and down the way the stars go," Peter answered.

"I thought it was second star to the right or something," Gwen responded, trying to remember how the story went, while at the same time questioning the authenticity of a book about childhood written by an adult.

"They're watching that pathway," Peter announced. "We can't risk them catching us there."

Gwen was acutely aware that this was not how she expected Peter Pan to talk, to look, or to act. After all, this boy was not a child but a teenager, and Gwen could hardly expect to believe he was the infamous Peter Pan that the adults of her world loathed. She didn't think she was being rude, only direct, when she asked, "Who are you?"

"Who are you?" he echoed.

"I asked first."

"But you care more, so you'll answer first."

Peter flew on, Gwen at his side and Rosemary trailing behind with Hollyhock. He said nothing more, totally content to let the conversation die on that note. Hoping to prompt something more from him, Gwen gave in. "I'm Gwendolyn Lucinda Hoffman. Who are you?"

"Peter Pan," he announced. His voice was full of pride, as if he never got tired of answering the question he had been so reluctant to address.

"I thought Peter Pan was a boy who never grew up."

"You thought Peter Pan was real, not just a character from a book?" Peter responded, awkwardly continuing in the third person.

"Well, no, I *did* think he was fictional—"

"Then I guess you don't always think right."

Peter zipped ahead, trying to leave her in the dust. "Peter, wait!" Gwen called, even though she realized he wasn't really going to abandon them.

"No. Keep up," he replied.

"How is it that you're so much older than in the stories?" Gwen asked. "I thought people didn't age in Neverland."

There was honest curiosity, and even a smidge of concern, in her voice, which must have been why Peter decided to dignify the question with a response. "Am I in Neverland tonight?"

It seemed like a trick question to Gwen. "No… I suppose not."

"That catches up with you."

Gwen had never considered this. How often did Peter Pan rendezvous back to the real world he'd abandoned? If he was constantly fetching children away from their drab futures as adults, Gwen could see how decades of travel between worlds would wear on him.

It was silly to doubt that he was Peter Pan. There was no denying the puckishness of his nature, nor the childishly handsome grace he carried himself with. He flew, utterly carefree, like a firefly meandering through the evening.

As they flew up to the moon, Gwen caught sight of his eyes, seeing the ivy-green color of his irises and their golden centers. His long hair was shoddily cut and windblown. When he looked Gwen in the eyes, she felt as if she were staring into a mirror, that she had found someone who reflected an aspect of herself she had hardly even been aware of.

Rosemary was giggling delightedly as she shot past them, ever closer to the moon, with Hollyhock bounding along in leaping strides. The moon seemed to grow to an impossible size, and Gwen lost track of how far they were from the buildings below them. The silvery, white light of the moon engulfed them. They seemed to be flying impossibly close to it, but Gwen was aware of how probable it was that they were doing the impossible.

"Are we really going to Neverland?" she whispered, finally allowing herself to believe it. She had left her house under the guise of going for Rosemary's sake, but now she questioned what impulse had really guided her. Rosemary danced through the air, content and lighthearted. Her little sister didn't need protecting or watching after, not in the sense that Gwen could possibly hope to provide for her.

Peter smiled, each tooth like a star. His smile seemed to radiate light. She knew how silly her question must have sounded, but he seemed happy to answer it. "We're halfway there."

It would have been hard for Gwen to explain what happened then but, fortunately, no one would ever call on her to explain it. Where she was going, everybody else had already experienced it.

The stars began to blow out, one by one, falling away from their static places in the heavens. Each and every one of them became shooting stars, dipping down or zipping away. Gwen couldn't tell which way was up anymore, so it was impossible to say which direction the twinkling stars were going. The only pinpricks of light that hung in the air now were the little granules of dust Hollyhock left behind before she landed on Peter's shoulder, tucking herself securely into his ivy-vine sash. The moon became all encompassing, and Gwen realized that she was being pulled toward it. She was no longer swimming through the sky, but rather being drawn through the darkness to that sole source of otherworldly light.

The world, what was left of it, sped away, and Gwen screamed with glee as she felt herself being whisked away in one direction after another, faster and faster. Soon, there was nothing left but the glow of the moon, and even that was illusionary. As Gwen's eyes adjusted to it, she realized she was drifting through the air in pristine daylight.

CHAPTER 11

THEY WERE ABOVE THE CLOUDS, WHICH POSSESSED THE SAME bright glow as the moon they'd been chasing just moments ago. Gwen took a big breath before diving through them, as if she thought she was about to submerge herself underwater. Following Peter and Rosemary, Gwen drifted down and emerged on the other side. The haze of the white cumulus cloud dispersed, revealing a paradisiacal island below it.

The stunning blue waters lapped against the sunny sand of the shore, and a multitude of greens wove together in a seemingly limitless jungle. The shape of the island was hard to comprehend as they rapidly approached it. They came at it from a direction known in Neverland as *weast*, which meant they soared to the jungle passing between Cannibal's Cove and the Mermaid's Lagoon. Shooting over the peninsula that divided the two landmarks, Peter guided the girls through a bright new day in Neverland.

They stayed above the tree line until they reached the grove, and Rosemary knew the final stretch well enough to lead them there. Rosemary hit the ground running with utter joy and ample laughter. Gwen slowed and stopped to watch her sister land, but she was seized by a sudden self-conscious thought. She didn't know how to land. She had hardly figured out how to fly, and now she was supposed to know how to gracefully stop? She felt as though she was on a bike with too much momentum to simply slam on the brakes. The more she panicked about it, the more her form faltered. Soon, it wasn't a matter of trying to land, but of recovering from her crash.

Her flying gave out, and Gwen thudded down to the soft bed of uncut grass, turning her fall into a somersault as she did so. The recovery would have been seamless, if not for the startled yell that she let out. With her big mouth open, it was soon full of grass and dirt. Rosemary laughed at her older sister, but Gwen could not object. She found herself smiling, even as she spit the grass out of her mouth.

Gwen was speechless as she finally touched down in Neverland, an impossible place she had long ago stopped believing in. Even the colors were brighter. The air was permeated with summery warmth. There was no doubt in her mind that she had just stumbled out of a bleak October reality and into a magnificent, eternal summer.

Summer! When was the last time that word had carried such an all-encompassing sense of promise and adventure? When she was little, summer had been synonymous with freedom. She'd lived through so many eternal summers, but those eternities had long since slipped away. As a child, how could she have comprehended at the start of any given summer that it would eventually end? Long into her childhood, she had suffered a beautiful object-impermanence in regard to the calendar and seasons. In the moment that school let out and summer swept children away on the wings of fantasy, it was an endless thing. Gwen had never questioned how the immortality of summer had escaped her as she aged, but now, for the first time since that indeterminate point in her youth, she felt the infinity of summer swallowing her again.

Surrounded by towering trees that seemed all at once exotic and Seussian, Gwen marveled at the way they stretched up toward the sky, their leaves like paint splatters of green against the blue canvass. While gazing up at them, Gwen caught sight of an intricate system of colored ropes that ran between the trees. She didn't understand what this was until Peter came swooping down. He pulled a slingshot out of his back pocket and swept up a rock from off the ground. While still in motion, he shot the rock off with remarkable precision, and Gwen watched in awe as it triggered a Rube Goldberg contraption amid the trees.

She couldn't quite follow the motion when it started, but the initial impact of the rock struck against a brassy bell. It echoed like a gong as the colored ropes unraveled, revealing themselves to be, not ropes, but tightly wound cloths. One after another, they were released and allowed to unfurl down to the ground. In electric blues, ecstatic oranges, and enduring reds, they fell to the floor of the grove. Still more sheets unfurled, engulfing and surrounding a small section of the grove they had landed in. Bubblegum pink, lime green, sunshine yellow, and the brightest shades of crimson and turquoise.

What was more, the initial brassy bell had released a cascade of smaller silver bells as well, and Gwen watched a massive oak tree as strings of tiny, glittering bells plummeted down, jingling like Christmas.

Gwen felt secure inside of an adventure, a rare sensation that she duly appreciated. There was safety in this moment, engulfed in this labyrinth of a cloth fort, but she could not imagine what the future might hold from one moment to the next.

The bells had heralded Peter's arrival, and a stream of children erupted from the Earth to welcome him home. Some came from camouflaged hammocks high in the trees, others bubbled up out of tree stumps, and still others from indeterminate places under layers of morning glory vines. From Gwen's perspective, they seemed to pour out of nowhere.

"Peter! Peter!" they all cried, overjoyed to see him again, skipping and prancing below him, waiting for him to land among them as they laughed.

Peter was still in the air, playing up his arrival with dramatic flourish and narcissistic pleasure. As he dove down, soaring within an arm's reach of the ground, zesty red poppies sprang up, trailing after him. He landed at last, laughing. As he struck a victorious pose, he was swarmed by the giggling children. Gwen watched in awe, but her little sister wandered to her side.

"How long has he been gone?" Gwen asked. From the looks of it, the children had not seen him in weeks.

"Just since yesterday," Rosemary said. "We only left to get you."

Two shirtless boys danced around him, making as much of a ruckus as they could. Two girls tugged on his arms, and a third nestled herself at his feet, wrapping herself around one of his legs. Hollyhock hovered, never straying far from Peter, but bouncing off each child's head.

"I have returned!" he triumphantly announced. "And I have brought Rosemary's storyteller!"

When he looked to Gwen, all wide eyes fell on her. The excitable faces of the children glowed with new enthusiasm as they surveyed her. In a second's time, they had all run to her. Deserting Peter, they approached her with a slightly more skeptical delight.

"It doesn't look much like a storyteller," the taller of the boys announced. Several of the children pointed and laughed at Gwen.

"How would you know what a storyteller looks like?" a boy with buck teeth asked him.

"What kind of stories does it tell, Sal?" a startlingly blond boy asked, leaning in much too close in order to stare at Gwen, unblinkingly, in the eye.

"Why don't you ask it, Newt?" Sal replied.

Gwen looked at the short, blond boy and tried not to be intimidated by the sheer intensity of his vivid blue eyes. "What's your name?"

"I'm Newt, and this is Sal."

"Newt's not a name for a boy," Gwen replied.

"It's short for Newton."

"Oh."

"And mine's short for Salamander."

"What?"

Taking Sal's advice, the eldest of the girls, a pudgy-faced child, no older than twelve, asked, "Excuse me, but what kind of stories do you tell?"

Rosemary piped up, eager to endorse her older sister. "The best stories, Bard! She tells fantastic stories about princesses and stars and race car drivers."

Sal and Newt exchanged glances before bursting into laughter. There was nothing inherently funny about this, but Gwen was fast learning that laughter was an adequate response to anything in Neverland.

"Then that settles it," Peter proclaimed. "She shall tell us a story tonight—the best and most fantastic story."

Gwen felt she was being unfairly put on the spot. "I don't know that—"

The children cheered, but a pigtailed girl asked, "And if she doesn't?"

"If she doesn't?" Peter echoed, as if it were a wholly irrational thought. "If she doesn't tell the most fantastic story we've ever heard, we'll tie her to a stake in the jungle and leave her!"

"Or walk her off the cliffs!"

"Or feed her to the lions!"

"Or dump her in the lagoon!"

The children were as happy to dream up punishments for Gwen as they were to meet her, and Gwen could not say she liked the way things were going. She shot Rosemary a mean glance, but her little sister did not seem to realize what she had committed her older sister to.

A third, dark girl had been far from quiet, but had not yet spoken. She had a drum at her side, secured by a strap around her shoulder. She began beating on it, chanting in a gibberish that her comrades were happy to join in on. Clapping, stomping, and dancing, they formed an untouching conga line around Gwen. Utterly out of her element, Gwen looked to Peter, but all he said was, "A story, Gwen-Dollie, or it's off the cliffs and into the cove!"

As Peter pulled out a homemade flute and began playing a whimsical tune for the Lost Brigade to march to, Gwen leaned over and whispered to Rosemary. "They won't really throw me off a cliff, will they?"

Rosemary, stoically looking at her sister, informed Gwen, "You'd better just tell them a good story."

CHAPTER 12

GWEN FOUND IT SURPRISINGLY DIFFICULT TO NAVIGATE THROUGH the labyrinth of sheets that constructed their fort in the forest. She was also confused as to whether she was in a forest or a jungle. Huge oak trees were rooted deep in the Earth, alongside palms and peeling Eucalyptus trees. Paper-thin leaves clung to tree branches as often as pine needles spread out over clustered branches. The children seemed to use the words jungle and forest interchangeably, depending on their moods.

Peter vanished with the smallest and nosiest of the boys just as quickly as he had arrived, leaving the rest of them to their own devices now that they were full of renewed energy. It wasn't long before the oldest of the girls, little Bard, decided what festivities were in order.

"I think," she began, with modest conviction, "that before the story, we should prepare a feast for Peter's return."

That simple proposal was all it took to animate her fellows, and they sprang into action, each dreaming up an equally frivolous role they might have in the planning of a feast. Everyone scattered to gather food, find torches, and decorate with flowers. Even Rosemary darted away into the woods in search of fresh eggs. Gwen felt a pang of guilt and inadequacy seize her as soon as Rosemary left her sight. She wasn't doing a very good job of watching after her little sister.

She sat, sifting through her emotions and finding mostly confusion. She'd never thought of confusion as its own, independent emotion. Confusion had always been an intellectual state that described the emotions she was feeling, but today, that was all she felt. Confusion and bafflement. There weren't even other emotions for her to be confused and baffled by. Instinctively, she reached into her satchel for her phone to check the time. It was out of cell range and not functioning. Gwen severely doubted that clocks were going to be of any use to her while she was here anyway.

Bard, the one child who had not run off to pursue some aspect of her own proposal, quietly approached her. Gwen sat in the grass, still spellbound by her surroundings, trying to figure out what animal off in the distance was making that cooing, whirling noise.

Bard picked a handful of the blood-red poppies that had sprung up in Peter's presence. She sat down near Gwen and bashfully looked up at her. "Can I put flowers in your hair?" she finally asked.

"Uh, sure."

She walked smartly behind her and began braiding the long-stemmed poppies into Gwen's light brown hair. Bard had a calming presence and prided herself on being very mature for an eleven-year-old. "Rosemary told me that you were a big kid, but I didn't think you'd be as big as Peter," Bard politely remarked. Bard suspected that Gwen was actually a little older than Peter—she was a very smart eleven-year-old—but she wasn't going to point that out.

"Uh, yeah," Gwen responded, feeling submissive at Bard's touch.

"What kind of stories do you tell?"

"Nice stories," Gwen said. "I try to tell nice stories."

"That's good. I had a brother who would tell me mean, scary stories, and I didn't like that at all. We haven't met properly though. I'm Bard."

"Hi, Bard. I'm Gwen, I think… I think I'm still Gwen." She was slightly unsure of that. Everything else had changed in the past day, maybe she had too.

Bard took Gwen's answer in stride. "It's a pleasure to meet you, Gwen."

She was intimidated by how calm Bard seemed. Feeling wildly out of her element, Gwen didn't know how a child could be so confident, or seem so knowledgeable. If she had any pretensions about the sort of rights or wisdom that came with age, it was time to forsake them. Neverland was not a place that lent credence or privilege to age. As counterintuitive as it seemed to ask a child for help or information, Gwen quickly realized that was the only way she was going to make sense of anything here. "What's going to happen, Bard?"

"Just about everything we can think of, and everything everyone else thinks of, too. The others are going to go get fruit and food and pick up all sorts of wonderful things for a feast tonight. When Peter gets back, maybe he'll play us a song or we will all dance until we fall down. If it's a real celebration, perhaps someone will even bring back some good mud for squishing toes in and making muddy feetprints. I think that Spurt went with Peter to get Neverland fruit for you in case you tell a good story, and I know that Newt and Sal are braiding ivy ropes so that we can bind you and throw you in the lagoon if you tell a bad one. But don't worry, I have confidence in you. If it's just a so-so story, maybe we won't even have to throw you in the lagoon at all, so long as you tell a better one tomorrow night. I like your pajamas."

Gwen was dazed by all this nonsensical information. She didn't rightfully process any of it, except for the final compliment, to which she groggily responded, "Thanks." Gwen had endured a sleepless night, and she'd left well before dawn. The sun was high overhead here, and she wondered what time zone Neverland was in. She was incredibly tired and let loose a yawning roar as Bard finished the loose, elegant braid. Taking a ribbon out of her pocket, she sweetly tied Gwen's hair with the tiny, ratty strand of pink that looked to have come off a present a long time ago.

"I think I might just… fall asleep." Gwen sighed, lying down as she felt Bard's hands leave her. It wasn't just the sleep deprivation; it was the overwhelming change of circumstances and confusion as well. She slumped into the grass; it was the sweetest bed she had ever encountered. It was lush but not wet, and it softly folded over itself. As she closed her eyes and nestled down into the ground, she questioned why she had ever slept in a bed. Clearly, the ground was a much better place to sleep. The best, in fact. Beds and mattresses, frames and sheets… these were yet more grown-up conspiracies. When she got home, she was going to get rid of her bed and just start sleeping in the yard.

Bard retreated, leaving Gwen to sleep in the sunlight. Meandering over to one of the trees where she knew the fairy Bramble would be sleeping, she knocked gently and roused him. With his groggy help, Bard covered Gwen and gathered some of the sheets to turn part of the fort into a tiny recluse for the sleeping teenager. Once that was done, Bramble darted off in the hope of finding more interesting endeavors now that he was awake, but Bard diligently sat just outside of the impromptu teepee, braiding poppies into a bright red crown for their honored storyteller.

13

GWEN WOKE UP TO THE SOUND OF POORLY STIFLED GIGGLING. Something was obviously happening, but she was too disoriented to comprehend her environment. Once again, she groped for her phone in an attempt to make sense of the world with it, only to remember it was no use to her. Her daytime dreaming had been a vague affair—she woke up thinking of Jay, but that thought quickly dissolved. Darkness encroached on every inch of the tiny teepee that had been constructed around her. She hardly remembered falling asleep in the grass, let alone tucked away in this tent. How had she slept through the entire day? Dozens of questions flashed through her mind. The only thing she didn't question was whether her adventure had been a dream. For as bizarre and unbelievable as it all was, it felt more real than anything else had in a very long time. Neverland's fairies and flying were fantastic, true, but Gwen felt so quintessentially alive when she encountered them. The metal lockers and plastic desk seats of high school had never endowed her with this intense feeling of life.

The giggling continued, ebbing and flowing as the nearby

children wavered between almost reining in their laughter and utterly losing themselves in it as their giggles infectiously spread to one another. It was getting worse. They weren't going to get tired of laughing in anticipation, they were just going to get more antsy and giggly until something happened. Whatever that was, Gwen was certain of two things. One, it undoubtedly involved her, and two, there was no way for her to avoid it.

Having no other option—unless she wanted to sit in the sheets and wait to be ambushed—Gwen crept out and prepared to be accosted in the open. To her surprise, she was not immediately swarmed, tackled, or otherwise attacked. She moved slowly. She could hear the children, and from the influx of giggling, she assumed they could see her too. Something was glowing ahead of her, but she could only faintly make out the light through the cloth curtain. Winding her way through the labyrinth of curtains, Gwen saw motion here and there, like hiding children darting behind the sheets, just out of sight.

Gwen's hair was coming undone, but Bard's little pink ribbon clung tight to the now falling-out braid. She felt strange, as she always did after sleeping through a whole day, jet-lagged or sick. Moving cautiously, Gwen felt her heart pounding in her chest, heavy and slow. There was no reason for her to be afraid, much less scared of children! At worst, they would ram into her too hard when they charged her. There was absolutely nothing to fear, and yet, Gwen was afraid. Her palms began to sweat as she crept about, and she felt herself woefully unprepared to face whatever startling force she was about to confront. Gwen couldn't remember the last time she had been so terrified. She loved it.

How long ago had her last game of hide and seek been? When was the last time she had played kick-the-can and attempted to sneak her way past her playmates? It had been too long since she felt this awful, jostling sense of doom over something totally harmless. Her gut told her she was being stalked, watched, and preyed upon, but her mind and heart could not have felt lighter. She had forgotten the tenacious and feverous joy of fear when nothing was at stake.

As she finally escaped the fort, Gwen spilled out into the unobstructed grove, the moon rising from behind a monolithic oak. The torches were staked in two rows, creating an eerie aisle up to a jaggedly broken, bulging tree stump, on which Peter was sitting.

He made a throne of the towering stump, leaning against its back and sinking into its mossy base. Kicking his feet up, he lounged with a nonchalant, princely presence. His eyes were on Gwen as soon as she came into sight.

Leaves rustled violently, and Gwen realized the children were tucked away in the trees. She saw Newt and Sal in one, lying on adjacent branches, their bellies against the bark.

Bard was situated on a rope swing, hanging low to the ground. She leapt down and approached Gwen, crowning her with the wreath of poppies she had woven while the girl slept.

Gwen leaned down and accepted the crown, but she moved like a zombie, stunned and uncertain how she was supposed to react to this whimsical stimuli. She felt she was playing a game unaware of the rules.

She drew closer to Peter, approaching and looking up at him from his high throne. Gwen couldn't begin to imagine what the tree had looked like before it shattered, or what monstrous force had toppled it.

As she passed them, the children scaled out of the trees, creeping through the darkness and following as her tiny entourage. Their giggling unified and harmonized, like a chant or song, but it was neither. It was only the rawest expression of joy.

They managed to calm themselves, and by the time Gwen thought to look back at them, they had already taken their seats, happily situated on the floor of the grove, surrounding her and facing Peter.

In her blue dress, polka-dotted pajama bottoms, and poppy crown, Gwen waited for something to happen.

"So," Peter began, his high and boyish voice booming to the best of its ability, "we gather for a story, and we will have a story from her or we'll have her head!" The children cheered.

Somewhat detached from her circumstances, Gwen was more troubled by the fact that they were constantly changing her form of execution than the fact that they seemed to be planning to execute her. Gwen suddenly wished she had thought of a story today rather than nap in the grass.

She looked up to the sky for inspiration, and it was freely given. Seeing the stars, as bright as they were numerous, Gwen had a thought for a story.

She didn't know what she was going to say from one word to the next, and yet the story seeped fluidly out of her lips. It was not her story, only one she happened to be telling.

"Once, not that long ago, there was a man named Eugene, who was an anthropologist, someone who studies strange, new cultures. Well, a strange new culture was discovered, on an island that no one even knew existed until some sailors were blown off course and landed there after a storm. They saw fires and huts, but they didn't dare venture onto land, for fear the inhabitants would be unfriendly, possibly cannibals who would devour them whole. So they sailed back home and told everyone of the island they had found.

"When Eugene heard about it, he made up his mind right away to head to that island and study the people there. He found the sailors and the captain who had landed there by accident, convincing them to set sail to that island with him aboard. The captain and his crew were reluctant to embark on the voyage, but Eugene paid them handsomely and they finally agreed, on the sole condition that they would not have to put foot on the island themselves. They were deathly afraid of the natives.

"So they set sail within a week's time, and Eugene bravely embarked on his mission, not knowing what he would find when he arrived. The journey took them several days of bad weather and treacherous seas, but he was sailing with an able crew, and they survived. On the final day, the weather cleared, and they approached the island under blue skies.

"They moored the ship in the sandy waters of a calm bay. Two of the crewmen rowed a dinghy to shore, but were too afraid to as much as step out of the boat. Eugene was left, all alone on the shore, with only his pack of rations and bushwhacking supplies."

"What's bushwhacking?" one of the girls whispered.

"Shush, Jam. It's what happens when you whack a bush," Bard informed her.

"He traveled through the jungle, slashing through the vines and brush and bramble, heading for the village and hoping he would be well received. He didn't have far to go—the islanders lived near the shore—and it was not very late into the morning by the time he arrived at the edge of their village.

"The people of the island, who knew their home as Moon Island and called themselves Astrians, were surprised to see an outsider. No one had ever come out of the jungle before, let alone wearing such strange clothes as the bushwhacking anthropologist did. They were dressed in clothes made of vines and leaves.

"Still, they welcomed the stranger into their village. They

greeted him warmly, touching his shoulders in greeting and shaking his hand when he offered it. They were a friendly people, and they were excited to meet the stranger. They prepared a great celebration, gathering their drums and lighting their torches. Eugene was given an elaborate robe to wear to honor him as their guest. Their storyteller told him the story of their people while others busied themselves within the village, readying the celebration. This delighted Eugene, who took notes furiously in his book, recording every detail the storyteller shared about the history of the tribe.

"He assumed, while he was listening to the storyteller, that the other villagers were preparing a feast of some sort as part of the celebration."

"We prepared a feast!" Newt blurted. Sal clunked him on head, and he was quiet after that.

"Evening fell though, and there was no food in sight. What's more, Eugene had not seen any of the natives eat anything all day. He had thought that odd during the day, but he had not wanted to remark. Now that dusk was setting in and the people still were not eating, Eugene began to wonder. As he began to think about it, he realized that he had not seen anything edible during his entire time on the island. He had passed no fruit trees; there had not even been animals. All day, he had not seen so much as a bird flitting through the trees.

"The chief prepared a bed for their guest within his own home, but Eugene was horribly hungry and could not stand the mystery any longer. By the glow of the fire pit, he approached the chief and finally asked him when his people ate.

"The chief looked at him quizzically, answering 'At night, of course. When else?'

"Eugene was relieved to know they would be eating shortly

now that night had fallen, but he still did not understand. 'But what do you eat?'

"The chief was very confused by his question, for he thought it would be obvious. 'The stars. We eat the stars.'

"Eugene could not comprehend this answer, but the chief gestured to his fellows, and Eugene saw them as they reached up to the sky to eat for the day. He wandered among them, watching as they stretched arms up to the cloudless night and opened up their palms only to close them around the stars. Mystified, Eugene stared silently on as he watched the islanders pluck the twinkling stars out of the dark night. Holding them in their palms and between their fingers, they fed themselves from the fruit of the night sky.

"At last, a young woman with long, dark hair and big, bright eyes took note of Eugene. She swallowed the star in her mouth and approached him, inviting him to join her in this strange dinner. Skeptically, Eugene followed her motions, reaching up to the star she gestured to. The rest of the village was clearing the sky of stars, but as they finished, there were still a few beautiful and twinkling stars left for Eugene. The brightest of all of these, he wrapped his hand around. When it disappeared, he was so surprised he almost let it go again, dropping it out of his palm before he could bring it back down to his mouth. He looked at it in his hand, shimmering and glowing, before swallowing it whole.

"It was smooth, but it tingled as it rolled down his throat, almost like a liquid. It tasted sweet, but unlike any food he had ever eaten before. He continued to eat, one star after another, until he noticed that his fingers were beginning to glow.

"Eugene felt something wrong inside of himself, something bubbling up within him that was unsettling and discomforting. Feeling as though he were about to be violently sick, he ran away from the fire pit to get away from his gracious and magical hosts. He dashed just a little ways into the jungle so that he could escape their eyes and let the feeling pass.

"Collapsing among the trees, he felt something inside of himself rising. It was not an urge to be sick however; it was the stars themselves trying to return to the sky. For you see, Eugene was not one of the star-eating people, and he could not stomach the celestial fruit."

"What's *celestial*?" Jam asked, even more amazed with that bold, new word.

"Shush, listen," the smallest girl instructed. She did not know the word either, but that did not impede her appreciation of the story. Gwen continued.

"He began digging a hole in the soft dirt, trying to push his glowing hands deep into the Earth, grounding himself so he would not be pulled away by the force of the stars lifting him up. No matter how hard he tried, Eugene could not fight it, and the stars consumed him as they pulled back up to the sky. He became the stars, the night, and the darkness.

"But even once they had returned to their place in the night sky, something was wrong with the stars because they carried with them all the pieces of Eugene that still belonged on Earth, pieces that resisted rising, pulling back down to the ground.

"So one by one, the stars that Eugene had eaten, that were now irretrievably mingled with his very being but returned to the night, began to slip out of the sky. They became falling stars, falling into the minds and hearts of people all over the world, shooting their way into music and paintings. That's how I know this story, because one of his stars fell straight into my head while I was dreaming, and that little piece of him told me, clearly promised, *Reach for the stars and they will be freely given.*"

Gwen held her hands in front of her then, waiting quietly for a reaction. The children held their breath, wondering if that really was the end of the story, and if so, what they were supposed to make of it.

Peter, still perched with regal nonchalance on his mangled throne of a tree stump, responded, "That was a good story."

The lost children got to their feet and burst into jubilant cries, following Peter's judgment. He impishly smiled. They wouldn't have to drown Gwen in the lagoon after all. The children were more excited now about having a feast than an execution anyway.

CHAPTER 14

THE FEAST WAS MAGNIFICENT. THERE WERE MORE FRUITS THAN Gwen ever knew existed, and some she was certain didn't. Sal and Newt had gone fishing and brought back trout they had delighted in disgustingly gutting. There was a thick vegetable soup that Bard had been responsible for, and freshly squeezed juice that little Jam had squished into existence using whatever fruits struck her fancy. Blink had even procured some milk from Miss Daisy, which Gwen assumed was a cow, although she was informed by the youngest of the boys, Spurt, that it was birds' milk. Gwen didn't know what to believe, or whether her belief had any bearing on the reality of what she was eating. She was, however, acutely aware that the egg-shaped fruit her little sister served her had twinkling, raven-black shells and a plain white yolk that tasted almost like marshmallow filling. In Neverland, everything that occurred appeared to be a quantum supposition of fantasy and reality, and simply believing in an event seemed to change its outcome.

Gwen was adorned with more flowery jewelry, including

daisy-chain bracelets and a wild zinnia that the dark little girl, Blink, had brought back for her. The massive flower had a hard time staying put behind her ear until Bard weaved it into her hair. Dinner was served in the jungle, at a crudely assembled banquet table made from the cross section of a fallen tree. The children rolled slices of tree trunks up to it like seats, and proceeded to make a grand mess of all the food they had assembled. Much as Eugene had been in her story, Gwen was a guest of honor and treated to the finest and most fantastic food the island could offer.

Their meal was illuminated by torches, which Gwen found were utterly without fire. What the children called torches were really just small platforms on tall, wooden poles. The reason they radiated light was because fairies had flown up to them to waltz and glow on the tiny dance floors. Before the children distracted her, all eager for her attention, Gwen saw Hollyhock dancing with a dapper fairy boy who glowed slightly more orange than gold.

Jam and Spurt grabbed her hands and dragged her to the table, asking a million questions between the two of them. Rosemary pushed through the throng of lost children to sit beside Gwen and beam with pride as the others enviously marveled over her big sister.

Gwen could hardly keep the children straight. The only ones she knew were the oldest girl, Bard, and the duo that was Newt and Sal. They seemed to go everywhere together, but it was easy to keep the two of them straight. Newt was short, and Sal was tall. Newt's short hair was blond, and Sal's mop of hair was brown. They both had blue eyes, but animated Newt's were piercing and bold, whereas lanky Sal had eyes of a mellow, marshy color.

In order to match all the children to their odd names, Gwen convinced them to tell her about themselves. They did so eagerly. In their world, coolness was measured by age, up until the point when someone became a grown-up. Older kids had a presumed level of wisdom, if only at checkers and storytelling. It didn't take much to win the respect of children, and by asking them in earnest about themselves, Gwen managed that much.

It was telling, what each child focused on as they vied for Gwen's attention.

Bard spoke modestly about her sewing and hopscotch records, letting her accomplishments speak for her, and added that she had once held a baby without dropping him to further her credibility as a caregiver. Jam spoke longest, despite talking the fastest. However, she managed to say very little about herself. Most of what she said had to do with her favorite parts of stories that she had read. By the end of it, Gwen did know that Jam liked princesses who saved themselves, witches who were sometimes good, and the name Eleanor. Jam was a very beautiful girl, with a round face framed by her pigtails, and a bookish glint in her bright blue eyes. Had she not been younger than Newt, Gwen would have mistaken them for twins.

As for Newt, he and Sal explained themselves together, stumbling over each other in their excitement to volley the conversation back and forth. From the gate, Gwen knew she couldn't trust anything they said. They constantly changed their stories, trying to one-up each other or weave each other into memories they weren't part of or hadn't made yet. There was no coherency to their stories, which made them unbelievable even in the environment of Neverland.

Spurt was the smallest of all of them, and he seemed peacefully offset from the two totally in-sync boys and all the girls. He was dark-haired and freckled, with a mouth full of funny teeth and a face full of expression. Spurt had energy, but no productive use for it. He spoke little, but he was constantly loud. His laughter was incessant, his screaming his primary means of communication. He raced from person to person, as if he were a shadow who couldn't make up his mind whom he belonged to. Gwen never got more from him than his name.

Blink, the tiniest of the girls, was far more composed, one of those children who had a no-nonsense attitude about their nonsense. Her brown eyes were soft against her dark complexion, and her attention was hard to break once it was focused on something. Blink stared at things curiously, with a steadfast devotion that ran counter to her name. Her tone was incredibly happy, but her face rarely reflected her joy. When given a chance to explain herself, she explained her future. She had a clear vision of her future as a musician, a champion swimmer, and a renowned scientist… but never did *when I grow up* creep into her explanation. Blink seemed to be under the impression that she could accomplish all that she wanted to within the realm of childhood, and for all Gwen knew, it was well within her capacity.

Rosemary interjected here and there to bring attention back to herself. She was full of positive observations and compliments, pertinent to the situation. Gwen listened whenever Rosemary volunteered that Blink was the best tree climber she had ever seen, or that Newt and Sal knew how to sword fight, but Gwen's attention began to drift as the conversation fractured into a whimsical cross between fish tales and duck-duck-goose. Her eyes were on Peter, who had slowly distanced himself from the feast and headed back to the grove.

Absorbed in their own antics, the young children did not much care as Gwen slunk away from the table. They continued boisterously, but she crept through the forest, stepping softly with her bare feet. Only the fairies noticed her leave, and of that bunch, only Hollyhock was interested to see where she was going. Her dancing partner, Bramble, had long since abandoned her to gorge himself on the food lain out as part of the children's feast.

It is an inescapable truth that every fairy in Neverland was terribly afflicted with one vice. On all other counts, the fairies were generally good and noble creatures, but each one had one failing, one Achilles' heel within their moral fiber. For Bramble, it was gluttony. He could never pass up a speck of food, and he had been known to abandon far more important endeavors than dancing in the pursuit of sweet food. If left undisturbed, Bramble was liable to indulge until his stomach ached with the richness and quantity of food he piled into it, leaving him no occupation but lying belly-up, inert and idle. Had Spurt not decided to chase after him and play cat-and-mouse games with the gluttonous fairy, Bramble might have eaten himself into that state at this feast as well.

Of course, being new to Neverland, Gwen did not know this about fairies. So she could neither have known what Hollyhock's particular vice was, or that it was the worst of all vices.

Wrath could find its outlets, gluttony could be satiated, and even envy could be tempered. What troubled other fairies were very simple vices that had limits and constrictions. Hollyhock was a different case though, because her vice was bred from virtuous desire and innocent incomprehension. Hollyhock was curious. There are few things as dangerous as curiosity, for it is never satiated and curious people are always coming up with more questions to ask. In a world constricted by the necessity of growing up, it was seen as imperative to human survival that the majority of people outgrow their curiousness, but in Neverland, they had quite a different view of the issue, and Hollyhock's curiosity was perennially left unchecked.

Her curiosity was what prompted her to follow Gwen, to see where she was going, hear what she would say, and observe how she would say it… even if Hollyhock already knew exactly who Gwen was going to go say it to.

CHAPTER 15

UNAWARE SHE WAS TRAILED BY THE GLITTERING HOLLYHOCK, Gwen approached Peter's darkened stump. Her feet were cautious against the cool grass of the grove, and she half expected the boy to order her away, he appeared so nestled in his own thoughts. Peter made no objection though. He didn't even look at her.

Only when Gwen came to the foot of his stump and finally said, "Hello," did he even give her a fleeting glance. Strolling around the stump and bending down so that she could stare directly into his askance eyes, Gwen prodded, "It's polite to acknowledge people when they greet you."

Peter looked at her and replied, "Consider yourself acknowledged."

Gwen stood patiently. When Peter gave her another quick glance, she asked, "May I join you?"

Without verbalizing an answer, Peter stood up on his stump and sat on one of its knotty edges. Gwen climbed up, her bare feet feeling their way across the dry bark and spongy moss of the shattered tree trunk. He seemed reluctant to let her up, but more at ease once she was on his level with him. She sat opposite of Peter and said, "You left the feast."

Peter had a handful of berries that he was absently eating, but he had not taken anything else with him from the table. "So have you."

"Why?"

"Everyone was telling their stories. I already know all their stories. It was boring."

Gwen pulled her knees up to her chest as she perched on part of the massive stump. The cuffs of her polka dot pajamas were already getting dirty. "But I never got to hear your story." Peter didn't seem inclined to respond to that remark. "I mean, you carried me off to Neverland, I've been here all day, and I haven't any idea who you are."

"I'm Peter Pan," he informed her.

"Just like in my stories?"

"Just like."

"Not quite."

Peter gave her a wary glance. Gwen knew age would be a sensitive subject, and she didn't dare do more than hint at it. Everything else about him was just the way she had once pictured it, in imaginings long since forgotten in the wake of algebra homework and driver's ed classes. Gwen didn't know what to make of him, and Peter offered no assistance on that front.

"This is a neat stump."

His toes wormed their way into a patch of fluffy moss. "It used to be a neater tree."

"It looks like lightning struck it."

Peter's eyes narrowed, as if angry, but he delighted in the mysteriousness of his answer, "It was a different sort of storm that killed it."

"Oh?" Gwen gave him a look of wild curiosity, prompting

an excited explanation.

"A horrible storm. Electricity can ferry so much information back and forth. That's why they attack with it. They think they can kill things and pinpoint our location. They can't though. Neverland is too smart.

"Who are *they*?"

Peter didn't even bother to look at her. "Don't be stupid," he instructed.

Gwen remembered flying to Neverland, and what he had told her as they flew up to the moon. "You said *they* were watching one of the pathways. What does that mean?"

Peter looked at her, as if her ignorance was insulting him personally. "Do you really not know what's been going on?"

"You're taking kids to Neverland. Parents are freaking out. What's there to get?"

Peter scoffed at her, watching his feet as he wiggled his toes. He continued to lounge in the lightning-shattered stump, offering no answer.

"Why did you carry me off to Neverland?"

"I didn't carry you here," Peter objected. "You flew. Hollyhock gave you a bit of dust, and you did the rest yourself. Anyone who wants to go to Neverland for the right reasons can get there."

"What are the right reasons?" Gwen asked. She could hear crickets in the grass nearby, but they sounded like they were neighing, not chirping. Usually slightly paranoid about bugs, Gwen didn't feel like she had to worry at all about spiders or worms out here. Whatever creatures crawled and crept across Neverland wouldn't be as disgusting as the bugs back home.

"You know—adventure, mischief, exploration, curiosity… good reasons. That's why so few adults can ever get here, even when they try to come destroy us."

Gwen surveyed the stump. It looked brutalized. "Adults

did this?"

Peter was more somber than she ever imagined he could be when he informed her, "We're fighting a war, Gwen. We're building a resistance."

Gwen laughed nervously, simultaneously trying to communicate that she didn't believe that in the least, and that she really did. "A resistance against what?"

"Against all the adults who think we should have no choice as to whether or not we age. Against everything that says magic can't be entrusted to people, that it has to be committed to organizations and groups, used to forward *grown-up* agendas."

Gwen had only recently been introduced to the idea of magic as a functioning aspect of reality. Her father had explained it to her in brief, never mentioning that there were other sides to the argument. Gwen tried to wrap her mind around this new perspective, but it was hard enough to imagine that this was somehow a politicized issue.

"But Peter, isn't it only natural?" Gwen timidly asked. "Haven't you figured out by now that everyone needs to grow up? Maybe a few of you can exist on the fringe of reality out here, but everything depends on the fact that people eventually grow up."

"Everything there is different from everything here. They have a system in place, but no one's going to tell me that makes it natural. Or even if it is, natural isn't the same as right. Normal isn't the same as moral. Everyone deserves a say in what happens to the world, and the only reason they don't have it is because kids don't know any better than to believe their moms and dads when they say growing up is such a wonderful thing. It's stupid… Do *you* want to grow up?"

"I think I might already *be* up," Gwen quietly confessed. The mere fact that she could argue the other side gave a dangerous insight to how deep the hooks of adulthood were in her.

"Nonsense," Peter said. "If you were grown up, you wouldn't have come here. Nobody who's grown up ever flies to Neverland. They might get here through other means, but they sure as snowsalt don't fly."

"I'm not a kid," Gwen said.

"Well then," Peter said, "if you believe that, I think the real question is… why *did* you let yourself be carried off to Neverland?"

He had stumped her, and Peter reveled in the argument he had won. Gwen knew what she had told herself about why she followed after Peter and Rosemary, but there were a hundred other reasons brewing in her heart and mind, all in conflict with each other. Gwen couldn't think of why she had flown off to this place—she could only dream up every possible reason someone in her position *might* have taken off for Neverland. She had told herself that she was going to watch after Rosemary and keep her safe, but her little sister was currently in the jungle romping around with six other children while Gwen sat, curled up on a stump, talking to a boy. Gwen had hardly seen Rosemary since they'd touched down in the grove.

"I guess so I could tell a story," Gwen answered, feeling as though she ought to produce an answer, no matter how flimsy. It was comforting just to have a response.

"It was an alright story," Peter told her.

"Didn't you like it?" Gwen asked. She resented his aloofness.

"It was good; it just wasn't great." He was so casual about it; Gwen couldn't stand it.

"Well, what kept it from being great?" All the other children had loved it, so Gwen wouldn't have minded even if

Peter hated it. Or at least, she wouldn't have minded as much. His seeming indifference was maddening.

Peter shrugged, as if it wasn't anything in particular, or anything important. Gwen waited, determined to make him to defend his position. "It was unrealistic," he finally retorted.

Gwen couldn't believe his audacity. "How could that possibly bother you?"

"It was just so obvious from the way you told the story that you'd never *actually* eaten a star."

"Well, of course I haven—" Gwen stopped, suddenly realizing that it was more than likely her point wasn't valid in Neverland. After all, if it *was* possible to eat a star, Peter Pan would know. She paused before it dawned on her what her response should be. "Will you help me eat one now?"

Peter looked at the stars and then back at Gwen. "Alright," he passively agreed, as if he were not about to facilitate a magical cosmic phenomenon for Gwen. "Which one do you want?"

Gwen had not thought this far ahead. She looked up at the sky, and for the first time in her life, she was truly baffled by the sheer quantity of the stars. At home, she had marveled over them, but they had been the dim and limited stars of a suburban sky. Even when she had been camping and seen the night sky in all its glory, Gwen had never been asked to pick between them. Now that she was asked to choose just one, she realized how many there were. "I don't know," she answered. "I don't want to take one that will be missed."

"It'll be back by tomorrow night," Peter promised. "If they didn't replenish themselves… well, just think how long ago people would have eaten all the stars out of the sky. It just depends on what kind of flavor you want." Peter gestured to the stars as he explained each one's particular taste. Gwen leaned close to him, to see as he pointed. "Sirius is sort of fruity and spicy, but Vega has this meaty, chocolate taste. If you wanted something creamy and sour, you could always try Rigel."

Gwen took this in, but she was busy searching for a star that jumped out at her. She leaned in the nook of the stump, scanning the sky like a kid in a candy store. "What about that one?"

Peter shifted on the stump, leaning closer to Gwen to see which one she was pointing to. "Eltanin? Eh, sure."

As Peter withdrew, Gwen tried to fish the star out of the sky. As focused as she was on it, she couldn't manage to grab it. Peter laughed at her. "You can't pull a star out of the sky while you're on the ground." He was in good spirits now, which Gwen appreciated even if it was at her expense. He put two fingers in his mouth, making a sound that purred and whistled at the same time.

Hollyhock, still watching from behind a heavy oak leaf in the tree above, didn't want to give herself away by darting down to answer the call. Fortunately, Dillweed had heard it, and came to Peter's aid. There weren't many fairies who answered to Peter with such devotion. Too many fairies were afflicted with sloth or pride, such that they wouldn't answer Peter's call, but Dillweed came readily, although somewhat unsteadily. Dillweed was given to drink, and that was his vice. There was no fairy who was quicker to rationalize a drink or find a reason for drunken revelry. The feast had made it particularly easy for him to justify a whole blossom full of honeysuckle mead.

He landed on Peter's shoulder, holding onto the boy's ear to steady himself. Smiling stupidly, the fairy steadied his double vision as Peter pointed. "Do you see that star, Dill? That's the one we need. Think you can bring it down for us?"

Dillweed nodded his pink face, but he felt compelled

to climb up Peter's extended arm rather than take off on his wings. Only once he had scaled to the top of the boy's finger did he leap into the air and set his fluttery wings into motion. Dillweed didn't have to go far to capture the star. He grabbed it in both of his hands, bringing it slowly back down. It seemed bigger to Gwen, once it was out of the sky. It was hard to tell how brightly it was glowing when Dillweed's shimmer encompassed it, but the silvery, white light of it was more intense than his faint red glow.

He handed it off to Peter, who in turn ruffled the fairy's mop of hair with a single finger. Dillweed chuckled drunkenly, a noise which sounded more like crystal ringing than any laughter Gwen had ever heard. The tiny fairy flew off and away, too inebriated to notice Hollyhock even as he passed her hiding place.

"Here you are," Peter said, presenting her with the cosmic fruit. He dropped it in her hands. "You can thank me later. Maybe you'll tell better stories once you eat it."

Gwen held it in her hands like a marble. It felt warm and viscous, like a tiny ball of warm Jell-O rolling around over the lines of her palm. She wanted so badly to eat it—to swallow it whole and let it worm and wiggle within her insides—and like all of her deep desires, Gwen questioned it. Something inherently told her to resist the path of easiest pleasure and quickest reward. Although Peter assured her that the sky would replenish its stars by tomorrow evening, Gwen was certain that eating a star would come with consequences. She didn't know how it would affect her, but she wanted to clear one thing up before she went any farther with this fantasy.

"I can't stay here," she declared.

"What does that have to do with eating stars?"

"I don't know," Gwen said. "But I need you to know that… I have to go home."

"Do we bore you so terribly?" Peter asked.

"Not at all," she answered. "This… this enchants me. Too much so. I need to go home, and I'm going to do everything in my power to convince Rosemary to go back with me too."

"You really don't want her to be happy here, do you?"

"No," Gwen responded. "I don't want her to be happy *here*. I want her to be happy in the real world. It's impossible not to be happy here, in paradise. It wouldn't mean anything."

"You think you can't be unhappy in paradise?"

Gwen delved into Peter's eyes, looking for emotion. She was sure it was there, but she couldn't decipher it. Peter's face remained childishly blank and impossible to read. He was still too much of a child to know the range of emotions that Gwen was coming into. He knew excitement, but he had never been impassioned. There was love, but he did not understand commitment. Somewhere in him, he had frustration, but his temperament had never broached anger in the consuming sense that adults gravitated toward.

Gwen felt as though she'd insulted him, and he hadn't even realized it.

Peter seemed to give the matter some brief thought and then triumphantly stood up on his stump. "I will need to return in a week's time to search for an ally who is traveling and hiding within reality. When I go, I will take you home, and Rosemary as well, if that is what you two want."

"Thank you, Peter."

"Now, are you going to eat the star or not?"

Hollyhock watched on, feeling as though she should warn her, but not having the gall to interrupt them.

Gwen smiled at him, finally plopping the bright marble into her mouth. It rolled on her tongue, and she softly trapped it between her teeth. Biting down on it, she found it was gummy and soft. Chewing it like a caramel, she found that aspects of it melted into her mouth. It tasted like hazelnuts and milk, but the flavor changed the longer she spent chewing it. There was a peppery spice to it, but she could not place it. The more she chewed the star, the more massive it became. It seemed to be expanding and inflating, gumming up her teeth and growing into such a sticky mess that she could hardly move her jaw. Gwen tried to speak, but her garbled words were unintelligible.

Hollyhock shook her head and fluttered away, knowing she should have warned the big little girl. The children had quieted down after their feast though, and nothing sparked her curiosity faster than children who weren't making noise. She left to investigate.

Peter leapt down off the stump, rolling into a somersault on the ground as he did so. His laugh was playfully vicious—the sort of laughter children make when trying to appear villainous for the sake of a game. Gwen began yelling, or rather making flustered noises, as she struggled with a mouthful of star.

"I told you," he cried. "I told you that your story would have been different if you'd ever tried to eat a star!"

Gwen moaned a little, hoping he would help her through this predicament now that he'd had his laugh. She felt claustrophobic within her own body when she was unable to move the mouth she so frequently used for communication, eating, and breathing.

She jumped down and stumbled to her feet on the ground, running up to Peter. Her mouth was now firmly fixed in a half-opened state. Peter peered into her mouth, and she watched as he leaned closer, his face illuminated by the light that was seeping out. His green eyes caught the glint of it, but their twinkle remained all his own. "Oh wow," he said. Gwen squeaked, unsure what that remark portended. "How much did you chew it?"

Gwen whimpered.

"You're a dumb girl." It didn't sound like an insult; it just sounded like a reality. "Didn't you realize it was turning to star goo in your mouth?"

Gwen objected with a whining grunt. He hadn't warned her at all.

"Come on," he instructed, waving her after him with his hand. "We need to wash that out before it supernovas."

A shrill, "Mahhhammmma!" was all Gwen could say to articulate how terrified and confused she was at the prospect of having a star explode in her mouth. She raced after Peter, also afraid that she might lose him in the dark of the night and be left to explode by herself.

He dashed into the woods, extraordinarily light on his feet. Gwen felt herself bounding through the forest with increasing ease as well, but it was hard for her to make a conscious note of it when she was so distracted by the star gunking up her mouth. It was getting warmer, but not yet uncomfortably so.

She couldn't have said exactly when they started flying, only that they lifted off the ground at some point. They didn't touch down again until they had made it to the stream.

In the middle of the slow creek was a tiny islet, hardly big enough for Gwen and Peter to both set foot on. They landed there however, and Peter encouraged her. "Have a drink and wash your star down. Put it out before it blows out."

Gwen kneeled down, her knees resting against the uneven pebbles of the river's exposed bed. She cupped her hands and lifted the fresh water up to her mouth, hurriedly pouring it in. She had drunk like this before, but never from a body of water. Sometimes, when she could not be bothered to get a cup down, Gwen had taken a quick drink from the kitchen sink in this manner. There was something novel about it. Her mother had seen her do it once though and been appalled. *Just get a glass, Gwendolyn… and don't wipe your hands on your shirt!*

As she regained the ability to move her jaw, Gwen swished the water around in her mouth and let it dissolve the last of the star, washing it away into her gut where it glowed much more peacefully. All and all, the slight burning sensation reminded her of the time she had tasted a sip of her grandfather's bourbon. She wiped her hands on her dress. They were only wet with water, after all.

Her mouth felt slightly numb, and Peter was still snickering at her. An idea occurred to Gwen, but she didn't know if she was confident enough in her flying to attempt it. Deciding it was worth the risk, she pooled water into her hands one last time, standing up quickly to sling as much water as she could on Peter. Under pressure, she could not directly take off. Before he could react, she got a running start, tromping three steps across the bitty island, into the shallow stream bed, and launching herself from there. The bottoms of her pajamas dripped water, but Gwen did not think about her soggy pants as she rose into the air, fleeing Peter as he pursued her back to the grove. Rolling through the air, all Gwen thought about was the sound of her amusement. She had never appreciated it before. In Neverland, even her own laughter was brand new and full of magic.

CHAPTER 16

WHEN THE CHILDREN WERE FINISHED WITH THEIR FEAST, THEY abandoned it without hesitation. What little food was left on their wooden plates and tin spoons was devoured by the fairies. After an evening of dancing, they were all delighted to nibble away the last of the fruit and drink up the last of the milk. All of them except for Bramble, who had eaten alongside the children and gorged himself into a swollen, tired state already.

They tromped, jolly and excited, back to the grove to find Peter. He was there, with Gwen, but by the time the children had all ambled back, they were too full and sleepy to think of anything but bed.

Spurt, after a wild day of incessant energy, was totally spent and almost fell asleep on the grass outside. Bard prodded him and took his hand, leading him to the hollow tree that would slide them down into their underground home. Newt and Sal, in a final burst of excitement for the day, raced each other down their separate shoots. Blink and Jam slipped down a tree, one after another. Rosemary tried to get

Gwen to follow, but when she approached the pine tree that her little sister disappeared down, she knew there was no way she would fit through the slender crack in the trunk.

Instead, Peter took her with him as he flew up to the branches of the giant oak tree. Gwen had not known how afraid of heights she was until Peter Pan asked her to walk across branches three stories above the ground in the dark. She followed him and was careful with her footing. Holding onto branches above her, she steadied herself as she crept toward the trunk.

"It's just like I told you," Peter announced, immediately worrying Gwen, since he hadn't told her anything. "Just let your breath out as you go down and you won't get stuck in the trunk."

Stuck? In a thirty-foot oak tree? That was a possibility? Gwen had never known she was claustrophobic until Peter tried to put her in a tree.

"Oh, and one more thing," Peter said. He didn't seem to be very focused on what he was telling Gwen, and she was worried there were actually many more things she ought to hear before she attempted to go down on her own. "Breathe out slowly at the very end, so you don't hit the ground at full tilt."

With that last remark, he jumped into the hole in the oak tree, vanishing silently. Gwen could hardly bring herself to admit how much this startled her. She looked down to see if any children were left in the grove to better explain this process. Surely, Bard could shed some insight or encouragement, or maybe Spurt was small enough to go down with her so she wouldn't be so alone in this? There was no one though, and Gwen resigned herself to diving into the tree alone.

With slow, delicate motions, she lowered herself into the hole. At first, she braced herself against the inner walls of the trunk, holding herself in place with her feet, hands, and stiff back. Once she was used to the feeling of being inside of the dark tree, all Gwen had to do was loosen up to begin falling.

As she whooshed through the darkness to an underground destination she did not understand, Gwen began to scream. Her dress fluttered up around her, and her hair became a tangled mess. She tried to stop herself again, but it was no use. The further down she went, the wider the trunk became.

At last she toppled out of the darkness and into a room full of mellow light. She put her arms up in front of her shocked eyes, clenching her eyes shut and bracing herself poorly for the fall. When she slammed against the ground, it was bouncy and soft. It did not feel like a ground at all. Gwen opened her eyes and saw that she had fallen directly on top of a bed. The children were all gathered around her, and they had obviously been waiting for her to fall.

"I told you moving the bed would be a good idea. I knew she'd fall," Newt declared.

Jam stared at her, confused and disappointed. "But she's a big kid. How do you not know how to go down a tree if you've been a kid for so long?"

Gwen awkwardly sat on the quilt bedspread, and Bard climbed up to comfort her. "But it's her first time," Bard justified. "My first time, I got stuck and Peter had to finish pulling me down. Have a cookie."

Bard gave Gwen a cookie, and in that simple gesture, the totality of the embarrassment she felt vanished. The children didn't care—and certainly weren't going to remember—that she had screwed up this first descent. From the look on Spurt's tired, freckly face, he had already forgotten everything that'd happened in the past two minutes. This was not like arriving in homeroom late or that time she'd shown up to class crying out of her left eye because she had flinched, forcing Claire to stab her in the eye while applying mascara. No one was going to remember this. As children, what did they care who had blundered or how? Tomorrow, one of them would do something equally stupid. It was inevitable, and they respected that.

The other girls climbed up into the bed. Jam and Blink nestled themselves against Gwen, and Rosemary dashed up behind her so that she could wrap her arms around her sister. Everyone was still watching her, but Gwen quietly stuck the cookie in her mouth and took a small bite. It was delicious, and still soft.

She broke the cookie in half, handing the smaller half to Rosemary and keeping the larger half for herself—it was her cookie, after all.

"No fair! I want a cookie too!" Spurt objected. Bard hushed him as she climbed off the bed, pulling another cookie out of her pocket. She handed it to sugar-hungry Spurt. As he ate it, she wrapped her arms around him from behind and carried him off. She was the biggest and he was the smallest, but it was still hard for her to properly carry him. She took him over to a tiny, woolly bed that was made up on the floor. It was a dog bed, but no one questioned why Spurt slept in it, or why he liked it.

"Will Gwen sleep with us or in the big bed?" Blink asked. Gwen kept waiting to see some sort of hesitance, reluctance, or indecision exhibited by Blink, but as far as Gwen could tell, Blink was the single most confident and direct human being she had ever come across.

"Yes! Yes!" Jam yelled, bouncing on the quilted bed.

"Gwen can sleep wherever she wants," Peter replied. Gwen heard his voice, but she did not see him. She began looking for him in the big, underground room. The walls were lined with the roots of all the trees that shot down into it, and the floor was made of the red-brown dirt. Vines crept all around the roots and ceiling, full of strange lilies that were more like lamps than blossoms. Thus the room was dimly lit with the yellow and blue glow of flowers that had lights in place of filaments.

There were places where roots did not cover the walls, where hollowed-out alcoves were filled with all manners of things. Ancient books with broken spines were piled in one tiny nook, alongside markers, crayons, and paper. There were dishes, most of them chipped, and a traveling trunk left open… revealing what was perhaps the grandest collection of dress-up clothes any child could ever hope to own. The largest and roundest of these alcoves had a little ladder leading into it, and Gwen saw that Bard and Blink were already tucking themselves away in it for the night.

Toadstools of epic proportions cropped up from the earthy floor, and they looked to be the perfect size for a child's seat. There was a small tree in the center of the room, not far from the foot of the bed. It was just a sapling, but Gwen could see some bird—or other creature—had already built a nest amid its green, heart-shaped leaves.

An apple core startled her as it fell from the ceiling and crashed down beside the sapling. Gwen looked up and finally saw Peter almost directly overhead, lounging in the hammock after having finished his apple. His arms were stretched out, his hands under his head. He glanced down at Gwen, smiling when he saw her look of amusement. He said nothing to her.

"She's too big!" Newt complained as Sal climbed up onto the bed. Newt was smaller, and he had to leap up acrobatically in order to get on top of the bed. "She won't fit!"

Rosemary perched on the headboard of the bed, like a happy little hunchbacked gargoyle. "Of course she will."

Jam pointed and gestured as she informed her bedmates, "Newt and Sal, you two can sleep on that side, and then Gwen can sleep to my right and Rosemary can sleep to my left."

"We want to sleep on that side," Sal announced, crawling over the bed with Newt.

"If she's on the left side, what if she kicks me in my sleep?" Newt added.

"I want to sleep next to my sister!" Rosemary said.

"I'm not sure I will fit…" Gwen admitted.

They squabbled just long enough to tire themselves out, and then totally reversed everything Jam suggested. Sal and Newt slept toe-to-toe with Jam and Rosemary, for the bed was big enough for small children to do so. Gwen slept next to Rosemary on one side of the bed, so she wouldn't have to worry about squishing anyone else. As the conversation died down, so did the lights, which would only glow as long as people were awake.

The tired Neverlandians fell right asleep, but Gwen held onto consciousness. She'd spent all day sleeping, and she needed to let her overworked mind unwind before it could ease into sleep again. She scratched Rosemary's hair, and Rosemary murmured, half-awake. Gwen snuggled away from Rosemary for a moment, but she grabbed her sister's hand. She wanted to be alone to think, she wanted to be close to someone for comfort, and she wanted to stay awake and be asleep.

Rosemary wasn't quite asleep yet. Whispering quietly, Gwen told her little sister, "Peter's going to fly us home in a week."

Rosemary mumbled a quiet protest.

Gwen kissed her sister's head and wrapped an arm around her. "We'll go home then, and it will be nice. We'll have to go home, Rose, but we can stay and play until then."

Rosemary didn't object. She only whispered, "Let's have an adventure tomorrow," before falling asleep and making a sweet little humming noise as she breathed through her nose.

CHAPTER 17

IT HAD BEEN YEARS SINCE GWEN HAD WOKEN UP BEFORE TEN IN THE morning without the belligerent assistance of an alarm clock. However, that was a function of how late she stayed up most nights, surfing the internet like an incessant series of waves she felt obligated to meet, one after another. There had been no cat videos or Facebook pictures of Jay to keep her up last night. She'd gone right to sleep, and had dreams untroubled by visions of school corridors and homecoming anxiety.

Consequently, she woke up right at dawn. She didn't know it was dawn, buried deep in the burrow. She initially assumed, from how well rested she felt, that it must have been noon.

The others were all still sound asleep, curled up in the strangest positions, as children are wont to do when sleeping. The only other soul awake seemed to be Peter. He was sneaking through the underground home, breathing on all the lily lights to wake them up to start glowing for the day. His belongings were shuffled and tucked away in every corner of the oblong, corner-less room. His knife was stuck in the wall, helping pin up a tightly woven tapestry, his flute was left on one of the toadstools, and the particular hat he wanted for today was buried at the very bottom of their traveling chest of clothes.

He had been quiet up until he rustled the chainmail in the trunk. Gwen wondered if that was what had woken her up. The other children weren't disturbed by it though. He looked like he was about to take off on some kind of escapade. Worry-free now that she had a return date for reality, Gwen wasn't going to let a single adventure pass her by in the next week.

She scurried out of bed, doing her best not to disrupt any of the sleeping children. Newt and Sal were pressed up against each other, back to back, the covers thrown completely off. Rosemary was snuggled securely in the quilt, but Jam was sprawled out underneath it, her mouth agape as her little chest rose and fell with each sleeping breath. Peter saw Gwen's intention to come with him, and he waited for her. "Nice Phrygian cap," she said, proud of herself for recognizing the red cap of liberty she'd learned about in her history class.

"No, it's a hat," he told her.

He jumped up and caught hold of one of the strong oak roots like a monkey bar. Pulling himself on top of it, he stood up. He had to hunch, but he stepped aside so that there would be room for Gwen to pull herself up as well. She had a much harder go of it. There were many years between her and the last time she'd done whimsical acrobatics like this. She managed to kick her feet up well enough to grab the root with her toes, and then kicked her legs over it from there. Peter extended his hand and helped her to her feet. "Just breathe in as we go up. Ready?" Gwen nodded, exhaling with Peter before they both drew a deep breath and shot up, holding hands as they headed for the top of the oak. Daylight trickled in from the top, but Gwen could just barely make out the shape of Peter's face as they rocketed up.

They stepped out of the tree and onto a limb, Peter stretching and yawning as he did so. He struck a triumphant pose, enjoying the morning as if it were his and his alone.

"Going up is a lot easier than coming down," Gwen announced.

"That's because you had my help," Peter told her. "You wouldn't have been able to get out at all if it weren't for me."

"I think that's a little presumptuous," Gwen answered, stung but not hurt by the implication of ineptitude.

Peter launched off the oak tree with a running start, throwing himself into the air and flailing in free fall until he started flying, halfway to the ground already. Gwen descended with more grace, still getting used to the sensation of flying, or at least the taking off and landing bits. It had become immediately obvious to Gwen that the hardest parts of flying were the transitions. Once you were in the sky, you felt as though you could continue that way forever. It was having the confidence to start or the restraint to stop that made it hard.

Peter landed on the ground of the grove. The tent and colorful clothes were packed up again, exactly as they had been when Gwen first arrived. "Where are we going?"

He strode across the grove and went over to where Gwen had been enclosed in a teepee for her nap the day before. The satchel she had sloughed off was still in the grass. "I don't know where you're going, but I'm going to the lagoon." He picked up the purse and handed it to Gwen. She took it, thinking that no adventurer should ever be without their full arsenal of trinkets and doohickies.

"If you're coming with me, then you're going to meet the mermaids."

CHAPTER 18

THEY FLEW IN THE FOREST, NOT OVER IT, BUT THROUGH IT. THERE wasn't much fun in flying high over the island when there were trees and vines to swing from, strange birds to call to, and the occasional perfect piece of whittling wood to be found. Peter had a very impish way of traveling, and took his time flying when he was not in a hurry.

They passed several fairies who flitted, chuckled, and gossiped as they witnessed young Peter and his companion heading for the infamous Mermaid Lagoon. When they passed by Hollyhock, Peter invited her along, but the orange fairy could not be tempted onto an adventure when she knew that Peter was only going to the lagoon. Fairies and mermaids were very different creatures, and although fairies could usually understand English, the way in which mermaids spoke somehow baffled and confounded them. Without a water nymph to translate, fairies and mermaids could have no natural communication. Consequently, Hollyhock found it terribly dull to go to the lagoon and only hear Peter's half of the conversation.

So Peter ambled on with neither a fairy nor any apparent concern for them. He flew happily from tree to tree, playing with anything that looked the least bit inviting. Gwen was content to meander in the same way, but she stayed closer to the ground, watching golden snakes slither away and inspecting the multitude of flowers she found deeper in the forest. She asked every question that flitted into her mind. For once, she felt free to admit her ignorance without facing judgment. Peter already thought she was foolish and stupid, and that didn't seem to impede his opinion of her. He answered every question with the same enthusiasm she asked it. He had just finished explaining the explosive nature of the pale purple popping flower when it occurred to Gwen that he might just be making everything up. By that time though, they were already at the lagoon.

They landed and moved slowly through the jungle for the last few hundred feet, giving Peter time to explain to Gwen as she walked at his side.

"If you've never met a mermaid before, there are a few things you should know about them."

"Like what?"

"Like they are the most cunning and conniving creatures you will ever cross paths with."

"Really?" Gwen asked, astounded. "I would have thought mermaids would be… I don't know, beautiful and sweet."

"Sirens, all of them. They'll do anything to get what they want. Mermaids have no qualms about the means to the end, so long as it's their end they get to."

"Well, what do they want?"

"It's always some kind of trouble… not that they'll ever tell you what they want."

Peter barreled through a clump of vines, hanging low in his way. Gwen followed after him, her curiosity compounding with every moment. "Are they dangerous then?"

"Terribly," Peter responded. "So there are three rules for whenever you confront mermaids. First, don't get too near to them; second, don't get too close to them; and third, don't *ever* get in the water with them."

"Alright. Easy enough," Gwen said, wondering if there was a working difference between the first and second rule.

"The best thing to remember," Peter continued, "is that mermaids will never tell you what they're after, and it's best to assume it's something dastardly. Whatever they want from you, whatever they want you to do, just don't."

"Well, if they're so terrible, why are we going to meet with them?" Gwen asked, not seeing what good could come of the encounter.

"Because mermaids know things, and they can learn things you and I couldn't ever possibly learn, even if someone spent a hundred years trying to teach us… and they have information right now that I need."

Peter caught sight of a papaya tree and reached up to pick its fruit. It seemed impossible for Peter to pass up ripe fruit, so he beckoned to Gwen and filled her satchel with a few. He found a mango tree, and tossed Gwen a few of those fruits as well.

"Will the mermaids tell you?" Gwen asked. "If you're so bent on thwarting them, what's to stop them from giving you misinformation to spite you?"

"They're very easy to coerce," Peter said, his mouth full of mango, "and the one good thing about mermaids is they can't lie."

"They can't?"

"Nope. Not even a tiny white lie. Mermaids don't go against their word, and they stick to the bargains they strike. But that makes them even more dangerous, obviously."

Gwen didn't see how that was obvious at all. If anything, it seemed like that would make them less of a threat, but there wasn't time to press the conversation further. They broke the tree line and found themselves on the edge of a small cliff. Crude steps carved into the cliff's face led down to a rocky lagoon. Below, the beautiful bay of blue-green water was so clear and still that it was easy to make out the silhouettes of the slender, aquatic nymphs swimming beneath the surface.

CHAPTER 19

PETER AND GWEN CLIMBED DOWN THE CLIFF'S WEATHERED PATH. From moment to moment, Gwen changed her mind as to whether she thought the uneven steps down were intentionally formed, or simply the fortunate product of nature. It didn't take them long to descend, and when they reached the shoreline, Peter climbed onto large rocks that led out to deeper waters. He settled on one that would keep them just high enough that the mermaids would not be able to reach out and grab them. Gwen crawled beside him. She knew better than to venture any closer than Peter did, but she stayed on her hands and knees, staring down into the water, searching it for the mysterious mermaids. Their shadows moved with seamless smoothness, and Gwen's heart raced. Flying and fairies were one thing, but mermaids presented a whole new strain of magic and fantasy.

Peter had picked up a few pebbles from the stony shore, and now chucked them gently into the water. One after another, he threw the small stones into the lagoon, letting them slip into the water and mark their point of entry with thin, graceful ripples.

Gwen gasped—out of delight or fear, she did not know—as the first of the shadows rose to the surface.

It was a gradual lift into a dead man's float. Gwen could only see the pale white flesh of the mermaid's back and the mass of rich, brunette hair. She lifted her head up slowly, as if only now coming to life, and then flicked it back with dramatic flourish, sending her hair flying behind her. As soon as she laid eyes on Peter, she smiled, all toothy and sly.

"Peter," Cynara cooed, swimming closer, "you've come to see us again."

Gwen could hardly keep her eyes on the creature as others surfaced. The red-headed Eglantine came straight up, keeping only her eyes above the water. She hung back, but eventually did rise up. "I wasn't expecting to see you today," Eglantine said, her accent soft and aquatic. They both seemed to have high, feminine voices. "You so rarely come around."

"I thought I would today though," Peter casually replied.

"Who's this you've brought with you?" Cynara asked, glancing only briefly at Gwen. The mermaids seemed far more interested in Peter, but the third and final mermaid surfaced closer to Gwen and stared at her with uncanny interest. The blonde mermaid remained quiet, but Gwen tried not to stare back, or betray how intimidated she was by her blue eyes. They were a lighthearted blue, surreal only in how human they were.

"This is Gwen."

"Gwen..." Cynara echoed, feeling the word with her tongue and hearing it in her own voice. "Is that so?"

"What is she?" the blue-eyed mermaid asked.

Peter didn't miss a beat, which was good because Gwen wasn't even sure how she could have answered the question. "She's a girl, Lasiandra."

That answer seemed to pacify her. Lasiandra retreated a ways, swimming to and fro as she followed the conversation. Her hair was much less voluminous than the other mermaids, and she seemed less engaging.

"What brings you to our lagoon, Peter?" Eglantine asked, her red curls bobbing in the water.

"What can we help you with?" Cynara sweetly cooed, pulling herself up just a little on the rock, making Gwen very uncomfortable. Kelp was woven together over her chest, slick and clinging to her wet body.

Peter did not react. "Have you been watching the sky?"

When she saw that she could not entice either of them closer, Cynara retreated into the water. Floating on her back, she splashed her tail playfully, her slender fins like whispers and spider webs as they fanned out and flexed in the water. Her scales glittered with a metallic sheen, catching the light and glittering beautifully. The whole motion gestured, *come here*, but as if that was not enough, she invited Peter in with her. "Of course I have watched the sky. I have seen it take shape and color every dusk and dawn, I've watched the clouds drift through it, and the planets amble by, murmuring their secrets to me and speaking of what's to come through their motion. Come into the water, Peter, come swim with me, and I will take you out past the horizon to the place where the stars sleep by day."

"Stars don't sleep," Gwen declared, although she doubted herself as she spoke. She was not trying to assert her own knowledge, so much as hoping Cynara would disprove her.

Eglantine laughed and swam nearer. "Silly girl. Peter, why do you have such a foolish girl with you today? The stars sleep the same as everything sleeps, and the moon rests with us in the time betwixt its set and rise. Deep within the waters, at depths you've never dreamed of, it sinks into our waves and plays with our tides."

They were enchantresses, and every coy word was designed to entice Gwen.

"You can swim with us too, Gwen," Cynara promised. "It's shallow… where your dreams sleep. You could see it."

"The water is fantastic," Lasiandra added, her voice sounding far more honest in contrast to the affected tone of the other sirens.

"No thank you," Gwen answered, knowing that this—much like the you-have-already won emails that piled up in her spam box—was simply too good to be true. Too vague an offer, too grand a promise. It wasn't worth finding out what the catch was. She was glad Peter had warned her. The mermaids and their propositions were appealing. People paid hundreds of dollars to swim with the dolphins and giant sea turtles in Hawaii, and here Gwen had a chance to swim with mermaids. If only she could have accepted the offer, confident that nothing would befall her!

"Oh, what a sore sort of girl," Eglantine said, pouting and turning all of her attention to Peter. "But you're more fun. You've got an adventurous heart, don't you, Peter? You'll come swim with us, won't you?"

"Not today," Peter answered. "There are other adventures to be had today."

Cynara was not amused. "When are you ever going to come with us, Peter? We have so much we could show you. We could teach you to read the skies for yourself."

"Why would I want that when I can trust you to read them so well?"

"I could tell you everything I know," Cynara promised. "I would, Peter, for you."

"But then what reason would I ever have to come back here to see you, Cynara?"

"You're welcome here any time. You don't have to come just to find out what the skies say."

"Aye, but today, that is what I need."

"You always need so much," Eglantine complained, floundering toward a rock and folding her arms over it. As she flicked her wet, curly hair away, Gwen could see the little bits of bright red coral, still living, that dangled as earrings from her ears.

"And you ladies always give me so much. I've brought you something today."

All three mermaids' heads picked up. They were beginning to grow tired of Peter until he made that announcement. "Have you finally brought us a sky glass?" Eglantine inquired.

"No, I've forgotten to look for one."

Cynara seemed upset, even angered by this. "If you knew what we could do with a sky glass, if you understood the power it would have in a mermaid's hands, you would not be so forgetful."

"You have not found one yet in all the expanse of the sea?"

"No glass is formed in the sea, Peter," Lasiandra reminded him. "But it is so plentiful on land."

"If I didn't know better," Cynara announced, coy and curt, "I would say you didn't *want* us to have a sky glass."

Everyone was quiet for a moment.

"Perhaps next time we meet, I will have acquired a sky glass for you," Peter answered. "But today, I bring fruit."

Smiles washed back onto the mermaids' faces. The announcement excited them and put Peter back in their favor.

"Land fruit?" Eglantine inquired.

"As if I would try to serve you any other, Eglantine."

Lasiandra seemed most enchanted of all. "Tell me you've brought me a mango, Peter. Tell me you've brought me a mango." Her tail fluttered enthusiastically beneath the surface, stirring up a froth of bubbles.

"Only papayas today."

Lasiandra's excitement was considerably diminished, and Gwen's heart sank a little when she saw the pretty mermaid's spirits fall. She wanted to share the mangoes hiding in her purse, but she didn't dare contradict Peter.

"Sorry, Lasiandra," he apologized as he pulled one of the papayas out of Gwen's pack and tossed it to the blonde mermaid. She caught it in her hands and held it tight, like a cherished treasure she was afraid to drop. Peter took a second papaya and threw it to Eglantine, but as he did so, Cynara begged, "Pass me one, too, Gwen. Hand it here."

Gwen reached into her satchel and was about to do so, but she briefly caught Peter's eye and remembered his instruction. Before she could bend down to hand it off to Cynara, Gwen responded, "Here, catch." Cynara caught it with ease as she gently threw it down to her, but there was slight disappointment in her eye.

Eglantine split her papaya open on a blunt rock and immediately began devouring its soft interior. Mermaids could stay underwater indefinitely, but they had no means to traverse land. Even if they climbed onto the rocks in their little lagoon, there was no conceivable way for them to scale up the cliff to the fruit trees that hung right above them, ever in sight and ever out of reach. The sea offered a rich feast of vegetables, kelps, seaweeds, and aquatic creatures, but nothing could compete with the sun-warmed sweetness of land fruit.

Cynara and Lasiandra also began to eat the bright orange fruits as Peter asked again, "Can you tell me what the sky has been doing, what the planets have been telling you?"

Although disappointed she would get nothing more out of him than fruit, Cynara was now willing to discuss the heavens with Peter. “The planets have been all unaligned for quite some time. There is disunity in the sky, and disharmony in the world. Pluto and Neptune will remain in the far corner of this wayward house for many years, but that is the way of this time. The war’s end is not in sight, and nothing you do now will end it.

“It is a turbulent moment, with Jupiter so far from its sister planets, and alone in its own distant house. Mercury is roaming quickly through the houses, but in little more than a week’s time, it will be alongside the other dark planets, just as Venus eclipses Mars.

“There is envy in the sky, Peter, and when the heavens are jealous, no good can come of it. The stars have stopped shooting. They are holding their breath and waiting to see what magic will govern them in the centuries to come. The sky will not help you, but it will not impede you. These bodies cannot assist in a matter such as your war, but they are firmly sided with you. When your stars and his align, you will have your chance to meet the minstrel. He still moves with the music of the spheres, for now. That music continues to play, but its sound is softening, Peter.

“You must understand that the magic is being drained from the mechanics of it. The constellations have left the stars and the man has left the moon. Your adversaries are emptying out the sky, Peter. They discover more and more every day, but they assign numbers and letters where once they gave names and legends. They are stripping the sky of its majesty. That is why the stars will not aid you in your battle—they are unable. They are too governed by physics and cannot bend to manifest their prophecies. They have whispered our destinies to us, but now it is in our hands to enact them.”

The mermaid bobbed in the water with playful mystery. Peter pensively considered her words. “Thank you, Cynara, this is… an interesting turn of events."

"The one you seek is on his way," she assured him. "His travels will be safe, and he will be invincible until he lifts his instrument again. The stars still love him, even if man has forgotten. If you want to find him, seek out the aviator, Peter. He is closer to the stars than you realize. The aviator has seen the whole world over from his place in the sky, and he will know how to find the piper."

"Will it really be that easy, Cynara?"

"Oh, by no means. Even if you find that minstrel, you'll still have to convince him to play his star-music once again… thank you for the papaya, Peter."

Cynara swam off, slyly smiling. She stayed on her back, but sank into the waters, her fruit still in her hands.

Lasiandra retreated, but she kept her eyes peeking out of the water. She still watched Gwen, hardly glancing at Peter at all during this encounter. Gwen held Lasiandra's eyes, but Peter seemed to have lost sight of her as she drifted back behind a low rock.

"Perhaps next time, you will come swim with us." Eglantine giggled. "Then you can speak to the planets yourself."

"Little boys cannot speak to stars; that's for those whose dreams are born beneath the saltwater sky."

"Silly, Peter," Eglantine replied as she, too, swam off. "Anyone can speak to the sky." She left the rind of her papaya floating, having already devoured all of its flesh. "The only hard part is getting it to talk back."

CHAPTER 20

PETER WAS IN A HURRY TO LEAVE THE LAGOON ONCE THE MERMAIDS were gone. Gwen was not entirely sure that Lasiandra had really left though. As she and Peter walked back across the rocks, Gwen thought she saw motion in the water beside them. Peter led the way, so his back was to her when she reached into her pack and pulled a mango out of her satchel. Gwen got quickly to her knees and leaned down to one of the low-lying rocks, placing the mango where it would be within a mermaid's reach. Gwen didn't know why she left it for Lasiandra, or if the mermaid would even find it there.

She got back to her feet before Peter could catch her in the act of… defiance? Kindness? Gwen didn't know what motivated her, and she didn't care to guess. Hurrying to catch up, she tripped over her own feet as she landed on the pebbly shore, landing on her hands and knees. She didn't hurt herself, but the contents of her purse's side pocket went flying, and it took her a second to gather them back up.

"What's the matter? Bugs get your feet?" he asked.

"Something like that," Gwen answered, not wanting to

decipher whether his expression was a permutation of cat-got-your-tongue, or if bugs legitimately ganged up on people in Neverland.

She gathered her things: her notepad, her coin purse, and her compact mirror, stuffing them all back into the side pocket. Continuing to riffle through her purse as they walked, she checked the mangoes to make sure they weren't bruised and shuffled through the side pockets to make sure she had everything she thought she needed. She had not yet taken inventory of her purse, and she couldn't recall what was jammed in it when she left home. Still, when she could not find her cell phone, she knew she must have lost it.

She and Peter had only just started up the steps back up to the bluff and jungle, so she asked him to wait a moment, running back to the place where she had tripped coming down off the rocks. Sure enough, her cell phone was lying there among the smoothed-over pebbles and rounded-down rocks. Peter was not in sight, but rather at the start of the path just around the bend in the cliff's face, so when Gwen noticed that the mango she left was gone, she didn't hesitate to venture a little closer to the place where she had left it.

Nervously glancing over her shoulder, Gwen reaffirmed that Peter was not coming back after her for any reason. There was something else sitting on the rock now. Her heart betrayed the excitement within her chest, but only Gwen could sense its nervous beating. She walked slowly, watching the water for any motion as she approached the rock. It was too low and close to the water's surface for comfort. The lagoon was as still as glass though.

Gwen picked up the token left in place of the mango. It was a glimmering coin, perfectly round and almost paper thin, shaped out of vivid, bright abalone. Like spilled oil in a rain puddle, the mother-of-pearl pattern was beautiful and fluidly random. Gwen felt its glossy surface, and then quickly pocketed it in her satchel. She didn't want Peter to question what was taking her so long. She had her phone and the strange totem from the mermaid as well.

It burned within her purse pocket, and Gwen itched to hold it in her palm again, but as she walked back with Peter up the cliff, she did not touch it. The coin remained in her purse, tucked securely away as she ventured back to the grove. She thought nothing of taking the mermaid's coin with her. After all, it had certainly been left for her, and she did not doubt that Lasiandra had wanted her to have it.

CHAPTER 21

It took Gwen a while to work up the audacity to ask about, what she presumed would be, a rather explosive subject. The following morning, after Gwen's encounter with the mermaids and the elaborate game of hide-and-seek that spanned across half the island, she finally asked Peter while in the underground home. "Are there… are there any pirates here?"

Peter smirked and continued peeling his apple, sitting on a toadstool chair. Jam hungrily gobbled up all the sweet skin of the apple, just as soon as he handed it to her. "Not anymore." He sheathed his knife at his hip, took a huge bite of the apple, and then passed it to Bard. As she munched the fruit, he stood up and began to speak. Hollyhock buzzed and trilled excitedly, rousing Bramble from the nap he was taking in the underground home's little tree so that he, too, could hear the story.

"The last of them were Captain Rackham's crew," Peter began. "They flew the skull and stars flag high on their mast, sailing a great flagship called the *Black Death*. It was a massive ship, with a hundred or more pirates all aboard it!"

"A hundred?"

"Maybe only a dozen," Peter amended. He continued, undaunted. "They swore that there was booty buried in our jungle, a chest, buried by the oldest of pirates, old Scarface himself, who was more like a god than a man to all the pirates who came after him. Rackham and his crew swore to find the rumored treasure.

"They sailed three times 'round Neverland clockwise, and twice counter-clockwise while they tried to make sense of their map. Finally, they came ashore and stormed the island. They found Blink and took her hostage, you know. They were convinced she knew where the treasure was buried."

Bard delicately nibbled on the peeled apple, watching Peter like a movie as he bounded around their underground home. Spurt was still asleep in his little dog bed, but the other children were waking up, happy to start the morning with one of Peter's stories. After a while, everyone but Spurt was awake and eagerly listening.

Hollyhock bounced up and down, adding her own commentary, seemingly for the sake of hearing her own singsong voice. Bramble listened, sleepy but attentive, to Hollyhock's version, while Peter related the story to the children. Peter told it exactly as he remembered it, so very little of what Gwen heard was true. Still, he got the feel of the story right, and that was what was really important.

"So then I flew up behind his first mate, who couldn't see me on account of the patch on his left eye."

"I thought you said the patch was on his right eye," Gwen interjected.

"It was," Peter replied. "He had patches over both of his eyes. That's why he couldn't see me."

Gwen shook her head, getting fed up with his impossible

story, but dying to know how it ended. "That doesn't make any sense. Why didn't you just say he was blind then? And if he was blind, why did you have to fly up behind him anyway?"

"Because I had to strangle him!" Peter declared. Hollyhock flew up behind Peter, pantomiming this part, dragging Bramble along to be her victim. "With the very rope he'd used to tie up Blink, I flew up behind him and just like that! BAM! I pulled the rope around his neck and nearly popped his head off. He dropped to the deck, dead as a doorstop!"

Newt and Sal cheered at this part. Spurt was still sound asleep in his dog bed. It was amazing, really, that the one who was usually the most high strung and noisy was the soundest sleeper as well.

"What about the captain, Peter?" Bard asked, smiling and chewing her apple. She had heard the story before, so she knew just which question to ask to get to her favorite part. She did love the part about what happened to the captain, mostly because it changed every time. No one could tell a story as well as Peter could, because no matter how many times he told it, and no matter how much it stayed the same story, the details were always radically different.

"The captain?" Peter echoed, "The captain! Well, Captain Rackham came up behind *me* and nearly cut me in two. He would have, too, if I hadn't seen his shadow creeping up. He jabbed his sword forward to stab me, but I flew up and out of his way, and his sword went right into his first mate."

"But his first mate was dead on the deck of the ship. He fell over when you strangled him," Gwen objected. In response, Hollyhock pinched her. "Ow," Gwen complained.

"Shush," Rosemary told her.

"This was before he fell. Once he was strangled and stabbed, then he fell over and was dead as a doorstop."

Newt and Sal cheered again.

"At that point, Bramble and Dillweed had already found the captain's treasure chest in his quarters, but they had gotten themselves locked in there. If I hadn't realized they were missing, they might have been locked in there forevermore, but I saw them glittering through the porthole window as I zipped around the ship, and I went back to the deck while the captain was still looking for me near the bow of the ship. Blink and I teamed up then, to roll a great barrel of rum across the deck, smashing it straight into the captain's door. We didn't have a key of course, but the rum exploded everywhere, the door broke down, and Bramble and Dillweed flew out.

"I saw the chest then, and knew just what it was. Blink and I ran in, and by that time, Newt was there as well to help us. The three of us pushed over the chest and dumped all the gold, pearls, jewels, coins, and riches out of it so that it would be light enough to lift.

"That's when Puddlebee—Rackham's parrot—found us, and began squawking as loudly as he could, 'Caw! They're in here! Caw! In here! The rotten children!' But Bramble was quick and boxed him between the eyes. Puddlebee snapped his beak at him, but Bramble flew faster than the parrot could. The dumb bird chased him all around the room, until at last Bramble flew for the chest and just narrowly turned back up and away. Puddlebee wasn't as quick and slammed right into the chest, knocking himself out and falling into it, which we shut up quick.

"Of course, the captain had heard his bird and was coming right for us. So, thinking as quickly as I always do, I lifted the chest and flew out of the quarters with it. I went to the edge of the boat and stood with the chest over my head."

At this point in the story, Peter felt it necessary to go over to Spurt and pick him up, dog bed and all. Peter was telling a fantastic tale of his own valor, and would not stand to have anyone sleep through that. Regardless, Spurt remained sleeping even as Peter carried him across the room and continued his story. Bramble and Hollyhock circled overhead, dropping a light film of fairy dust over the sleeping boy.

"When Captain Rackham saw me there, he came running as fast as he could on his limpy peg-leg. He swore a vicious streak and screamed at me not to throw it overboard, thinking all his treasure was within it.

"I waited until he was spitting distance away from me… *and then I heaved the chest overboard!*"

Peter then chucked Spurt, tossing him squarely to the bed. Jam and Blink scrambled out of the way as the freckly little one slammed against the bed, finally waking up with a start and a gasp. Wide-eyed and awake, the first thing Spurt saw was Peter storming toward him, yelling, "And the fool was so scared for his gold, that he dove in after it!"

Peter launched himself onto the bed and tackled the newly awakened Spurt, who began howling with joy, kicking and screaming right back. Newt and Sal exchanged the briefest of glances before yelling in unison, throwing themselves onto the bed to join the wrestling and tickling.

This continued for several minutes, in which all the girls picked sides and began screaming for a victor within this senseless and directionless fight. Even Gwen found herself rooting for little Spurt, yelling, "Just wiggle away from him, Spurt! He can't grab you if you get behind him!"

"I'll strangle you all!" Peter cried, but he couldn't even swat back Hollyhock and Bramble, who were flitting and pinching him as much as they were pinching the other children.

Eventually, the ruckus died down, with no obvious winner. The only two who continued fighting were Sal and Newt, who seemed to have forgotten that when they joined the ruckus, they were teammates. Rosemary pulled them off each other, kissing both of their foreheads when they each declared that they had both been mortally wounded.

Peter smiled at Gwen. “What do you think, Dollie-Lyn?”

Gwen had already decided how she would respond to all this. The story had been full of incongruities and inconsistencies, so she announced haughtily, “I don’t believe a word of it,” and promptly sat down on a toadstool, affecting the most incredulous air.

“But it happened!” Spurt insisted, even though he’d slept through the whole story and didn’t know what he was advocating for.

“It did, Gwen!” Rosemary assured her.

“How would you know? You weren’t there.”

“I can prove it,” Peter replied, rolling off the bed and pulling out a painted cardboard box from beneath it. “We still have all the booty.” Sure enough, the peeling cardboard was loaded with all the treasure described.

“Where’s the flag?” Gwen asked, still not satisfied.

“The what?”

“The flag,” Gwen repeated. “Everyone knows that when you kill a pirate captain, you take his flag. That could be anyone’s booty. I want to see the skull and stars flag.”

The children looked at Peter. They’d never heard that you had to take the flag before. In fact, Gwen had made that rule up on the spot, in the interest of making things hard for Peter.

He looked disarmed at first, as if Gwen had taken the wind right out of his flagship sails. His expression recovered quickly though, and the smirk flickered back.

“Well, let’s go get that flag then.”

CHAPTER 22

THE PIRATE SHIP HAD LONG SINCE BEEN ABANDONED, AND BARD and Spurt felt it would be better to stay and watch over the underground house. Others were reluctant, but willing, to venture to that possibly haunted ship that had rotted and bobbed in Cannibal's Cove since Peter defeated its crew. Gwen was more scared of the prospect of running into crocodiles, but Peter assured her there had only ever been one fearsome crocodile in Neverland, and it had gone the way of the pirates.

Jam and Blink were as adventurous as ever, and Rosemary wasn't going to pass up the opportunity either. Gwen wondered, as they embarked, just what she had gotten herself into, but she had no way or desire to back out of it. Newt and Sal were already singing a made-up sea shanty.

They flew out, Hollyhock and Peter leading the way. High over the trees and into the clouds, they bounced their way back down into the foggy cove, which was still full of midmorning haze. The ship's mast was broken and toppled over on itself, and the ship's body was covered in dark, mossy growth. Every inch of metal was coated in heavy, red rust, and when they set foot on the soggy deck, it squeaked as if the wooden boards beneath their feet were moaning.

"First one to find the flag is the winner!" Rosemary declared as she took off into the disarray of discolored sails.

Newt and Sal followed after her, while Jam exclaimed, "No fair, you got a head start!" Blink calmly searched the deck, thinking that the flag might have blown down to the ground after all this neglect. Hollyhock kept to Rosemary's side, having a tremendous confidence in the little girl's ability to find the missing flag.

Gwen's arms swelled with goosebumps, which she rubbed down with her palms. It wasn't even that cold, but there was a distinct marine chill that haunted Cannibal's Cove. Her lacy yellow dress—a new one she had found in the traveling trunk of mismatched clothes—did not feel like appropriate garb for this occasion. She pulled her hair back with the ribbon Bard gave her upon her arrival in Neverland. "So this was the last of the pirates?"

"Yep," Peter answered. "I defeated the very last of them, and not another ship's sailed in since." His triumph did not mask the melancholy of his voice. There was a nostalgic look in his eye as he surveyed the decaying ship; it had once been a grand stage for his heroic feats and gallant antics. Now, it was only a memory, and its glory was confined to a story he couldn't even remember well enough to tell coherently.

"Why did the pirates stop coming?" Death hung on the air and troubled Gwen, but it was not a human sort of death. It was the death of dreams and ideas, of fantasies and spirits.

"What would have brought them here," Peter asked, a bitter spite sneaking into his tone, "once they found out there was more money to be made on Wall Street than in gold doubloons? Why be crooked pirates scheming for treasure they wouldn't know how to spend when they could be honest businessmen with two cars in their garage and a summer home upstate?"

A nervous laugh left Gwen's lips. Peter was talking about reality, and it surprised her to see how uncomfortable that made her.

"Why spend your whole life on the high seas looking for treasure," Peter asked, talking to the clouds as he scaled a rope up what remained of the half-crumbled mast, "when you could have a promised paycheck in exchange for all the life you'd live between nine-and-five."

He stared at Gwen. Her heart still rested with that reality, and he seemed determined to make her feel guilty for it, wanting her to burn with dread as she considered what the alternative to Neverland really was.

"But that's not nearly as exciting," Gwen said.

"No, it's not, but it's life, and people live it."

Rosemary's piercing cry cut through the fog. "I found it! I found it!" She came running out of the mist, the faded black flag fluttering as she held it over her head.

"No fair!" Jam insisted.

Blink continued searching the ship, unfazed by the discovery of the flag. The dark little girl hunted through the fog, knowing there had to be even more interesting things left to rot among the waterlogged boards of this old ship.

"We should play out the story!" Jam announced.

Rosemary didn't miss a beat. "Can I be Peter?"

"No, you're a girl. Peter has to be Peter. You can be the captain, but I'll be Blink and you'll tie me up—"

"But Blink's here!" Rosemary argued. "Blink has to be Blink."

"Blink can be Bramble though."

"We want to be pirates!" Newt exclaimed.

"I don't want to get tied up." Rosemary pouted.

"Somebody has to though, and Blink's the tiniest, so she should be a fairy."

"Why can't Hollyhock be Bramble? She is a fairy!"

"Hollyhock's not playing, so it has to be Blink."

"I don't want to be a fairy," Blink said. "I just want to be me."

They trailed off into discussion, batting ideas back and forth, only to shoot them down and squabble more about the technical details of their reenactment. Jam was full of instructions that no one ever seemed to want to follow. Eventually, it devolved into a simple game of tag.

The young children ran loops around the slick deck, sometimes slipping and falling, but never seriously hurting themselves even when they did hit the deck. Peter quickly joined the game, and Gwen happily took part in it as well.

She wanted to run and race over the old ship, and not worry about the implications of letting it and all it stood for rot within Cannibal's Cove. It was easier to focus on avoiding Blink's tiny hand and quick, racing feet than to remember the two-car garage and nine-to-five job her father had. She wondered if her father worked with old pirates, gathering magical treasures to transmute them into economic solutions for their country.

Gwen heard something rustling, like chains in the galley below. While Jam wailed and Peter laughed, no one else seemed to notice. Something shifted in the bowels of the boat, and Gwen's attention was drawn to the door down into the hull of the ship. Were pirate ghosts a thing in Neverland? She glanced back at Peter, reassuring herself that he was there. What was the worst that could come of exploring the ship with Peter there to protect and defend?

She went to the hull's entrance and found that its rotting door easily swung open. As she peered into the darkness, she could hardly make out the shape of the warped steps leading down. She saw a small, red light blinking in the otherwise total darkness, and she was instantly confused. It looked like a tiny LED light, like some electronic device low on batteries or an alarm clock flashing as it sounded. Neither of these things had any business in Neverland.

It shifted closer to her, and the stairs' floorboards moaned under great pressure. Gwen didn't dare venture into the darkness, but she leaned in closer to see…

A scaly snout emerged out of the darkness, its unpolished, jagged teeth as sharp as its eyes. The crocodile lunged.

Its low reptilian roar was lost in the sound of Gwen's scream. She flung herself backward and away from the humongous beast. Falling down in her attempt to get away as fast as possible, she scrambled to her feet as it pushed its way through the doorway and onto the deck. It amazed her that the massive creature had even fit in the stairwell.

"Get up, Gwenny!" Peter cried. She saw that the other lost children were already high in the air, out of the crocodile's reach. Scurrying to her feet, she tried to fly up and join them. The children were all gleefully calling to her, horribly excited and screamingly alive, with only a playful sense of danger.

Her feet stayed firmly on the ground. Even when she jumped up, Gwen felt herself pulled back down by tenfold the force of gravity. She couldn't fly when her heart was racing with fear, when she knew too well that crocodiles could kill you and death was the end-all of life and joy. No one else was afraid. It was only because she comprehended the consequences that Gwen could not find the focus to fly.

She ran across the deck to the steps outside the captain's quarters. The crocodile was slower than her, but it was pursuing with passion. Gwen was too panicked to do anything but stay a few steps ahead of the scaly monster.

"*Fly*!" Peter yelled.

"I can't!" Gwen cried. She felt tears coming to her eyes. She was inept and scared; she felt younger and smaller than anyone there, a baby among children. She was going to die in the jaws of the crocodile because she couldn't muster the whimsy to fly.

Hollyhock zipped down and began doing laps around Gwen's head until they were both dizzy. Bramble did jumping jacks in her hair. Even with all this fairy dust, she still couldn't leave the ground.

Peter sank down, away from the mast and down to the side of the boat. "Jump, Gwen-Dollie, just jump over the edge and fly over here!" Gwen ran to the edge of the boat and got up on the ship's railing. She almost could have leapt into his arms, he was so close. The crocodile was after her though, and when it came snapping at her heels, Gwen locked eyes with Peter and leapt with all the confidence she could muster.

Covered in fairy-dust, she was weightless in the air for a cruel, short moment before she plunged down into the saltwater below. Her startled, screaming gasp drew in a horrible mouthful of dank seawater, and as she flailed alone below the surface, she heard the deafening crash of a gigantic reptile joining her in the chilly water.

23

GWEN THRASHED THROUGH THE WATER SO FRANTICALLY THAT she didn't know whether she was sinking deeper or floating up. She felt her arm jerked up in someone's firm hold, and as she finally managed to break the surface, Peter swept her up into his arms and carried her high into the air. She wrapped her arms around his neck and held herself as close to him as she could. Saltwater dripped from her hair, her dress, and her eyes.

"Can you fly now?" Peter's voice was little more than a whisper.

Gwen shook her head against his chest, sad and ashamed.

Peter flew her back up to the ship, setting her on the deck's railing where she would be safe from the crocodile now that it was floating below in the water. Gwen looked down at the creature with fearful hatred. The other, carefree children were throwing pebbles at it. Jam was even so bold as to pull the crocodile's tail and fly away, screaming euphorically before it could catch her between its teeth.

"Is that the same one?" Gwen asked.

"If these are my eyes, then, aye, that's the ticking crocodile," Peter muttered.

"I thought you said it was gone?"

"Oh, we chased it away. We sent it after those awful suit-and-tie pirates. It must have come back home once it'd eaten its fill of their nasty bones and briefcases." Peter landed and peered over the ship's edge, his chin in his hand.

"It didn't make a sound!" Gwen felt cheated—she would have been prepared for the crocodile if only it still ticked. "No ticking, just blinking… What's that thing on its neck?"

Peter's eyes narrowed as he looked to Gwen. "What blinking thing?"

"Some sort of device on the back of its head. It's got a little red light that blinks."

His face remained stony, even as he became pensive. Gwen didn't want to interrupt him. He startled her when he leapt off the boat and flew down near the crocodile.

Peter and the crocodile had a long history that was both unpleasant and playful. They danced around each other, snapping, diving, darting, and dipping around as Peter tried to get a better look at the light. He flew back up like a firework, exploding into a dramatic pose as he landed on the ship's deck. "It isn't good," he announced.

"What is it?"

"It's a tracker. They must have caught him and planted it on him before turning him loose again. They knew he'd eventually come home."

Gwen looked back down. The crocodile seemed harmless from afar, more like a bit of driftwood than a danger. "What does that mean?"

"It means we have to get that device off him and destroy it."

"Get it off him?" Gwen laughed in disbelief. "How do you

plan to do that without losing a limb? It's huge! We couldn't fight it even if we all teamed up."

Peter nodded and sighed. He was in a state of dread that Gwen had not seen from him before. "We'll need help." His unblinking eyes watched the crocodile. He seemed caught in a problem that was much more twisted and more subtle than that posed by the carnivorous creature below. "We'll need the mermaids."

CHAPTER 24

PETER PUT TWO FINGERS IN HIS MOUTH AND WHISTLED IN A strange fairy-like pitch to get the attention of his entourage. The lost children came to an abrupt halt and held themselves in the air as Peter called out his orders.

"The grown-ups that are trying to find Neverland have some sort of foul device on the back of our beloved crocodile's neck! We need to get it and destroy it, lest it transmit our location to those wretched adults!"

While the crocodile's attack had struck the children as a terribly funny, exciting thing, this news seemed to perturb them into focus. There was no more laughter, although Jam did ask, "What does 'transmit' mean?" Her question went unanswered, because Peter was already giving everyone their marching orders.

Blink, being the fastest flier—aside from Peter, of course—was sent to fetch the mermaids from their lagoon. It was high noon, so they would most certainly be sunbathing on the rocks. Bold Jam was in charge of keeping the crocodile on the surface and near the ship. Happy to play the damsel in distress, Jam willingly flitted just out of the crocodile's reach as bait. Hollyhock and Bramble were put on a stealth mission since they were light enough to land on the crocodile and observe its device unnoticed. Rosemary, Newt, and Sal flew off to the shore to find heavy rocks and other things they could drop on the crocodile's head if needed.

While everyone else accepted the situation without question, Gwen was all tripped up on the logic of it. "How could a transmitter work here? I kind of thought… well, technology didn't work in Neverland." After all, her cell phone had lost reception the moment she'd arrived.

Peter was busy unwinding rope from the mast. "Technology is their magic, Neverland is ours. It's all magic. It all works." He looked back at her with slight irritation. "Well, don't just stand there and be a girl; help me get this rope down."

She immediately assisted him, embarrassed that he had to ask her to make herself helpful. Peter left her side and began scouring the deck for something, opening all sorts of rotted chests and barrels. "What will it mean if the transmitter gives them the location though? People can't come to Neverland unless it's for the right reasons… right?"

"Knowing how the crocodile got back here might give them an idea for how they can invade. But they don't have to be here to do damage." Peter's voice was bitter as he called back. "If they know where we are, they can attack from afar. They've done it before."

"When? How?" Gwen was confused, but as she finished unwinding the rope and loaded her arms full of it, she approached Peter.

"About eight years ago. Remember the tree stump? They fried it—and a lot more—in an electrical storm attack."

He kicked open a wooden crate, finally finding the net he was looking for. A thin smile crossed his lips, and it was a welcome sight to Gwen. Together, they untangled the net. As the lost children returned with their various rocks and heavy branches, they, too, helped untangle the net. Bramble and Hollyhock gave a report back to Peter on the nature of the device, and just about the time Jam was getting cranky and tired of being bait, Blink arrived with the mermaids.

When he saw the beautiful faces of the mermaids bobbing in the water, Peter ordered his lost children, "Wait here on the deck."

"*I'm tired!*" whined Jam, still taunting the crocodile on the other side of the boat.

Peter took note. "Rosemary, take over for Jam."

"Wai—" However, before Gwen could object, her little sister was already flying down to play bait for the crocodile. Peter took off, hovering down near the mermaids, but not too close.

Gwen, curious and confused, did not want to just wait around on the deck. Emboldened by a new sense of purpose, she left the lost children to gape at the mermaids from a distance. She threw herself into the darkness of the hull, no longer afraid now that the crocodile was in the open sea. It was perilously hard to see, but fortunately, Gwen wasn't the only curious one.

Hollyhock came after, and Gwen welcomed the glow of her tiny friend. She trod the steps carefully until she came down into the first floor of the hull. From there, she headed directly to a porthole. She pushed the grimy, round window open with a careful hand. Peering out to see the mermaids, she heard the tail-end of their clandestine conversation.

"The tracker can lead them to Neverland. We need your help to get it."

"Peter," Eglantine chastised. "Our kind has been here longer than you have—or ever will be. No one can come to Neverland unless they are led by a creature that holds its magic."

"They will have the means to bomb us again," Peter warned.

Cynara laughed. "Then they will bomb Never*land.* The reality-dwellers cannot even scour the depths of their own seas, let alone come after us in ours. This poses no threat to us."

"You don't want it to come to that."

"Of course not," Cynara declared. She sounded genuine to Gwen, but with mermaids and their sly voices, it was always impossible to tell. "But you are in no position to bargain with us."

"We've stated our price," Lasiandra replied. "Either deliver it to us or worry about the crocodile on your own."

"Alright, alright," Peter reluctantly ceded. "I have a sky glass with me, see? Bring me the transmitter and it's yours."

The mermaids giggled, their aquatic voices ringing with an ominous joy.

"Now you're being agreeable."

"We'll bring you the transmitter."

"We promise!"

As they sealed the deal, Lasiandra caught sight of Gwen, spying on them from the porthole window. Gwen gasped as Lasiandra's eyes met hers, and she ducked out of sight. Realizing Peter would be back to the deck in a moment's time, Gwen hurried back up the steps to rejoin the other lost children waiting for him.

CHAPTER 25

IT WAS A LITTLE FRIGHTENING TO WATCH MERMAIDS WRESTLE WITH a crocodile. Gwen found herself fearing for the reptile in its three-against-one fight. It was hard to follow exactly what was happening while the girls continually dipped underwater and darted through the foam and opaque waters of their struggle. A thin arm would appear here, a head would pop up there, and a splendorous tail would surface just long enough to splash down again. The water frothed with action, and the mermaids seemed to enjoy having an audience of lost children cheering them on and baiting their egos.

Finally, Lasiandra got around its front and held its front feet while Eglantine clamped onto its tail and back feet. This demobilized it enough that Cynara could wrap her arms around its snout and begin singing to the ravenous creature.

The children were instantly quiet, entranced by the sound of the mermaid's song. The rippling voice gave rise to a song whose notes ebbed and flowed like the tide. Even Gwen was captivated by the song. Although it was spoken in a watery tongue with lyrics that carried no meaning, something about it struck Gwen as familiar, as if she had heard it long ago and it was somehow a quintessential part of her own childhood. It haunted her like the tune from an old music box, and Gwen began to think that it was just that. She remembered hearing this song before, as a child, and falling asleep on an early summer evening after her mother wound her music box and put her to bed.

The crocodile could not fight the lullaby, and it was subdued quickly by the mermaids' charms once their physical strength had overpowered its ability to fight them back. Peter had said that mermaids were dangerous creatures. Here, Gwen saw the evidence of it. The beast did not seem asleep, only in a trance. However, Eglantine rose to the surface and pulled herself up on the great beast's back to yank the tiny transmitter from off its neck.

The crocodile roared in pain as this was done. A bloody spot appeared between the scales, and the children all cheered as it reanimated, swimming desperately away to some place where it would be safe from the vicious mermaids' reach. They hadn't even needed the rocks, rope, and net the children had gathered.

"Here it is, Peter!" Eglantine called. "Come down and get it!"

"Throw it," Peter told her.

"I might break it."

"Good. I want it destroyed." Peter was adamant. He was not going within arm's reach of any of them. The mermaids bobbed peacefully in the water, but they fooled no one. The children had all just seen what they were capable of.

"Bring us the sky glass first."

"Yes," Cynara chimed. "We've told you we'll give you the transmitter when you give us the glass. Come down and give it to us."

Gwen watched as Peter pulled nothing more than a shard of mirror the size of his palm from his pocket. "I'll throw yours down when you throw mine up."

Eglantine sighed. "Oh, very well, Peter." She cocked her arm and tossed the transmitter up as Peter sent the mirror down to her with perfect aim. It landed in her outreached hands, and the transmitter clattered to the deck of the ship. Cynara and Lasiandra swarmed Eglantine, while all the lost children gathered around the transmitter.

"Blink, give me the rocks."

Blink had them ready in her hand. Peter laid the transmitter down on the flattest rock, and drove a sharp-edged stone straight through the electrical device, which appeared no bigger than a USB drive to Gwen. Peter brought the rock down with a fearsome cry, seeming to drive his hatred for all things grown-up down with the rock as well.

The huddled children scattered as the tracker exploded. Peter let out a yell of pain, and a small fire blossomed within the broken, sparking pieces of the transmitter. It sizzled, and Jam—the only one wearing shoes that day—stomped it out.

"Arrghh!" Peter cried, holding his burned hands in front of himself. The explosion left his palms swollen and pink, but Bramble and Hollyhock began kissing his fingers to help heal the hurt.

However, a much louder commotion had cropped up below the ship.

"No, let me see!"

"You did see!"

"He threw it to me! Give the sky glass back!"

"You can't even use it yet; just give it here!"

Peter forgot his burns as he went to overlook the mermaid fight. The lost children quietly asked questions among themselves, and the whole band watched as the mermaids greedily wrestled each other for their precious mirror, a commodity that could not be reproduced underwater. As they fought, growing ever nastier about it, the mirror finally slipped out of someone's hand—it was hard to tell whose—and flew against the hull of the ship. Upon impact, the thin mirror shattered, its pieces falling quickly to the water.

"NO!" the mermaids screamed in unison. They dove underwater to search for a reasonably sized shard they would not find, but not before they started blaming each other.

"Look what you've done!"

"You're such a fool!"

"Lasiandra, you've lost it!"

It was a pitiful thing to see, but when Gwen turned to Peter, he was smiling at their small tragedy. He was relieved.

CHAPTER 26

THE WEEK WAS WEARING THIN WHEN PETER DECLARED THAT THEY were going to track down Old Willow. This announcement seemed to be entirely spontaneous. It evoked the most enthusiastic response from the lost children. The morning had been dull and uneventful, so Peter rightfully deemed it time for an adventure.

The children scrambled and redressed. The boys flung off their shirts to go bare-chested as the girls helped each other put their hair into braids. The underground home was turned upside down in an attempt to find the bows, arrows, walking sticks, and other tokens they had collected from Old Willow and her tribe. Hollyhock and Dillweed proved to be especially good at turning up the long-lost relics and toys, which were hidden under beds, in drawers, and strangely stuck to the ceiling.

"Come on!" Peter rallied. "If we want to find them before dark, we'll have to start tracking the redskins now!"

Spurt ran yelling across the room, hooting and hollering, pounding his palm against his mouth.

Gwen was incredibly uncomfortable with this. "Don't you think that's, you know, inappropriate?" Gwen asked. "I mean, calling them… *redskins*?"

"No," Peter answered as he scaled a rope up to his hammock. Gwen watched him as he dug through his things. Alongside the hammock in which he slept, Peter had woven nets of twine that hung from the ceiling, full of the many trophies from his previous adventures. He found his headband, an embroidered leather band that he slipped proudly onto his head before climbing back down.

"But, referring to them, just by a color, don't you think that's… offensive?"

Peter shook his head, flinging his hair out of his face. "They call us kids. That's just an age."

His mind was completely untroubled by an issue that Gwen had spent the past few years tiptoeing around, for fear of falling into its contentious and controversial pit. "I just don't think we should call Native Americans that."

Peter laughed, and Gwen could tell it was at her expense. "Do you think you're in America right now, Gwen-dolly?"

"Well—no."

Peter's smile stayed strong. "Then they aren't Native Americans, are they?"

As usual, Gwen was without answer.

Once they had dressed, the children gathered gifts for the redskins. Jam neglected this part of the process so that she could cover her face—and everyone else's—in war paint. She even forced Gwen to sit down so she could smudge lines of bright red pigment all over the older girl's cheeks and forehead. As Jam smeared it on, Gwen couldn't help but think of Claire and all the times she had forcibly applied makeup to Gwen's face. Claire's mascara brush and eyeliner pencil were much more uncomfortable than Jam's warm fingers.

With all the hubbub, Bard was the only one to ask, “What are we going to see Old Willow for?”

Peter took down the skull and stars flag they had recovered from Rackham’s ship, which had been nailed up to the wall of the underground home for the past few days. “Because we’re expecting an ally,” Peter replied, “and she’ll be able to help us find him.”

“Another lost boy’s coming?” Newt asked. Hollyhock zipped over to Peter, eager to hear more about this ally. Peter had spoken very little of him, and although Hollyhock had a few theories as to who it might be, she leapt at any opportunity to hear more about him.

“Not quite a boy,” Peter replied, “but he’s definitely been lost, so it will be hard to find the piper without redskin trackers.”

“Piper!” Jam exclaimed, her excitement increasing tenfold.

“Oh boy! Really, Peter, really?” Spurt was overjoyed. “Is he going to play music for us?”

Bard put her hand to her face and pensively remarked, “We better bring nice gifts then.”

The lost children packed up and set out through the forest, creeping and stalking in a direction Jam referred to as *nouth*. Gwen trailed after Jam, who seemed the most confident in her navigational abilities. Newt and Sal wove through the brush, looking for tracks or signs of the redskins. Bard and Blink carried a wicker basket between the two of them, filling it with all the fruit that the others picked as they explored the forest. While Hollyhock and Dillweed scouted ahead and flew among the others, Bramble remained stowed away in the fruit basket and was carried along as he secretly feasted.

The trek became so fun in its own right, that half of them forgot they were even trying to seek out the redskin camp.

They ate fruit, collected interesting sticks, and wandered through the forest happily until early in the evening.

As the sun began to set over Neverland, Peter hushed the brigade of children and scaled to the top of a tree. The others flew up to see what he saw, immediately recognizing the smoke of a redskin fire drifting up from the plains just beyond the forest.

27

THE CHILDREN CREPT TO THE EDGE OF THE FOREST WITH WIDE-eyed caution. Even the fairies stayed low, tucking themselves into the children's pockets so that their glow would not be seen. The prairie grasses grew yellow and tall on this side of the island. A cackling bonfire flickered and burned, unattended. Three tall teepees stretched up toward the dimming, golden sky, but not a soul was in sight. Gwen's heart began to thump in her chest with the rhythm of a horse's gallop.

Scenes of old westerns flashed in her mind, and she waited for a similar scenario to unfold. Grinning, Gwen couldn't help but remember the last time she had played cowboys and Indians in the schoolyard. It had been such a long time ago, yet the memory was still so vivid for the sheer joy of the game. She didn't know how to feel about that happy, innocent memory of caricaturing Native Americans.

"Is it safe, Peter?" Spurt asked, his whisper so loud that the entire group heard it.

"Where are they?" Jam whined.

"Maybe they're out hunting," Bard proposed.

Blink was more skeptical. "They might have heard us coming and set a trap."

No one wanted to step out from the trees and brush alone, lest the redskins attack.

"What do we do, Peter?" Rosemary asked, tugging on his arm.

"We'll go out all at once so if they try to ambush us, we'll outnumber them. Gwen and Rosemary, you two hang back, just in case of an emergency."

"What do we—?" Gwen began, but Peter was already marching forward toward the teepee camp. The others scrambled alongside him, pushing their way over the last creeping ivy vines and shrubberies. Rosemary was the first to yelp; she and her sister hung back and saw the trap spring into action a split second before the others felt it close up around them.

All the children screamed as the ground lifted from beneath them and they were swept up into a booby-trapped net. As soon as they triggered the trap, the net sprung and gathered them all up like fish, worming and writhing, squished next to each other. They were a puddle of children, mewing and moaning for help, suspended between the trees. Even the tiny fairies were having a hard time squirming their way out.

"What do we do, Gwen?" Rosemary frantically asked.

"I don't kn—" Yet again, Gwen was cut off. This time, it was as a dark hand clapped down over her mouth. She began screaming, but with all of her friends caught up in the rigged trap, no one could respond to her muffled cries. A strong arm wrapped around her, and Gwen found that she could not break away from the redskin brave who had a hold of her.

In another tongue, he called out something. Gwen

saw another man spring from hiding among the bushes as Rosemary ran by. He lunged at her little sister, but Rosemary was quicker. She dove out of the way, grabbing the tomahawk at his side. It was right at eye level for the small girl, so she pulled it off his leather belt as she raced past him. The redskin holding Gwen yelled something again, but Rosemary was already up in the air, her quick flight disorienting the brave who was after her. She got up just high enough that she could swiftly come back down behind him, holding the tomahawk to his own neck. She kept the blunt end of it to his throat, for the moment, and latched onto his back, yelling, "Let my sister go!"

The sound of old laughter, breaking down an ancient, smoky voice, interrupted the sobriety of their fight. From out of the forest came a final redskin. He was an old man, with deep-seated wrinkles forming a somber expression on his face, even as he laughed and smiled through them. His hair was a dark, stony grey, mingled with a once-youthful black. He wore a brilliant feather headdress and a bright woven robe. "Running Fox, have you met your match in this tiny girl?"

"She is like the little jackrabbit!" he objected.

The elder waved dismissively at the other brave. "Let the sister go, Storm Sounds. The newcomers have beaten you, though we have trapped our old friends."

Storm Sounds let go of Gwen, and she turned around to look at him. He bore a stoic expression, as if already working on setting the same deep lines in his face as those of his elder. Rosemary released Running Fox and graciously handed him his tomahawk back before hugging him and bursting into a fit of giggles.

"Chief Dark Sun!" Peter announced, yelling over the mutterings and squabbles of the other children he was presently clumped with. Dillweed had managed to worm his way out of the entrapment. He was now working on pulling Hollyhock out from where she was squished between Jam and Newt. Everyone else was quite unalterably trapped.

"Ah, Brave Peter," the chief replied, looking up at the trap. "Peace be in your travels."

"Never!" Peter defiantly cried. "Now, will you let me and my comrades down, or must I cut our way out of your fine net?"

Dark Sun chuckled and told Running Fox, "Let down our old friends so that they might join us at the fireside tonight."

"We come bearing gifts!" Sal yelled.

"All the more reason to welcome them," Dark Sun replied. Sound Storms helped his fellow brave as he untied the knots and rigging that suspended the seven children overhead. "But who is the jackrabbit and sister? These are new faces to me."

"Jackrabbit comes from our white man land, and she has brought her sister, the storyteller."

Rosemary marched right up to Dark Sun and stared at the tall, old man's painted face. "I've never seen a redskin before."

"Rose!" Gwen hissed, appalled with her imprudent little sister.

Dark Sun smiled at Rose, but asked, "What is the storyteller's objection?"

"Don't mind her," Peter replied, struggling to orient himself without elbowing, kneeing, or otherwise injuring the others. "She's just a stupid girl."

"Mighty words to speak of a girl on the ground, when you are suspended in a net." Dark Sun walked over to Gwen with a slow gait. "From down here, she and the jackrabbit look like the smartest of all of you."

Dark Sun put an arm around Gwen, taking a paternal stance beside her. Patiently, he waited for Running Fox and Storm Sounds to finish undoing the trap, lowering the net of children slowly to the ground. They flooded out in a scrambling frenzy as soon as they were back on the forest floor. By that time, Running Fox and Rosemary had already become fast friends, and she was carried on his shoulders as he and Storm Sounds accepted apples from Bard and Blink, whose basket of fruit had mostly survived the exciting and sudden detour up into the trees.

Peter approached the redskin chief and crossed his arms to bow, solemn and respectful. Dark Sun returned the gesture. At that point, Peter seemed to feel comfortable enough in the old man's presence to tell him, "We have come to speak with Old Willow, that she might help us find the man I seek."

"Then you shall speak to her," Dark Sun promised, "but first, let us gather around the fire and share in food together, if we are still friends."

"We're still friends! We've still got all the stuff you gave us!" Newt announced, brandishing his bow.

"Then we will eat and tell the old tales. Perhaps make some new friends, too."

Gwen felt strangely comfortable in Dark Sun's presence, and she did not hesitate to return his smile when it came so readily to her lips.

28

THEY GATHERED AROUND THE FIRE, EVERYONE SEATED CROSS-legged in a semicircle around the flames. Gwen folded her legs into lotus pose, and although many of the children tried to imitate her, Peter alone managed the yoga pose. The open plains were just cold enough that being gathered near the fire felt like the best thing in the world. Gwen watched the logs crackle away into blackened ash, and she couldn't help but think of Jay's charcoal drawings.

Chief Dark Sun insisted that Gwen and Rosemary sit beside him, but because Gwen did not understand why she had this honor, it made her uncomfortable. Rosemary, on the other hand, had no qualms about the chief's invitation.

Gwen had been expecting to meet with a whole tribe, so it surprised her when no one else joined them. Confused though she was, it was Rosemary who had the frankness to address the issue. "Where is everyone else? Aren't there more redskins, Chief Dark Sun?"

The chief smiled sadly; it was an expression that fit well on the folds of his old face. "No, our numbers have been greatly diminished. Captain Rackham, the man of the sea and its demons, laid siege to our tribe after the great sickness. We are the only red man left on this land."

"Oh." Rosemary sighed.

"But that is an unfortunate story. We will tell brave and good stories tonight, for we are with brave and good friends."

They heard Storm Sounds speaking in their redskin tongue and looked back to the teepee from which he was emerging. He held the hand of an ancient woman, who had once been tall but was now hunched over and buried under the weight of a leather dress and dark woven robes. Her hair was equal parts a strong black and an unabashed silver, as if stars had fallen into her hair and streaked it as they melted away. Storm Sounds led Old Willow as though she were blind, but she surveyed all the faces of the children gathered around the fire. Her eyes lingered on the unfamiliar sisters. "To what do we owe the honor of these visitors?" she asked.

"Brave Peter and his fellows have come to seek help from you, so tonight we tell great stories of our people and share in the evening's blessings," Dark Sun told her.

"We come bearing gifts!" Sal announced again.

"And fruit," Bard added, feeling the need to make a distinction.

"The fire is making me hot," Jam complained, writhing as she sat next to Gwen.

"Then come take my spot on this side," Peter suggested as he got to his feet, approaching Old Willow. Her face remained inexpressive as he neared, but he presented her with a bouquet of flowers and herbs that she took and held like a baby in her arms. "I have gathered the greatest treasures that grow in Neverland's forests," he announced, "for Neverland's greatest medicine woman."

Her eyes twinkled to see the distinctive flora nestled in

the crook of her arm. "I hold in my hands our friendship, Brave Peter. It is a good thing." She passed the bundle of flowers and herbs to Storm Sounds, and he set it aside gently as Old Willow kneeled down and took a seat on the ground. Jam had scurried over to the other side of the fire where she could feel the evening breeze, so Peter sat down next to Gwen. Bard pulled out a pale pink peach, swollen with ripeness, from her wicker basket. She took a bite from it, and then began passing it around the circle, giving everyone the opportunity to have a bite of the succulent fruit. As the little peach traveled, Blink and Rosemary unfolded the pirate flag they had carried with them and presented it to Running Fox.

Blink announced, "We have brought this for you."

"It is the flag of the man who killed your brother," Peter told him. "We present it to you, in memory of Brave Flying Hawk. A great warrior is not forgotten among us."

Running Fox accepted the flag, folding it back up and keeping it pressed to his lap. "Those who do not forget are not forgotten," he answered, his voice deep and calm. "You honor my brother. You have the respect of his spirit, and the respect of the earth in which his body is buried. Thank you, Brave Peter."

"*Itcha Nu H'jow Talwa*," the medicine woman announced. Everyone echoed the phrase, as close in unison as they could. Gwen did not know the meaning of it, but she felt as if she were a part of something profound as she tried to fathom Running Fox's pain, and the spirit of camaraderie that existed between all of Neverland's inhabitants.

The peach that Bard had started around the circle was finally passed to Old Willow, who pulled the pit from it and ate the last of the fleshy fruit. Bramble had followed it all the way around the circle, hoping to steal a bite of it, but no one had paid him any heed. Disgruntled, he returned to the pile of kindling that Hollyhock and Dillweed were playing in. "What is it that you seek from this old medicine woman?" Old Willow asked.

"I am looking for the piper again," Peter told her. "I have spoken with the mermaids," Peter told her, "and they told me to find the man who flies by means of machine. His sympathies are with the children and the stars, and if I find him, I will find the piper. I do not know where in the white man's expansive land he will be. There is no better tracker than a red man. Will you teach me how to track this aviator, this master of white man flight?"

Old Willow nodded, considering his request. At her side, she had small, leather pouches attached to the belt of her dress. She began digging into these tiny pockets, pulling out a sparkling black egg. Cracking it against her peach pit, a ghostly white yoke oozed out and congealed around the pit. Flattening it in the palm of her hand and shaping it into a ball, Old Willow wrapped the peach pit in it and sprinkled a strange amalgamation of dusts and colored powders before completely enclosing the peach pit in the mysterious egg. "You have lofty goals, Brave Peter, you remind me of He Who Dreams. You do well to come to us for help. The red man was not born a great tracker, he learned it from Deer." Old Willow then threw the modified peach pit into the heart of the fire. As the egg coating cooked and burned, it began to color the fire a beautiful blue-green.

Jam *oo'ed* in delight, and Spurt snuggled as close as he dared to the hot flames.

"Deer was silent, Deer was quick, but Deer was not a hunter. He ate only of the land. He was peaceful, but strong. There was nothing in the forest he did not hear or could not find. No one knew how he managed to seek out whatever he desired, no matter where in the forest it was. Every time the red man saw Deer, he asked, 'How do you find what you desire, what magic do you have?'

"But Deer never answered. He would run back into the forest, and the red men would chase him. If Deer would not help hunt, he would be hunted, as is the way of the earth and its life."

Gwen watched the blue-green fire eat away at the peach pit's wrapping. As it burned away the encasing, it happened upon the explosive powders that Old Willow had mixed in with the pit. Sparks flew up and danced in the flames, forming sights that took shape and began to magically illustrate the story. The children's eyes left Old Willow's taut mouth to follow the dancing picture of Deer in the fire, leaping on legs of flickering flames as he danced up toward the smoke.

"One day, a young boy hunter was learning his arrows in the forest when he saw Deer. He pulled his bowstring back and fired an arrow, wounding Deer but not killing him as a better archer would have. The young hunter ran to him, finding that Deer could not get to his feet. He bled on the forest floor, wounded but not dead."

The fire grew red again as the powdery sparks showed the scene Old Willow described, Deer lying motionlessly and the young hunter running to his fallen body.

"Finally, Deer spoke to a red man. 'Little Hunter,' he said, 'my sons are waiting for me, hidden away in the forest. It is almost the time of winter. If they stay here, they will freeze and die. You have killed me, and I cannot return to them. Please, find my sons and tell them that they must leave for the warm place without me.'

"The young hunter was confused, and he did not know how he could fulfill Deer's request. 'Where are your sons?' he asked. 'I will do so, if you only tell me where you have hidden them.'

"'I cannot tell you where. The places of the forest have no names known to the red man, and my directions would only confuse you,' Deer replied. 'But if I were well, I would run to them as easily as I breathe the forest air. My feet know the way to my sons, and if you take my hooves, they will lead you to them. When I die, take the hooves from my feet and the bone from my body. Make a rattle, and the token will guide you to my sons so that you can tell them of my fate. Take me back to your tribe then, Little Hunter, and my body will in turn care for your brothers under the winter moons.'

"He died then on the forest floor, with the promise from Little Hunter that Deer's children would be told of his demise and warned to flee the desolation of the cold winter. Little Hunter took his knife and cut the hooves from Deer's body, so that he could make the rattle Deer described. He went back to his tribe to tell the other hunters of his kill, and they helped him carry it back to the village. While his brothers took the pelt and meat from Deer and prepared for the coming winter with it, Little Hunter made his rattle with the hooves and bone of Deer. When it was completed, he went back into the forest to find Deer's sons. If he failed, they would wait for their father and be trapped beneath the winter moons, rather than go to the warm place and return in the spring. There would be no more deer."

Gwen watched the fiery effigy of Little Hunter, moving gracefully through the flames of the fire. She was captivated by the magic, and so engrossed in the story, that she almost didn't notice when Peter flashed a smile at her, enjoying the story every bit as much.

"With his rattle, Little Hunter stalked through the forest." Old Willow continued, her voice still smooth and sweet for one so old. "Deer's hooves were quiet, but they jangled louder as Little Hunter drew near to the brier where the young sons were waiting. They came out when they heard their father's hooves, but Little Hunter explained to them that their father was dead and they needed to leave for the warm place without him. With heavy hearts, the young sons of Deer dashed off, not to be seen again until the moons of spring had come to warm the earth again.

"However, Little Hunter had finally found out Deer's secret and knew how he could be such a skillful tracker. Deer's feet were magic, and they would lead him to all that he sought out. Once the red man knew this, he could use Deer's hooves to help him track as well.

"So, when you ask that we help you track that Chief of Sky, you are asking us for what Deer gave our ancestors." Old Willow pulled a clinking, clanking rattle from out of her robes. Dark, hard hooves were tied to the long bone that made noise with every little motion. She handed it to Bard to be passed around to Peter. The lost children marveled over it, each giving it a little shake and listening to its clopping sound before handing it off. Old Willow smiled as the instrument finally ended up in Peter's hands. "This gift is happily given to you, our friend and ally. We know that you will use it to defend our land and preserve what is left of our home. Someday, when our tribe grows large again, Brave Peter, it will be for your efforts and the fight you lead."

CHAPTER 29

DANCING, DRUMMING, AND GENERAL REVELRY FOLLOWED. Confident he had what he needed to succeed, Peter's guise of respectful regard for the redskins toppled down into joyful camaraderie. Hollyhock buzzed around the fire, while Bramble buried himself in what remained of Bard's fruit basket. Nibbling on everything, he ate from each of the fruits until he had made himself happily sick. Blink and Storm Sounds played fantastically together on the taut skins of their drums, and Running Fox led a dance line around the fire, teaching the children a call-and-repeat song in the redskin language. Unaware of what they were saying, the children all gaily chanted back whatever Running Fox sang, overjoyed to be shouting gibberish at the moon.

Old Willow closed her eyes, nodding with a placid smile on her aged face.

Even Gwen joined the dance, letting go of all her previous apprehensions. Hollering and hooting the same as the others, Gwen lost herself in the moment. She continued to dance, stomping, kicking, and waving her hands freely, until she felt a powerful hand on her shoulder. Dark Sun stopped her, his stony face barely conveying the joy he actually felt. Gwen broke away from the other dancing children, and felt wonderfully small as she looked up at the chief.

Her eyes were wide and attentive, curious in a way Gwen knew she had been at some point before. In contrast to Dark Sun, Gwen was young, childish, and small… it had been a long time since someone had given her a single look that not only made her feel that way, but appreciate it.

"You remind me of my daughter, Storyteller." The others continued with their jubilant ruckus. Bramble began chasing Hollyhock around the fire, leaving a trail of popping, glittering dust that explosively sparkled in the flames. Dark Sun had Gwen's full attention. "She was almost as old as you when I lost her. My Tiger Lily would have inherited this tribe when it was still strong, and she would have made it stronger. She smiled as you smile. Perhaps your souls danced together in the world before this one."

Gwen nodded, appreciating the sentiment but feeling a little overwhelmed by it. "Chief Dark Sun…" she began, "What happened to Tiger Lily?"

"She was kidnapped by Captain Rackham. He tried for years to trap her, but through her cunning, she always avoided him. It was only when she fought him to save Running Fox's life that he finally captured her. He took her away a long, long time ago, and he sold her to the world that you children have fled."

Gwen gasped and covered her mouth. "That's terrible!"

Chief Dark Sun nodded solemnly in agreement. "Brave Peter has seen her since, and she survives well on her redskin strength, but she has been too long in that world to ever return home, and she is dearly missed." Gwen only noticed the modest feather headband he was holding when he finally placed it on top of her head. The red-and-yellow band fit snuggly around Gwen's forehead, and she wore it with immediate pride. "It is good to see her smile worn by another, to know that there are still brave girls too smart to walk into the traps before them."

Dark Sun winked at her, and Gwen indulged the impulse that told her to hug him. He kissed her head sweetly. She knew he was thinking of his own daughter as Gwen thought of her own father. She had not missed home much at all during her time in Neverland, but this show of affection flooded her with the memory of everything that home and family was.

Gwen wanted to return, desperately. Not to her mother and father, but to her mommy and daddy. As the redskin chief hugged her, Gwen knew she had felt this feeling before, but long ago. What had become of her father's ability to instill this sense of protection and love in her? Some time back it had dawned on her that her dad was Robert K. Hoffman, just another human being like she was growing up to be. He made her feel like an adult, in all the worst ways, and Gwen's homesickness was not for a place or a person, but for a point in time within a relationship that she would never reclaim.

When Gwen let go of Dark Sun, she noticed Peter looking at her from across the fire pit. His expression was unreadable.

Rosemary came running up to her then, taking their lingering sentimentality and scattering it to the wind. "Gwenny! Old Willow wants to throw the bones for us!"

"What?" Gwen asked, hardly hearing her sister over the sound of the others' drums and chants.

"I don't know what it means, but we're going to go in her teepee! A real teepee, Gwen!"

She looked over at Old Willow and saw the woman looking back at her, still sitting by the fire as if waiting for Gwen to join her.

"Go then," Dark Sun encouraged. "Old Willow will have wisdom for both of you, I am sure."

Rosemary swept up Gwen's hand and dragged her away from the redskin chief, excitedly chattering things that could not be heard over the sound of the call-and-repeat song Running Fox was still leading.

Old Willow said nothing, but stood up slowly, her walking stick balancing her like a cane. The feathers tied to the end of it were as majestic as those in her hair. She walked back to her teepee, Rosemary and Gwen trailing after in silent awe. No one seemed to notice the sisters sneaking away.

CHAPTER 30

THE INSIDE OF THE TEEPEE WAS DARK, BUT OLD WILLOW WALKED through it comfortably, as only one can in their own home. She lit tallow candles and began burning incense. Soon, the inside of the dark teepee was visible and smelled of otherworldly spices.

Gwen felt the hard earth beneath her feet. Within the tent, there was only dirt, no grasses left growing. Old Willow spread out a blanket in the center of the conical room and invited the girls to sit down on the wooly spread with her. The girls did so, and Gwen immediately began tracing the sharp, geometric patterns in the red-and-blue blanket.

"It is good to see new faces banding with Peter," she said, her voice as thick as molasses. "He needs more children on his side, more who are aware of their choices."

Rosemary eyed all the strange jars and pouches that littered the floor of the teepee and hung from indefinable places above. "Growing up is a choice, isn't it?"

"In more ways than one," Old Willow answered. "After all, even if you do choose to age, that doesn't necessarily mean you have to grow up. Here, my daughter, give the bones a shake and let us see what they say about you."

Rosemary remained happy, but Gwen could see gears turning in her mind now. She was as pensive as an eight-year-old could be as she considered bigger questions than most children were ever given a chance to answer. She took the leather bag and shook it, jostling the dry bones within. Rosemary handed the bag back to Old Willow, who dumped it out between them on the blanket. Gwen watched, her eyes panning over every chunk of bone and the strange symbols etched on them. Like uneven dice, they fell and settled, waiting to be read.

"Mmhm." Old Willow sighed. "What an interesting life you will lead, Little Jackrabbit. Let no one discourage you or sway your decisions. Your heart is the purest of those around you, which will guide you smartly, even as you surround yourself with others more knowledgeable or even more quick-witted." Old Willow touched the bones tenderly, prodding them without moving them. The two that had fallen farthest from the rest of the pile were of particular interest to her. "I have never seen this blessing bone with this curse bone before. It is uncommon that these two should go together…"

"Curse bone?" Gwen asked, concerned for her younger sister.

"Everyone has a curse, and everyone has a blessing," Old Willow said. "We walk through life with the good and the bad. There is no escaping the reality that both find us."

Equal parts timid and bold, Rosemary asked, "What's my curse?"

"Yours is the curse of a long life," Old Willow replied, her voice serious but not dark. "Everything you know now will someday change, and everyone you love will someday be gone. Your life will fill you up with memories, some of which will be very hard for you to carry."

Rosemary considered this, her little lungs breathing deeply as she contemplated the prophecy. Gwen watched fear creep into her little sister's body, and then a shudder ran down her own spine as she listened to Rosemary's young voice form the question, "Are people I love going to die?"

Old Willow had frightened her with reality, and now tried to comfort her with it as well. "Everyone dies, Little Jackrabbit, everyone… but yes, that is something you will come to know for yourself."

"What's her blessing then?" Gwen asked, her voice betraying how desperately she wanted to move away from this subject. Was Rosemary going to outlive her? Was that part of what Old Willow was communicating? Gwen suddenly envisioned her little sister as an old woman, burying her, growing older than Gwen would ever be…

Fortunately, Old Willow had that answer ready. As the fatty candles trickled down and cried wax, they illuminated the medicine woman's face. "You will die—and live—without regret."

"Huh," Rosemary mused, looking at the bone Old Willow's squat finger pointed to. It looked like a finger bone, etched with a symbol like the sun.

"Few people, let alone anyone who lives as long as you are destined to, can claim that. Your life will be long, but it will be good, Little Jackrabbit. Make your own choices, and you will stand by them until the day that you die."

"Wow." The word escaped Rosemary like a whisper, but it was a quiet exclamation.

Old Willow reached down past the collar of her leather dress and pulled out a long necklace that hung around her wrinkly neck. It contained on its black leather chain a single, turquoise pendant. "Take this, my daughter," she said, placing the jewel around Rosemary's neck. Rosemary graciously accepted it, immediately grasping the bluish gem in her hands, feeling its smoothness and admiring its aquatic color. "I am old, and I will be dead someday, but you are young and will live countless moons. Keep life in that gem, and tell the story of the redskin who gave it to you so that people do not forget that we were once a great people, too, on this land."

"Oh my gosh, thank you so much." Rosemary threw herself to her feet. "I'm going to go show Peter. Oh my gosh, this is so cool... redskin jewelry!" She took off in a gleeful fervor, racing out of the teepee without so much as a goodbye. Her head was buzzing with what the Medicine Woman had told her.

Gwen snickered at her sister's enthusiasm, having no other response to it. She felt slightly uncomfortable to be left in Old Willow's company alone, forced to face her scattered bones on her own. The redskin woman was piling the bones back into their leather bag, still kneeling on the blanket just in front of Gwen. Once finished, she reached over to a wooden chest and began sifting through its contents.

"I notice you flinch at that word," Old Willow remarked. "You don't like to hear voices say 'redskin,' do you?"

"I was taught it was inappropriate."

"In the world you come from, yes. Things are much more complicated over there, aren't they?"

"Terribly."

Old Willow pulled a pipe out of her wooden chest. As she sat across from Gwen, she lit it and began smoking. After a few puffs, which she seemed to find deeply relaxing, she extended the long pipe and offered, "Would you care to join me?"

"No, thank you," Gwen replied, shaking her head to communicate how totally she did *not* want to share in whatever Old Willow was smoking.

Old Willow did not seem offended, which relieved Gwen. "May I ask why not?"

For once, Gwen didn't go out of her way to be tactful. "It smells bad." Old Willow threw her head back and laughed, blowing smoke out of her mouth as she did so. Gwen felt compelled to reinforce her excuse. "I don't really like—er, I don't have an interest in—smoking anything or, you know… doing drugs."

Old Willow grinned, her white teeth beautiful against the vivid colors of her painted face. "You really are still a child, aren't you?"

Had it been said under any other circumstances, Gwen would have taken it as an insult, but here… Old Willow announced it as though Gwen had just proved her character in the best way possible.

"Children are so straightforward. They know better than to get involved in what is openly unattractive to them. And they are not yet so disillusioned with the weight of the world that they seek to relieve themselves of it."

"Do you wish you were still a child?" Gwen asked.

Old Willow put the pipe aside. "At my age, everyone does."

Gwen didn't doubt it. She thought that adults were always envious of youth. She suspected that was the reason so many adults were such bullies with their authority. Jealousy, plain and simple.

Gwen rephrased her question. "Do you regret growing up?"

The medicine woman picked up the bag of bones again and began playing with it in her hands, slowly tossing the old bits and turning them within their cloth. "It is not for redskins to remain children. This land does not give us that gift as it does you. It was not a choice for me to grow up. But if you're asking whether I would have remained a child if I could have… certainly."

Old Willow's answer would have been melancholy had she not been so peacefully resigned to the reality of her circumstances. Gwen thought about her own childhood, the time before she had started growing into her present sense of teenage identity. She had not wanted to remain a child at that time, but she had not wanted to grow up either. Childhood was all she had ever known, and Gwen mistakenly believed at that time that nothing could ever seriously change… but how things had! Nothing, no game, no belief, no attitude she'd had in childhood had been left untainted by adult perceptions and expectations. "I used to play cowboys and Indians all the time when I was little," Gwen said. "Now I don't even feel comfortable listening to the others say *redskin*."

Old Willow looked at her tranquilly. "What is your question?"

Gwen refocused, trying to find the train of thought that was lurking behind her words. "How did I lose that?" Gwen asked. "Why did I have to, and how is it all still here, untouched by everything that taught me it was wrong to play cowboys and Indians?"

Gwen had been bottling so many feelings and thoughts since she arrived in Neverland, afraid to share them with Bard or Peter, lest she appear too grown-up for their liking. The truth of the matter was that she was thinking like an adult though, in so many respects. She was years ahead of the other lost children, and that had brought far too many shades of grey into her life. Once, she resented that Peter had come to take Rosemary away. Now, her only regret was that he had not come and taken them both away sooner. As thoroughly as Gwen enjoyed Neverland, she felt that some of its magic was lost on her, and forevermore would be.

"You already know the answer to that," Old Willow replied. "Girls like you… they never ask questions they don't know the answer to."

Gwen would worry about deciphering the logic behind that remark later. In the meantime, she acknowledged its truth. Deep inside of her was an answer, and Gwen began speaking in the hope that if she tried long enough to articulate it, eventually she would.

"You redskins are like the mermaids and the fairies… you're not real. Not back in the real world. You're just this fictional, romanticized version of a real culture of people who mostly have the short end of the stick these days. But it's like everyone's so afraid of you because you are more real than mermaids and fairies and magical creatures….You're nothing like Native Americans, but a little like their history, and that inbetweeness of real and make-believe scares people. Like we're going to forget the difference between real Native American people and the Indians in our western movies."

Old Willow nodded. "There is a time and a place for everything, and if there is no place for redskins in what you call 'reality,' then this is where we will be… until they choke us out as well. There are those who would not have us even exist here. People think that only the serious is important. They forget how essential it is to remain whimsical."

"Is that what Peter is fighting for?"

"Peter is fighting for many things," Old Willow answered. "Because he knows what he believes."

Gwen curled up on the rug, hugging her knees to her chest. She envied Peter's confidence and whimsy. The world was simple for him, and he had all the answers his heart desired. "Some days, I don't even believe what I know," she confessed.

Old Willow's smile was soft and subtle, but her eyes remained hazy and strange. Gwen seemed to be able to prompt nothing from her unless she asked a direct question. Even then, she didn't know how much sense Old Willow's answers made… or whether it mattered that things didn't make sense when she was sitting in a teepee in Neverland. Gwen realized there was sometimes very little correlation between whether something made sense and whether it was true.

They could still hear the drumming and chanting at the fire. Gwen was growing tired, and was overcome with the desire to creep into a cozy bed and sleep away all of her doubts, exchanging them for the lighthearted dreams everyone around her seemed to be living. Before she did so though, she knew she could not leave Old Willow's tent without a few more nebulous answers for her to consider. Straightening the headband Dark Sun had given her, Gwen sheepishly asked, "Will you throw my bones, too?"

CHAPTER 31

OLD WILLOW'S FACE REMAINED PASSIVE AS SHE HANDED GWEN the leather pouch. Feeling as though her fate were in her hands for a brief moment, a sense of power filled Gwen as she shook the bag and jostled the ancient bones. When she handed it back to Old Willow, the medicine woman dumped them out between them and watched them scatter.

They fell simply… except for one. It was rounder than the others—it must have been, to roll so quickly and so far—unevenly running to the edge of the blanket as if trying to flee its brother bones. They watched it, not daring to interrupt its course, and glanced at each other for an explanation once it had finally come to a stop. "Which bone is it?" Old Willow asked. Gwen cautiously crawled over to pick up the stray bone, but by then, Old Willow had already searched the bones and answered her own question.

Gwen picked it up between two fingers, not wanting to touch it any more than she had to, and set it gently down in front of Old Willow. "This one," she softly answered.

Old Willow didn't need to look at it. "You are very

different from your sister. Similar though you may seem, you have very different spirits. Your heart is too confused, and following it will lead you to conflict. Whatever decision you make will bring with it untold chaos."

"Is that my curse?"

"Your curse rests within that. Follow your heart, and it will break. You are not your sister. You will make terrible decisions, which will ultimately bar you from all that you want and seek out. Acting on your heart will defeat you."

It was a wretched condemnation. How had Rosemary left with such a small curse as to merely know she would live many years beyond her time? This was so much worse… to think that every time Gwen felt confident in herself, she would be on the verge of making a terrible and regrettable mistake? She wished she had never let Old Willow throw the bones for her.

"So every time I follow my heart, I'll know I'm dooming myself?" Gwen was bitter with the woman now.

"Oh no," Old Willow replied, sparking a hope which she then immediately crushed, "because you will never know if the choices you are making are really in line with your heart's desires. Should they be, then yes, you will thwart yourself with them… but you will not know."

Gwen felt her spirits sinking as though they were a physical thing, pulling all her blood and warmth down with them. "Then what's my blessing?" Her voice had become sardonic, thinking that no blessing could make up for such a curse.

Old Willow held her eyes with an iron-fast intensity, which caused Gwen to look away, down at her own pink toes. The thick, warm voice of the medicine woman spoke. "You will always be happy."

She looked up, utterly confused.

Old Willow smiled at her naivety. "There is a tremendous difference between what you want and what will make you happy. But you will never be able to judge the difference through the haze of confusion that haunts your heart. All you will know, when all is said and done, is that you are happy."

Gwen did not know how to feel about that. It made it sound as though everything she did, all that she worked for, would be utterly in vain. She would never get what she wanted... Was the solution then to stop wanting? To just let the future take her where it would? That was impossible, Gwen knew, if only because she was a sixteen-year-old girl. Desire was inescapable, and choices abounded. As if the nebulous nature of decisions and their consequences were not convoluted and unknowable enough, Old Willow reminded Gwen that her heart beat a paradoxical rhythm. Even as it contracted with one desire, it was certain to relax with another. If someone cut her, surely indecision would pour from her veins in place of blood.

"Thank you," she said quietly, standing up.

"There is something more here," Old Willow remarked, prodding the little bone fragments. Gwen couldn't help herself. Although she did not sit back down, she waited for the old woman to tell her the last detail of a future she did not want to know, let alone live. "I see two others, deeply knit into the fabric of your future. They are a boy and a man... both of whom you will love."

Gwen stared at her. Old Willow was giving her a chance to walk away with only that much information. The old woman's eyes betrayed greater knowledge, and Gwen could not resist the temptation to question what more was knowable about her future. "And?"

"One will stand beside you until the day you die. The other, you will lose forever."

Gwen towered over the grey-haired woman, but felt small as Old Willow's eyes held her with such confident ease.

Gwen swallowed, finding her voice. "And you already know which one is which."

Like a statue, Old Willow did not need to gesture or speak in order to affirm Gwen's suspicion. The girl's remark was just that though—a remark. There was no question in it. Old Willow would not give the answers for questions that went unasked, so she remained silent and seated as Gwen bid her goodnight.

She turned from the woman, but did not look back for fear the redskin elder would see her quivering face, even as Old Willow gave her parting words, "Lily on Fast Waters, that is who you are, my daughter. A blossom caught in a chaos of a conflict that exceeds her. Goodnight, Lily on Fast Waters."

Gwen bit her lip and snuck out of the tent, throwing herself into the rich smell of the campfire and nightfall. The scent of Old Willow's incense and pipe stayed with her, as if clinging to her skin the way the bone's prophecy clung to her heart.

The children were scattered, no two of them focused on the same thing. Jam threw more kindling into the fire without reason, and Bard had usurped the drum, now banging on it as an amateur musician. Even Newt and Sal had broken away from each other to etch shapes in the dry dirt and run around teepees.

Rosemary, however, was curled up near the fire in a beautiful woven blanket. Wrapped up like a little inchworm, she seemed to have fallen asleep beside the enticing warmth of the fire, using her poofy hair as a pillow.

Gwen walked over to her little sister and put a hand on her back, rubbing the way that their own mother used to when the girls were going to sleep in their beds. Ages and ages ago, their mother had stopped doing that for Gwen, but she could still do it for Rosemary.

The girl stirred and looked up endearingly at her big sister. “Hey, Rose,” Gwen said, wanting nothing more than to gaze at the familiarity and love in her eyes.

Rosemary hunkered back down under the blanket and mumbled. Gwen answered, “You have a good time?”

An affirmative mumble and happy nod served as answer. Her eyes closed, Rosemary then asked, “Gwen?”

“Yes?”

Secure in her decision and confident in her desires in a way Gwen would never be, Rosemary peacefully said, “I’m going to stay in Neverland.”

CHAPTER 32

It was hard to say whether their meeting with the Redskins was the emotional highpoint or emotional low point of Gwen's time in Neverland. The adventure of seeking them out had been so enjoyable, but the joy of it had dissolved into the dusk, confronting Gwen with make-believe realities, which suddenly had a tremendous and surreal bearing on her real life.

The days blended together for Gwen. Every new day brought unique adventures and a constant stream of activity. There were sword-fighting competitions, pilgrimages to the Neverbird's nest, and daily flights up to the treetops to scan the horizon for approaching ships and seafaring pirates. Despite this, the evenings had a comforting routineness to them, and it was hard for Gwen to gauge how many days and nights had really slipped by. There were no calendars, no clocks, and no cares in Neverland. Gwen found herself losing time like she lost socks in the laundry. It had to go somewhere, and yet, there was only ever the present moment. How long had she been in Neverland? A week, two? A month? The distinction hardly mattered, and Gwen excused her ignorance by promising herself she would leave when the time came for flying home.

A deep-seated sense of melancholy stayed with her, and the other children could only tempt her so far out of it with any given game. On her last day in Neverland—the day before Peter would fly back to meet the aviator and find the mysterious piper—Gwen woke up in the premature morning. Unwilling to remain in bed listening to her sister breathe and Sal squirm at the other end of the bed, she snuck out of the underground home to find a little solitude. Even Peter was still sleeping at that point, sprawled out in his hammock high above everyone and well beneath everything.

Gwen had mastered the art of escalating out of the wide, old oak, breathing in sharply to propel herself up to the hole at the top of the trunk. For as much as she had resisted Neverland, in a very short time, she had learned its ways well. Although Gwen had never seriously considered the possibility, on this final day in Neverland, there was a very real suspicion in the back of her mind that her motive for coming with Peter was out of childish and whimsical self-interest, not concern for her little sister's well-being.

Now she lazed in the grove, lying on her back and fiddling with the strap of her satchel bag. She didn't want to be found by the others when they woke up, but she also didn't want to lose herself exploring for a more private place. Consequently, she had resolved to work quickly through her existential crisis.

Putting a time frame on solving her philosophical dilemma was anything but helpful. In an attempt to make it easier on herself, she tried not to think about the internal dread she had regarding her future, and focused instead on Rosemary.

Her sister had become convinced, unshakably convinced, that she needed to remain in Neverland. Gwen had come with the intent of wooing her back to reality, but the last threads of that hope had vanished following their meeting with Old Willow. Rosemary would not be talked out of it; not in a day's time, not in a week's time… not in a month's time. Gwen faced her reality with shaking bones and an unsteady heart—she was going to have to return home without her sister.

There was no way to drag her back by force, so Gwen did not have to consider the issue of whether she would resort to that. Rosemary would have to fly home in her own time, and Gwen would have to trust that, in the meantime, all would be well. There was still an ember of hope glowing within her that Rosemary would break down when she saw Gwen preparing to leave, and she would choose to go with her out of the same love that had compelled Gwen to chase her to Neverland. Even so, she wasn't going to bet on it.

Gwen briefly debated staying longer, knowing that if she left Rosemary here alone, she would go native in much more totality than if her older sister remained present. If she remained, she might be able to eventually shepherd Rosemary home a little sooner, but Gwen dared not remain in Neverland. Staying for Rosemary's sake would come at too deep a personal cost.

There was little that Gwen was certain of, but she knew this—she could not remain in Neverland. Writhing in the grass, trying to dissolve into the ground, Gwen wanted to slink away from the part of her that desperately wanted to stay. Some aspect of herself that had never felt so relieved, so at peace, so at home, was screaming that she should remain, and Gwen knew that any desire that screamed so senselessly was not to be trusted or indulged.

She couldn't stay and watch over Rosemary because

she knew Neverland would adopt her as well, and then the both of them would consign their future for their place in paradise. Gwen had to get out while she still had the will to do so. Someday, the reason would occur to her and this decision would make sense. She had to trust that all the adults she knew had made the same choice, and she would one day look back on this week as a happy vacation, a reminder of the possibilities.

When I am older, it will make sense.

But Gwen knew that was a lie. The older people grew, the less sense the world made to them. They buried themselves under invented complexities and self-imposed ambiguities. Staying made sense because it used the sensible arguments of a child's logic. Leaving never would, and yet Gwen would always be able to justify it with a vague and dreamy notion that it was the *right* thing to do.

Gwen found her mind constantly wandering back to homecoming and Jay. When she wondered whether Jay had won the homecoming king nomination, it made her feel stranded in Neverland, away from everything. Neverland surrounded her with a constant sense and smell of spring, but Gwen missed Jay's smell of fresh-crushed charcoal. Had he asked someone to the dance while she was gone? And what about Claire and Katie? What if they had dates now too? What would it be like if her best friend was going with Michael Kooseman and she had to go just with Katie?

She sat up and began picking through a tiny patch of weeds, looking for a four-leafed clover. It was something to do, and Gwen thought it might distract her for a minute. Almost instantly, she came across one, something that she chalked up to the nature of Neverland. It was a pretty little keepsake, and Gwen hoped it might bring her some form of luck anyway.

Digging into her purse, Gwen shuffled through its

contents to find the tiny notebook she could use to press the clover. The sunlight caught the beautiful glow of something else and her attention was diverted. Slipping the clover into the pocket of her beige dress instead, Gwen pulled Lasiandra's gift out of the bottom of her satchel.

It was like abalone and sequins, glinting every color of an aquatic rainbow as it played with the sunlight. It reminded Gwen of a coin, a large, half-dollar coin. She wondered what she was meant to purchase with it.

As she slipped it back into her bag, she also found her compact mirror in the purse's pocket.

Gwen glanced around, but not so much as a fairy was up and stirring at this hour of the morning. Did mermaids sleep at night the same as people did, or were they always busy, watching the night sky at those hours? If she went to the mermaid's lagoon now, would the beautiful creatures be there? Peter had a standing invitation to return, but no such offer had been extended to Gwen, unless this token was evidence to the contrary. Did she really want to leave Neverland tomorrow without having seen Cynara and the others at least once more?

Enough of the morning had been given up to idle speculation and melancholy mysteries of the heart. Gwen was finally asking herself questions that had answers, and she knew where she could have them answered.

CHAPTER 33

GWEN REMEMBERED THE DIRECTION SHE HAD TO GO IN ORDER TO reach the lagoon. She never doubted her navigational abilities. Much like flying, it took a certain confidence within the wanderer in order to avoid getting lost in the jungles of Neverland.

On her way there, she bushwhacked noisily, tripped over roots, flew up into trees, and made all manner of noises. Gwen had forgotten how to be quiet in the past week. It was never necessary, and she was expected to be, like any child, noisy and full of ruckus. This wouldn't have mattered, if she had not woken up Bramble. Away from his proper home, he had stumbled onto a squirrel's secret stash of nuts in a small hollow last night. He'd eaten his fill of them and then some, only to pass out in the early hours of the night. He was easily awoken and recognized the gait of a lost child, who walked with more melodic steps than redskins or pirates ever did.

Pulling his leafy shirt back down over his swollen belly, Bramble waded through the nut shells he'd left in the wake of his private feast to see who was up and out so early. When he saw Gwen, he flew after her.

Gwen did not notice Bramble until he flitted into her peripheral vision. She recognized him by his orange glow, even if she could not make out his features. "Oh, hello, Bramble."

He asked her where she was going, but of course, Gwen did not understand his fairy words. While the fairies were quick to learn English, they simply did not have the vocal capacities to speak it any more than humans could speak the fairy language. Bard and Blink knew a few fairy words, but only Peter could recognize their language well enough to reliably translate. All Gwen had discovered so far was how to tell the difference between their agreements and disagreements.

Guessing at his question, Gwen answered, "Peter and the others are still asleep in the underground home. I wanted to go for a walk when I woke up early."

Bramble repeated his question, thinking it very unlikely that Gwen would simply take off in a random direction just because she wanted to go on a walk.

Gwen suspected that he was curious about just that, but she did not want to tell him where she was going. The fairies could be incurable gossips, and she didn't want to have to talk to Peter or the others about the mermaids. The way they enchanted her…she felt criminal for indulging the desire to see them again. However, Peter had never told her not to visit them; he had only told her not to get too near or too close to them.

"I'm looking for a mango tree." It was the truth; it just wasn't the whole truth. Gwen didn't want to show up without land fruit, and she knew at least Lasiandra liked mangoes best. Bramble buzzed happily at this announcement, and Gwen took it as a sign that he would help her search, and perhaps be distracted enough by breakfast that she could lose him.

Sure enough, Bramble was quick to spot a mango tree that sported voluptuous orange and green fruits. They hung pendulously from the branches, and he immediately flew to them to catch Gwen's attention. She stood directly under the high tree, so Bramble pulled and tugged at the ripest of the fruits until one of them dropped down to the girl. She sprung to catch it and just barely managed. Bramble loosened another two for her before rubbing his palms together in eager desire for his breakfast. He began gnawing immediately on a juicy mango, still attached to its branch, and didn't concern himself with Gwen as she wandered away.

Mangoes tucked into her satchel, Gwen finished trekking to the edge of the jungle, descending the stony steps of the cliff's face to the aquamarine lagoon below. She did not see the swirling shadows of the mermaids this time though, and she questioned whether she would see them. Gwen didn't want to hike all the way down the cliff for nothing, but she didn't want to risk missing an encounter with the mermaids either.

Everything as it was before, Gwen picked up some pebbles from the shore and climbed out on the smooth, grey rocks to sit on the very same boulder Peter had first led her to. She made herself as comfortable as possible before she began plinking the pebbles into the water, one at a time.

At first, she waited long intervals between pebbles. She tossed them in different directions, hoping that one of them would catch the eyes or ears of some mermaid. She chucked the last few farther and more hurriedly, losing patience after the first few minutes. Still, she sat pensively a moment more before resigning herself to the fact that none of the sea-dwellers were coming to see her.

She wandered back, but lingered at the shoreline. Feeling around in her purse for the majestic token Lasiandra had left her, Gwen pulled it out and examined it. What did it signify? Why had Lasiandra wanted to leave it behind for Gwen? Not knowing the answer to these questions any more than she had known the solutions to her philosophical musings back in the grove, Gwen decided to leave the scale. No good could come of her keeping it; it was too confusing.

She set it down on the pebbly shore, watching the very next wave splash over it. As soon as it did, the thin, round scale was gone. A sudden sense of grief caressed her heart as Gwen realized that she would never see that magical gift again, but it was probably for the best. If she was going to depart from Neverland and truly leave all this behind, it would be better not to take such tangible reminders of it back with her. It was bad enough that she was keeping the headband Chief Dark Sun had given her.

She walked away, turning her back on the mermaid lagoon. She did not expect to hear a harmonious, high voice call out, "Gwen?"

CHAPTER 34

SHE TURNED AROUND AT THE VERY SOUND OF THE VOICE, BEFORE she even knew that it was her name the voice was speaking. Lasiandra waited by the edge of the water. Her hands against the sandy floor of the lagoon, she propped herself up in the shallow, lapping waters. Her tail flexed and splashed, the paper-thin tips of her fins catching the sunlight at a dozen different angles as they fell and rose out of the salty water. "You came back."

Lasiandra was intimidating in her serenity. She lifted the scale out of the water, holding it up in her hand. "Yes, I did," Gwen nervously answered. "How did you know I was here? I threw some pebbles in the water, but no one came."

Lasiandra's laugh was like rolling water. She pushed her wet, blonde hair out of her face. "You put my scale in the water, of course. Didn't you know that's what it was for?"

"Oh. No."

"Silly girl, didn't Peter at least tell you what mermaid scales do?"

"Ah, no… he didn't know that. I, well, I mean, it didn't

come up…"

Lasiandra thoughtfully tipped her head. "He doesn't even know you're here, does he?"

"Um, no."

Lasiandra smiled at Gwen's nervousness. "If you're so afraid to speak with me, why did you come all this way to leave my scale in the water so it could scream at me to come hither?"

"I don't really know."

Lasiandra giggled. "Well, why don't you at least take the scale back? I left it just for you. Maybe when you do know, you can call me again."

She held out the scale, trying to guile Gwen closer to her.

"No," Gwen answered, shaking her head. "I'm leaving Neverland tomorrow, and I don't imagine I'll be back to see you again."

"You don't *imagine* it? What does that mean?" Lasiandra playfully mocked. "But don't worry. I can hear my scale screaming from anywhere. Waters are not so different from one another, and they are all connected. Whatever water you put it in, I will come."

"Why?" This didn't make much sense to Gwen.

"Because I like you," Lasiandra told her. "We could be friends."

Gwen took a step closer.

"You're afraid of me." Lasiandra did not seem insulted, only disappointed.

"Shouldn't I be?"

Lasiandra relaxed, her face thoughtful. She didn't answer directly but told Gwen, "I won't hurt you." Gwen walked closer but stopped short, clutching her purse to herself. She was close enough to see the shifting, swirling contents of Lasiandra's eyes. Like tide pools, they twirled within themselves, mesmerizing and beautiful. They were the color of the midday sky. "I won't hurt you," she repeated, her voice hushed now.

Gwen reached her hand out to the scale Lasiandra held out for her. The motion was slow, jittery, and full of apprehension… but Peter had told her—mermaids never lied.

She brushed against Lasiandra's wet fingers as she took the scale from her.

Gwen dropped it into the side pocket of her satchel where it would be safe for the moment. Still staring Lasiandra in the eye, her heart skipped a beat when she whispered, "Come into the water with me, Gwen."

She didn't mean to draw a breath in as sharply as she did. She took a step back. "I don't think that's a good idea."

Lasiandra retained a relaxed posture. True to her word, she hadn't hurt Gwen. "Peter told you not to, didn't he?"

Gwen looked back at the cliff. She could leave, but instead, her eyes went back to Lasiandra. Her head gave an honest nod.

"Then surely he also told you that we never lie." The innocence in her voice seemed somewhat forced. Her tone dropped, and she spoke much more earnestly. "I promise I won't hurt you. I won't let anything happen to you. The other mermaids aren't anywhere near the lagoon, Gwen. It would just be us. I promise you won't get hurt."

Gwen trusted her, and it scared her to realize how quickly Lasiandra was winning her confidence. She looked for shallow excuses, trying not to dismiss the deep distrust she couldn't rationalize. "I don't want to get my clothes wet."

"Then take them off." Lasiandra rolled over, propping herself up by her elbows and watching her fins flick the little lapping waves along the shore. When she saw the surprise on

Gwen's face, she said, "It's just us girls. You can dry in the sun and put them back on afterward."

Gwen looked back at the cliff, half-expecting to see someone racing down it to save her from herself, but nobody was coming. As Lasiandra had so simply pointed out, the two girls were alone in the lagoon.

Gwen lifted her satchel off over her head and set it down on the shore. She swallowed, and began undoing the buttons on the front of her sundress. Lasiandra was quiet, as if not daring to speak for fear of diverting Gwen from the course of action she was now pursuing. As she dropped the dress down with her purse, Lasiandra swam a little further out, where the waters were just deep enough for her to comfortably tread water.

Indecisively, Gwen stood in her underwear. Lasiandra called back a simple reminder, "It's just us girls."

Slipping out of the last of her garments, Gwen waded into the water and left all of her clothes where they would be waiting and dry when she reemerged from the water.

The lagoon was pleasantly warm. She wouldn't have imagined it would be such a mellow, sweet temperature. "Come swim with me!" Lasiandra gaily called.

Gwen swam sloppily out to the deeper waters that Lasiandra was retreating to. Her feet no longer touched the sandy bottom of the lagoon, and she chased after the mermaid. Gwen kept her face out of the water, trying to remain oriented and follow Lasiandra as she drew Gwen farther and farther out.

Before Gwen could get any closer, Lasiandra dipped down under the waters, seamlessly falling out of view and into the blue mystery of the lagoon.

Gwen gasped and watched for her, her heart beating a little quicker with every second that Lasiandra remained out of sight. She jerked her head in every direction, but Lasiandra was certainly underwater. Gwen couldn't bring herself to duck her head under. There was one thing she knew she needed, and that was air. The idea of submerging herself did not sit well with Gwen.

A shadow darted by, and Gwen saw the watery silhouette of Lasiandra so near to her she should have been able to touch the mermaid, but she stayed under. Treading water and half-hoping to lightly kick the mermaid, Gwen watched the dark form circle her several times. Why wasn't she surfacing? What was she doing under the water?

A hand touched her leg. Reflexively, Gwen yelped, even though she knew it couldn't be anything beside the mermaid who had sworn not to hurt her. The hand was gone as quickly as it had appeared. It was almost as if Lasiandra had accidentally brushed against her, but it happened again. Gwen felt a hand slip over her knee just a second before the quick mermaid was behind her. Fingers brushed across her bottom, and a tail caressed her bare feet in a single sweeping motion.

She gasped deeper though and rigidly stopped moving altogether as she felt a hand on her inner thigh. The hand did not leave her thigh until another hand was already placed just below her belly button.

Gwen panicked at this intimate examination of her body, quickly paddling backward to get away from the mermaid. Lasiandra surfaced. "Is something wrong?"

Gwen studied the innocent look on the mermaid's face. Lasiandra seemed confused by Gwen up close. "No," she lied. "Nothing's wrong. I was just wondering when you were going to come up again."

Lasiandra and Gwen treaded water for a brief, silent, and unendurably uncomfortable moment. "Are all landmaids like you?"

"More or less," Gwen answered. It occurred to her that this was probably the first time Lasiandra had ever really seen a girl. Unclothed before her, Gwen was putting a different sort of anatomy on display for her. Did mermaids wonder why people covered their legs? Mermaids never covered their tails.

Gwen tried not to let this sudden realization become an awkward thought. Lasiandra stared at her, unremittingly interested in the shape and form of her body, and yet it didn't feel inappropriate, only unusual. There was nothing sexual in Lasiandra's expression, and for all Gwen knew, Neverland was a place completely devoid of all sense of sexuality. What business would mermaids have knowing the details of what Gwen had learned so long ago in middle school health class? This realization raised questions for Gwen, though, too.

"Lasiandra, where do mermaids come from?"

The mermaid flicked back her blonde hair, glittering with drops of water, and retied the rubbery kelp strings of her halter top. "Falling stars. When they fall on land, they burn out, but when they fall in water, they sink slowly and solidify for several days. They break open when they hit the ocean floor… but if it's far enough down, they'll have a chance to hatch before they crash to the bottom. These are the eggs mermaids are born of." Lasiandra explained it with graceful ease while staring at the sky. She rocketed her eyes back to Gwen. "Why? Where do people come from?"

Obviously, Lasiandra had no understanding of sexuality, something which seemed radically foreign to Gwen's mind since she had received the sex talk nearly five years ago. Gwen didn't know if it would have been a good idea or bad idea to explain the mechanics of human origins, but Gwen did know that she was not going to be the one to broach the subject with Lasiandra. "Hospitals," she answered. "They're big buildings where sick people go to get better and couples go to get babies."

Lasiandra's ears pricked up. "Couples? Why would it take two to fetch something as small as a baby?"

Gwen swore within her mind, realizing she'd given away more than she intended to. "People tend to go together. It's exciting." She tried to shrug it off as if there was nothing more to say.

Lasiandra's mind seemed removed from the conversation, as if she were trying to decode what Gwen was saying and draw a more concrete truth out of it. The mermaid asked no more questions though. "Come swim with me. I have such wonderful things to show you, Gwen."

"I don't think I can keep up."

Lasiandra swam closer to her and turned around. "Hold onto me. Ride on my back, and I will take you to the most fantastic places you've ever imagined could rest underwater."

"I can't breathe underwater like you can," Gwen reminded her.

Gwen felt Lasiandra's webbed fin brush against the bottoms of her feet as they both treaded water so near to each other. "I know that, silly girl, but here." Lasiandra's soft hand took Gwen's and put it on her shoulder. "Just squeeze my shoulder when you need to come up for another breath and we'll surface."

Lasiandra's shoulder was slick and cool, but there was nothing inherently inhuman about it. Gwen put her other hand on Lasiandra's other shoulder. She pulled herself close to her, pressing her body against the mermaid's bare back. Bracing herself with her knees, she bent her legs and held on as tightly as she could. Gwen tried not to let the position bother her any more than it bothered Lasiandra. She had never been so close to someone while naked, but Lasiandra didn't even have a perception of what sexuality was. Consequently, she mistook Gwen's shy nervousness for a fear of betrayal, not a discomfort with intimacy.

"I won't hurt you," she repeated. "I swear by the sky and the stars and all that they speak. You do believe me… don't you?"

"Yes," Gwen answered, a little apprehensively.

"Good." Lasiandra flexed her tail, making sure she still had her full range of motion even with Gwen piggybacking on her. "I think honesty is the most important thing, don't you?"

"It is important."

"It's the *most* important. Without it, how can you trust? How can you love?"

The fear had run its course through Gwen and left her mind clear. She thought about everything that Old Willow and Peter had told her while in Neverland. Mermaids couldn't lie, and they knew the future through the unhatched stars and planets within the night sky. Knowing all this, a question occurred to Gwen. "Am I going to regret this?"

Lasiandra did not answer before she dove underwater, swimming away with Gwen on her back.

35

GWEN HAD GRABBED A MASSIVE, STARTLED BREATH BEFORE SHE was plunged underwater with Lasiandra. At first, she scrunched her eyes shut, but after a moment's time underwater, she realized how silly it was to blind herself to whatever Lasiandra was swimming by.

The water was astonishingly clear. Gwen could not see so far ahead, but Lasiandra shot through the water with a baffling swiftness, bringing Gwen to the shadowy landmarks she saw in the distance. Gwen never would have guessed how deep the waters were within the lagoon. She had assumed it was akin to any other cove or bay, but it seemed it was infinitely deeper. From the bottoms of its unseeable depths, a massive, totally submerged mountain erupted up from the sea floor. Staggering upward, peaking only feet below the surface, Gwen tried to comprehend its size as Lasiandra swam around it. The scraggly surface of the dark mountain made it look volcanic—dangerous, but dormant.

As they came nearer to it, Lasiandra reached out and tickled starfish and anemones, putting them all into wiggling flux. A rainbow of sea life vivaciously launched into motion, baffling Gwen as she shot by it. Squeezing Lasiandra's shoulder, she felt their direction immediately shift as they began bolting for the surface. Exploding out of the water, Lasiandra then swam on the very surface, allowing Gwen to push herself up into the air and breathe as much as she needed to before pressing herself back down against Lasiandra and taking off again.

They left the lagoon. Lasiandra swam out toward the open ocean, and Gwen felt the warm ocean current cutting against her bare body. There was so much freedom in the feeling. Gwen just wanted to bury herself in the water and never surface again.

They swam, exploring the totality of the sea's majesty, weaving in and out of brilliant schools of fish and past creatures so impossible in appearance that Gwen didn't know if they were a product of Neverland or merely the foreign depths of the ocean. An octopus scrambled by, a great, green stone of a turtle crossed their path, and a terrifying, grey creature dashed in and out of sight before Gwen could determine whether it was a shark. Any time Gwen was about to run out of breath, she only needed to squeeze Lasiandra's shoulder to bring her back to the breaking point between the sea and sky. There was nothing but the surface to divide the one infinite canvass from the other, and nothing else to interrupt their spanning beauty.

Eventually, Lasiandra swam back to the lagoon. Gwen did not know how long they had been gone, only that it had seemed far too long and not nearly long enough. She brought Gwen right up to a low rock so that she could climb out of the water and begin drying on the sun-warmed stone. Gwen wrung out her long hair, but she could do nothing more to expedite the process of drying off. The warm breeze and glow of the sun did their work fast enough on their own, and Lasiandra and Gwen talked in the meantime. Lasiandra still had questions.

"What are boys like?" she asked, flipping casually beside the rock Gwen was spread out on.

"Well, you know Peter," Gwen replied.

"But they can't all be like him. I mean the kind you find where you come from."

"Oh, they're not so different." She stared up at the clouds that were slowly drifting in from the ocean. Flat on her back, Gwen bore her body up to the sky and mused on Lasiandra's question.

"But they must be interesting, at least some of them. Aren't there any you care for?"

"Well, there's one," Gwen answered, folding her hands over her bare stomach. A smile eased onto her lips.

"What's his name?"

Gwen hadn't given him much thought since she landed in Neverland. Suddenly, homecoming dances, parties, and math classes seemed like the most trivial of events. "Jay," she answered.

"That's a letter, not a name."

"It's his name," she assured her. "Jay Hoek."

"Tell me more."

Gwen's giddiness was rediscovered within herself as soon as she said his name out loud. She was happy to tell Lasiandra. "He's a year older than me, but I'm in his algebra class because I skipped a year in math. We pass notes in class, but I don't know… He's really handsome. He's got this dark hair, but bright blue eyes… eyes almost like yours. He's on the football team, but he's not, like, a huge guy. He's just a really cool boy who's funny and knows all these bad jokes. He hasn't been seeing anyone since he broke up with his girlfriend last spring, but the homecoming dance is happening after next week and I'm sure he'll ask someone."

Gwen was suddenly aware, not just of how much she missed Jay, but of how much she missed having Claire and Katie to talk to about teenage girl things. She wouldn't have even minded if Jay asked swim-team Jenny to the homecoming dance, so long as Claire and Katie would be there for Gwen to gossip with about it. Fortunately, everything would be back to normal by tomorrow. Gwen would go home and restore her grip on reality. There was too much she loved about it to leave it behind, and the potential that it housed seemed even more limitless than the miracles of Neverland.

"Do you love him?" Lasiandra asked.

Gwen smiled at the sky. For all the times that she had talked with Claire about Michael and Jay, "love" had never come up. It was a crush. Wasn't that the appropriate term to use for teenage romances and young, fluttering hearts? Things were more poetic out here, beyond the reach of reason and prudence. She didn't answer Lasiandra, but she did realize the answer. *I think I do love him*, Gwen thought, still beaming at the sky.

Lasiandra spoke then, striving to sound nonchalant and betraying herself with her own casual tone. "Mermaids can grant wishes, you know."

Gwen turned her head and saw Lasiandra playing with her hair, disengaged in an attempt to feign disinvestment. "Really?"

"Mmhm. Your heart's desire. We can call your deepest dreams down from the stars they fly to."

"So I could just ask you for anything?" Gwen asked, her idle curiosity quickly taking on a life of its own.

"That's not quite how it works." Lasiandra stroked the surface of the water with her hands, as if treading water humanly. "In fact, you couldn't tell me what it was. You'd just have to ask me to fetch it from the stars—whatever you want most in the world."

"And just like that, you could give me whatever I truly wanted?"

"Well," Lasiandra admitted, "I couldn't just *give* it to you... but if you were willing to return the favor, and fetch me my heart's desire, well, certainly that would be a worthwhile exchange."

Gwen laughed, this time out of anxiousness. "And what's your heart's desire, Lasiandra?"

"Oh, I can't tell you," she emphatically responded. "Not any more than you could tell me what yours was. It breaks the spell if you say it out loud. My dreams hide out of reach on land, but I could tell you where to find them. All I would need is a sky glass. I'm sure you've seen them somewhere in your world, the beautiful glasses that show you what is? We could do it for each other, Gwen, and have everything we want together."

The mermaids' greed for mirrors was somewhat explained by this. Gwen couldn't begin to imagine how all these things were tied together, but clearly mirrors became powerful magical tools in the aquatic hands of mermaids. She had an unsettling urge to hand over her compact to Lasiandra.

The proposition smacked of being too good to be true. Gwen believed it was possible, but she doubted that it could come without a price. She remembered what Peter had told her about mermaids and their mysterious desires.

"It's a nice thought." Gwen stood up on the rock, feeling fully dry at last. "But I don't think I'm ready for my heart's desire."

"How can you not be ready to have what you want?" Lasiandra demanded. Gwen walked over the rocks, minding her balance as she trekked to the shore, and Lasiandra swam to keep up with her. Gwen shrugged her bare shoulders as she made her way back. There was no answer for why there was quite literally nothing Lasiandra could offer her to sway her. Lasiandra, obviously surprised and frustrated by this, announced, "Isn't there something you want?

Considering that thought and remembering the wisdom Old Willow had imparted, Gwen answered, "Oh, I'm sure I want something… I just don't think I know what it is."

"Then all the more reason to get it from the stars, Gwen. They know what you can't see. Why follow dreams you don't understand when you could catch them here and now with my help?"

"I guess I just like the idea of finding out what I want the old-fashioned way."

"But when will you know what you want, Gwen?" Lasiandra begged, trying to get the landmaid to see how foolish she was being.

Gwen smirked as she stepped onto the shore. She was perfectly dry now; the sand didn't even stick to the bottoms of her feet. "When I'm older," she answered, confident in that much.

Gwen redressed and shook out her hair, which was still slightly damp. The sky had completely clouded over at this point, and there was no longer a sun to bask in. Once she was fully clothed, Gwen pulled the three mangoes out of her satchel and gave them all to Lasiandra in gratitude for guiding her through Neverland's waters.

Lasiandra took them hungrily, but there was no longer a playful spark in her eye. Her smile had fallen, and her charms were no longer employed to guile Gwen into security and familiarity. Gwen could not know what was running through the mermaid's mind, but she saw the stilted, half-hidden look of melancholy, and knew that this was not how the beautiful Lasiandra had intended for this meeting to go.

"Goodbye, Lasiandra," Gwen said, waving as the mermaid laid back and slowly swam away, her hands full of the mangoes she balanced on her stomach.

"Until we meet again, Gwen."

"I don't think that we ever will."

"Oh, we will," Lasiandra replied, her feminine voice only partially obscuring her bitterness. "The stars have whispered that much to me. We will meet again, under circumstances you cannot yet conceive."

"That doesn't sound good." It wasn't the words, but how Lasiandra spoke them that put Gwen on edge.

"Oh, don't worry. You've swam with me in the depths of Neverland's waters, you've brought me mangoes, and I've given you my scale... you can believe me when I tell you what the planets themselves know—we are going to be great friends, in the end."

It was an amicable promise, but Gwen had never heard anything that sounded so much like a threat.

A shudder struck Gwen squarely in the spine. "The end of what?"

Lasiandra's smile preyed on Gwen's mind. "Silly girl, have you forgotten that there's a war going on? You'd better hurry back before it finds you, Gwen."

And just like that, Lasiandra disappeared into the depths of her oceanic territory. A distant roll of thunder startled Gwen. When she looked back up at the sky, which no longer matched the cheerful blue color of the water, the grey clouds ushered her to the conclusion that it was time to go.

CHAPTER 36

GWEN LEFT THE LAGOON SLOWLY, CLIMBING UP THE STONY STAIRS embedded in the cliff face with no great relish. Her encounter with Lasiandra had left her feeling unnerved. An ominous doubt followed her, even once she was back to the top of the cliff. Catching her breath, Gwen stared down at the lagoon, too clear and transparent for comfort.

The woods had seemed bright and welcoming on her way to the lagoon, but returning, Gwen found that the jungle's canopy dimmed what little light was left in the cloudy sky. Strange creatures cackled and cooed. Impossible birds with trailing plumage flitted between high branches, and furry creatures darted between rustling plants. Everything seemed to be scurrying for safety or warning of some impending trouble.

Her pace quickened, and quickened still, until Gwen found herself outright running. Dashing through the forest, she ran, more afraid because she did not know what she was trying to outrun. Everything in Neverland had gone perfectly for nearly a week and a half, and Gwen tried to dismiss her paranoia as the over-worrying impulse of grown-ups. There was no reason for her to suspect anything was wrong, but in Neverland, it was funny how the less it made sense for something to happen, the more likely it was to occur.

Tromping past overgrown roots and thrashing through bushes, Gwen realized she was not returning on the same course that she had come from. This was an unfamiliar stretch of jungle, and she was still a long ways from the underground home. She was turned around and confused, and another crack of thunder sounded before she finally ran into Bramble.

More accurately, Bramble flew into her. In a confused haze, his flying was erratic at best. He was combing through the forest though, frantically flitting. Bramble was the only fairy Gwen ever recognized, aside from Dillweed and Hollyhock. "Bramble!" Gwen held out her hands and let the unsteady fairy land in them. He stood in her palm, putting a hand against her thumb to support himself. His stomach churned, full of mango and unhappy about the exertion of his panicked flying. "What are you doing out here?"

The question seemed to go over his foggy head. His little form heaved up and down as he took in winded breaths, tired from coming so far so fast. His eyes made a faint jingling noise every time he blinked. "Bramble?"

He looked up at her, finally, and a look of shocked understanding seemed to register on his face. He exclaimed something, but the only word of it Gwen recognized was the whizzing-noise-word that fairies used to refer to Peter. The rest of it just sounded like an underwater bee-buzz. Much to her dismay, Bramble picked up and flew back in the direction he had come. "Wait, Bramble! I don't know how to get back!"

Having lost her confidence, Gwen had lost her ability to navigate the magical jungles of Neverland. Lifting off her own feet, she resolved to keep pace with Bramble, but lost sight of the tiny creature almost immediately. She flew in the direction he had vanished in, but her confidence was rapidly diminishing. She could have flown up above the tree line and searched for the meadow, but her nerves kept her pinned close to the ground. Faltering as she flew, she tried not to doubt what she had come to believe was an innate ability. Should she have gotten more fairy dust from Bramble before he took off? Would that have helped? She didn't dare fly any higher than she was prepared to fall, but such a precaution did not aid her in the whimsical endeavor of flying.

A flash of lightning electrified the sky, shooting light through the forest with a jarring pang. The boom of thunder followed immediately after. The sky was grey and the clouds shifted like a swarm of dark fish in a pond. Gwen feared she would be caught in a storm, but not a drop of rain had fallen yet.

All at once, Gwen found herself in a meadow. She had never been here before; she knew that. Wildflowers cropped up in sporadic clumps, and the long, green grasses were uncut at her calves. The tree line had suddenly broken. One minute, she was racing through the forest, the next, she was floating here. Pausing to catch her breath, she ironically felt safer in this open area than in the claustrophobic security of the forest. She landed gently, unthinkingly. Turning her head to the sky, she saw the faint grey clouds blowing and rolling away. Darker clouds seemed to be coming to take their place.

On the other side of the meadow, Peter burst into the clearing. Bramble was leading him, guiding the boy to poor, lost Gwen. If Gwen had understood the fairy language, she would have already known that.

"Gwenny!"

"Peter?" Gwen shouted. She ran to him, and between her bounding strides and his quick flight, they met in the middle of the meadow, cornflowers and lilacs growing up around them. Perhaps if he had been on the ground initially, she would have hugged him. Peter lingered in the air for just a moment though, and by the time he landed, the impulse to hug each other had melted away into urgent discussion. "What are you doing out here?" His voice carried the sort of anger that only accompanied concern.

"I got lost in the woods; I was trying to come back. Is something wrong, Peter?"

Bramble flitted back and forth, pacing in the air, objecting to Peter and Gwen having this conversation now, rather than when they were safely underground.

"The opposition, they've launched an attack. We've got to get to cover."

"What? No, it's just a storm." Gwen didn't understand what Peter was telling her, but she had already made up her mind that she didn't believe it.

"Gwen-dollie, we've got to go. There's—"

The sky was suddenly drained of light. The thin, grey clouds that had blocked the sun were eclipsed by darker, brooding storm clouds, and as the daylight faded, small, grey flecks began to rain down. As they drifted softly, Gwen knew it wasn't rain. Her attention was as captivated as Peter's was, but she did not understand what it was the way he did. "Snow?" she asked quizzically, looking at the grey and dirty powder as it started to fall around her.

Peter held out his hand and caught a flake of it, crushing it in his hand. It left a smoky residue on his palm. "Ash."

The winds picked up, and more of the ash furiously fluttered down. It became larger, and Gwen could hardly comprehend the charred flecks of paper that were plummeting down. Peter zipped up into the air, jumping more than flying, to grab a large square of it. He came back down immediately, a look of horror on his face.

"Peter, what is it?" Gwen pled, hoping that her fear was born of her unknowing, that if she only had answers she wouldn't be afraid, but from the look on his face, she knew that answers would only bring more fear.

The invisible hand of the wind grabbed the paper from out of Peter's hold. It blew straight to Gwen. Catching it, she realized it was a page from out of a newspaper; the title read—ISIS ATTACK ON ERBIL; HUNDREDS DEAD.

She had seen newspaper headlines before, but this news did not belong here. Not in Neverland. It was too dark, too terrifying of a thing to read amid the lilacs and cornflowers. Again, she begged, "What is this, Peter?"

The page was torn out of her hand by the vindictive wind. Peter answered her, with a word she had never feared so greatly. "Reality."

CHAPTER 37

"We've got to go. Now." Peter's voice, usually so carefree even in its demands, genuinely scared Gwen by sounding so authoritarian now. She didn't fear Peter—she couldn't fear Peter—but whatever instilled this sort of militant disposition in him was certainly to be feared.

He grabbed her hand and yanked her with him. Gwen stumbled as she adjusted to his run. "It'll be faster to fly," she announced, leaping into the air.

Gwen knew that they had to get to safety as quickly as possible, and her first thought was to take to the air. In that moment, the idea was so instantaneous she couldn't doubt it at all. She found herself lifting into the air, before she could even process Peter's screaming, "No!"

Instantly, she knew why he hadn't taken to the air. Flying had always given her a totality of control over her motion. Ungrounded by gravity, she became capable of any kind of movement she could imagine. Gwen had never attempted to fly in a reality storm.

A hurricane-grade force immediately began sweeping

her away, spinning her in all directions as if some invisible monster was whirling her around. The ash, newspaper scraps, and whatever else reality was blowing in began circling around her, as if latching onto the magic of her flight and making it the center of its swirling vortex. "*Peter*!" she screamed.

"*Gwenny*!" Peter grabbed her by her foot. "Come down!"

Her motion was totally out of her control. The storm had claimed her and hijacked her flying. "I can't! It's impossible!"

"That's irrelevant; just do it!"

Gwen heard him, and cleared her mind quickly of her precept that she was incapable of the impossible. It was impossible to break away from the storm, but that was no excuse. She focused on Peter's hands, wrapped around her ankles, and gave herself over to that force and that force alone. She tumbled down before she could gasp at the sensation of falling. Picking herself up off the ground, she let Peter grab her hand again. This time, they ran.

The wind was still whipping at them, and Gwen could hardly see with all the hair blowing in her face. What she wouldn't have given for a hair clip to keep it out of her eyes! Fortunately, she did not have to watch where she was going when Peter dragged her along. He became her eyes, and she trusted him more than she ever had her own sight. So much motion and chaos surrounded her that she became blind in a way she didn't know she could be, not from a lack of vision but by an excess of it. There was no time to make sense of any given color or shape. The forest floor that they ran over was not made of dirt, sticks, leaves, and shrubs, but rather splotches of green and blurs of a color formerly known as brown.

"Where are the others?" Gwen cried, realizing with a guilty pang that she was not the only one she needed to be concerned for. What about Rosemary, the little sister she had purportedly followed here to look after?

"They're where we're going."

Despite how loud he spoke in order to be heard over the shrill howl of wind, Peter was not yelling. He was not calm, but he was competent, and if he felt any fear, he did not manifest it in his features. Gwen saw how confidently he navigated these woods… as if running through them was a game he had played before and would play again, unerring even when he played for great stakes. In anyone else, she would have taken this bold fearlessness as maturity, but in Peter, it was something else entirely. It was as if, in times of great danger, he could totally disengage, reminding himself, *It's only a game and I want to win.* When Gwen saw the faint smile that had crept onto his lips, she did not trust her eyes, but that sight told her that Peter had pushed consequences out of his mind, that he was running not for the fear of danger… but for the desire to do what he aimed to do.

All the while that they ran, Bramble clung to Gwen, clutching the collar of her dress with his hands and crouching on her shoulder. He whispered sweet reassurances to her, but Gwen neither heard nor understood the fairy language he was spilling into her ear.

It was dark beneath the canopy of trees and the sky beyond shrouded-in clouds. Gwen felt as though night was setting in, but it never got any darker. As they ran, the perpetual grey kept them caught in a daylight-darkness they could not escape.

A different kind of howl began offsetting the noise of the wind—a sound like static and a painful ringing in her ears. She wanted to believe it was some auditory hallucination, induced by the stress of the moment and the desire to hear something else—anything else—besides the violent wind. It grew louder though, coming closer and approaching with unrelenting speed. Gwen felt, perhaps rightfully, that if that noise touched her, it would surely kill her. The tone of it changed, and there was nothing to compare it to but the sound of a radio out of range, trying desperately to pull AM commentary down when the signals source was a world away.

With a shrieking crash, the noise stopped and the earth shook. As they ran over the uneven ground, this earthquake was all it took to throw Gwen off her feet. With a disoriented scream, she sprawled out and tried to brace herself for the fall as Peter's hand slipped out of hers. He had only stumbled, but as soon as his fingers had disappeared from hers, Gwen cried, "Peter!"

Bramble was tugging at her collar now, trying to pull her up himself, or at least suggest to her the importance of getting back up. "They haven't got us yet, Gwenny," Peter told her, giving her a hand and helping her onto her feet.

Sure enough, they were all still in one piece. They took off running again, but could not outrun the fury of the falling ash. More paper began to rain down, no longer drifting but flinging itself through the air. Entire sheets of newsprint blew at them, and Peter batted them away as they rampaged toward him on the wind. Some of them were still on fire, burning as they whirled down. Gwen stayed close to Peter, investing all of her confidence in him and his ability to keep her safe through this onslaught of unwanted reality.

As they broke the tree line and finally reached the grove their underground home was built beneath, the fairy broke away and took off in another direction. Gwen called out after Bramble, but Peter assured her, "Don't worry. He'll be safer once he's with his own."

They stomped through the grove, which was now covered in a singed layer of newsprint. The paper was caught in the branches of trees and littered the grove. Peter gazed at their oak tree and looked almost delighted by the challenge it presented. "Follow me," he demanded. "Don't fly any more than you have to, just one branch to the next."

He leapt up to a low branch himself, but before Gwen could pursue him, a scrap of flaming newspaper blew into her. The wind wrapped it around her left forearm, and she began yelling, trying to fling it off. The paper clung to her skin, burning and searing her arm as she tried desperately to peel it away. At last, she managed to tear it away, but the pain did not go with it.

"Gwen!" Peter called.

"I'm coming!" Gwen knew she would have to ignore the pain for a moment. She would have to pass it off to herself as the burning strain of exercise, not the wound that it was. Following after Peter, she flew from one branch to the next, climbing whenever she could. The wind still struck her, as if punishing her for disregarding gravity, but by the time it hit her, she always had a firm hold of her next branch. Pulling herself up in these increments, she watched Peter and chased after the boy, knowing this was one of the last places he would ever lead her.

He waited for her at the top of the tree where they would be able to slide down into the security of their underground home. When she climbed up to that final branch, Peter helped pull her up. He didn't say anything—he wouldn't, not until they were safely underground—but Gwen followed his somber-curious eyes and, for the first time, looked at her arm.

It was red and slightly enflamed, but it did not look like a burn… not with the printed black letters singed on her skin. Her left forearm seemed covered in a wordy tattoo, somehow transferred to her flesh from the burning newsprint. Gwen did not consciously read it, but absorbed words like *obesity, heart disease,* and *epidemic*, as she stared in horror and awe at the invasive wound reality had left her with.

There was no time to contemplate it. Peter shepherded her to the hole in the tree and gave her a little push. Gwen was guided by his gestures, her body still hers to move but only with the intention and direction of Peter's hands. She slipped down into the tree and fell as she exhaled one long breath that slowly became a panicked scream.

CHAPTER 38

THEY REMAINED IN THE UNDERGROUND HOME, SOME COWERING, some curious, for the duration of the bombing. The place transformed in Gwen's eyes; it was no longer a playfully hidden fort that housed them, but a wartime bunker. Shelter, protection… Gwen had never stopped to think that Neverland would need to be outfitted with defenses, but then she had never stopped to believe anyone when they spoke of this conflict as a war.

There was no disguising the noise. It didn't sound like anything other than the explosive assault that it was. The little tree that grew in the middle of the room shook violently with every impact above them. Even underground, the children could feel the earth shake with restless tremors.

In reality, a bombing would have inspired nothing but fear. However, among the lost children of Neverland, it brought the entire spectrum of human emotion.

Sal and Newt were demonstrative in their excitement. The two of them had climbed up onto the big bed, trying to gauge and guess when each new strike would hit. Perfectly confident in Peter and his ability to provide them a safe haven underground, they feared nothing from the bombs. They leapt up and fell back down onto the bed with every strike, laughing and making moaning, dying noises. Gwen found this alternately macabre and relieving.

Blink quietly watched the ceiling, her neck tilted back and eyes fixated on the earthy roof of their home. She stared as if the rest of the world was visible to her, and she really could see beyond the dirt ceiling to what was happening on the surface level. Quiet and thoughtful, either she could not be disturbed or she already was, deeply.

Spurt's usual energy became jittery anxiety. He was uncomfortable, almost claustrophobic, within the room when he knew that he could not leave it for reasons he could not comprehend. Surprisingly, his feeling of entrapment subsided once Bard took him in her arms. Sitting in his little dog bed, she sat him on her lap and wrapped her arms around him, explaining everything that was happening as well as she could manage, remaining calm and collected. She was the eldest of the children, but the way that she took hold of her smallest comrade suggested a maternal instinct well beyond her years.

Jam mirrored Sal and Newt's animated sense of energy, but it was a whining, inpatient guise for her worry. She asked questions of everyone. She paced around, dragging her feet and making faces, complaining that the fairies were gone, and always wondering aloud, "Is it over yet?" even though she was well aware it wasn't. Rosemary stayed with her, trying to glean confidence from the one child who didn't seem to have any at the moment.

Gwen listened to Bard tell Spurt about all the bombings she had sat through without a scratch, and her fear slightly ebbed away. Bard talked and talked and talked, which started

Gwen thinking about how long the young girl must have been here on the island. Forever young in Neverland, who was to say if Bard had come here a year ago or ten? Or perhaps even longer ago. What if she had come here years before Gwen herself was even born?

The other children had all been through bombings like this before. Rosemary and Gwen were at a distinct disadvantage for dealing with this. Rosemary's entire morning was spent safely underground, so she did not fear the event as Gwen did. Like so many of the other children, she took her cues from Peter. His lighthearted nonchalance dismissed the majority of the lost children's concerns.

He was not somber, even as he dealt with Gwen's burn. There was a shade of seriousness to his voice and motions, but even that did not obscure his carefree nature. On the wall of the underground house, there were drawers that Gwen did not realize were drawers, inlaid seamlessly into the earthy wall, covered again with a fine layer of dirt. Misshapen and oddly sized, Peter opened them up by their rock-knob handles until he found one that had what he was looking for.

With a transparent, blue bottle and a thick, white handkerchief, Peter came back to Gwen. She'd sat down on one of the taller toadstool seats, its spongy, orange-and-white top compressing slightly under her. She held her hand up, not letting anything touch her forearm, not moving it at all. The pain reminded her of a summer long ago when she had unknowingly ventured too near a wasp nest in the park and left with no less than four throbbing stings. Gwen had never been badly burned before, and she numbly wondered if this was what it felt like to be burned, or what it felt like to be touched by the sort of surreal flames that could only rain down on Neverland.

Peter soaked the handkerchief in the blue bottle's

contents, which smelled like equal parts oranges and honeysuckles. Gwen winced, preparing to feel the pain of an antiseptic, but when Peter draped the damp cloth over her burned forearm, it only felt cool and calming. It continued to smell sweet, lightly perfuming her arm and the room.

Rosemary was curious and somewhat frightened by the inflamed skin and strange words now printed on her older sister's arm. They discussed it quietly, but the others came to gawk when they grew bored of the bombing and the present emergency. When Jam eagerly asked, "What is it?"

Peter answered simply, "The reason we stay down here until it's over."

Gwen took the damp cloth off in order to flip it over, as per Peter's instructions. As she did, Rosemary struggled to read the words. Bard, the only other child who knew how to read, seemed to know better than to desire to know what Gwen's arm said.

"Let me kiss it and make it all better!" Rosemary declared, doing so before Gwen could object. To her surprise, the pressure of Rosemary's lips against her burned skin did not hurt, but actually did make it feel considerably better.

"Me too! I want to kiss Gwenny!" Spurt announced, leaping away from Bard to do so. It became an incredibly popular idea. Soon, Gwen found that all the young children had kissed her arm with a joyful desire to help her. Perhaps the strange, perfumed medicine was finally reaching its full effect, or maybe there was something to be said for the medicinal value of affection.

She looked to see where Peter had wandered to and saw him up in his hammock, whittling away at some new project. As wood shavings fell to the floor, he seemed preoccupied with his own work and apathetic to Gwen's condition, now that he had done his part to help her through it. While the others dissolved into a flurry of conversation and playful speculation as to how Gwen got her tattoo-burn, she watched Peter until he turned himself over in his hammock and looked back. "It's over."

The assault had subsided. Several minutes had ticked by without another quake of any size. A military, somewhere far away and close to home, had depleted its arsenal for the time being. Whatever damage was done was done, and the children waited for Peter to shoot up the oak tree before they scrambled into their own tree shafts to follow after.

Gwen was slow to animate, but Rosemary tugged at her, pulling her older sister along until she remembered how to move on her own. She glanced at her tattoo burn; the dark lettering had faded only slightly after Peter's treatment. "Come on, Gwen!" Rosemary insisted, getting ready to ascend to the grove.

A jarring feeling hit Gwen, as if reality had struck her and was struggling to climb over her. "Rosemary," she began, uncertain what rubble or decay would be left from the attack. "*This* is why we can't stay."

Rosemary smiled sadly, as if amused and disappointed at her older sister's response. Gwen had never seen such a knowing, pitying look from her sister. Little Rosemary! How could that girl look at her as if she knew so much more than her older sister?

"No, Gwen. This is why I have to stay." Rosemary stepped into the hollow tree, sucking in a huge breath that inflated her cheeks and shot her up to the surface before another word could be said.

Reluctantly, Gwen followed suit and zipped up the oak tree. She possessed no desire to return outside, having just survived the firestorm of reality that she'd been caught in.

Peter was still standing on the oak tree branch outside of

its entrance hole. He leaned an arm against a higher branch, propping himself against it morosely as he surveyed the ravaged landscape of his Neverland.

Gwen gasped, trying a moment too late to suppress the noise. Peter glanced at her, the unhappy look of his face unchanged by her presence. He turned his attention back to the smoldering countryside.

Neverland, so bright and green, had been buried under a layer of ash grey newspaper, but Gwen saw now the purpose of that malicious paper. She'd been a proud girl scout once, and had earned her campfire badge stoking fires. She knew it took kindling.

Covered in flammable, ashy newspaper, the land had been easy to raze once the real bombs detonated. The pine trees drooped down, their branches weighted with dark ash. Palm trees had become toothpicks. Entire natural orchards seemed to be wrought iron sculptures in the distance. The fires had put themselves out, but birds circled en masse overhead: songbirds, hawks, ravens, two peacocks, and their golden cousin the phoenix. Their screeching cries and tweeting laments were echoed by creatures of the Neverland forest-jungle. It all seemed distant and dreamlike to Gwen. The sky had cleared of clouds, but the outpouring of sunlight only gave a glow to the destruction.

Silly girl, have you forgotten that there's a war going on? You'd better hurry back before it finds you, Gwen.

Lasiandra's words sounded in her mind for the first time since she had left the lagoon. The mermaid had warned her, but Gwen could not abate the suspicion that she had not made it back in time. She might have been safe from this storm within the comfort of the underground home, but there was no denying that the war had found her. With a painful longing to revise the past, Gwen wished that she had departed from

Neverland yesterday, or the day before, or never come at all. Her heart was torn in half a dozen directions, every piece of it screaming for something other than this sight of wartime ruin.

Laughter distracted her. Taking her eyes down to the grove, Gwen saw the children. Already, they were discovering the strange oddities of a burned environment. She could barely make out Newt and Sal chasing after Jam with charred sticks, all of them scream-laughing with glee while Bard and Blink picked at charred flowers for black bouquets.

Feeling her burn wound throb under its bandage, Gwen angrily muttered, "They don't know better. They don't understand the way we do."

Only as she spoke did she see what was in Peter's eyes as he watched his compatriots below. There was no rage—no frustration with their childish irreverence. There was envy.

His jealousy of the children turned to anger with little prodding. "Who's we?" he remarked, his curt tone conveying his bitterness.

Wishing she could redact the remark for reasons she did not yet fully understand, Gwen answered, "You, me. Us. We see it differently than the kids do. We know what it is, because we're ol—" She stopped, not wanting to finish the word when she became conscious of what she was really saying.

"We're what? We're older? Like the people who did this?" He looked back to his friends in the grove. "Of course they know better, better than us, at least. They're what will breathe life back into everything the bombing ravaged. They're not the ones moping in a tree. It's us. We've forgotten better. That's all."

"I'm sorry."

Peter didn't look at her. His words cut through his teeth, making it clear that he was not apologizing to her, but to the island he called home. "Me too."

A shrill cry from below took their attention away. "Peter!" Gwen might not have been able to recognize the other children's sound of panic, but she knew Rosemary's voice anywhere.

"Rose!" she called, compelled to answer the call even when it was not directed to her. She and Peter leapt off the tree branch like synchronized divers. Shooting straight to the ground, Gwen surprised herself by how seamlessly she managed to pull out of her freefall and into flight. She didn't even stop to think about it, the instinct to get to Rosemary just carried her.

The others gathered around Rosemary in a nervous circle, but they parted to let Peter and Gwen in. The girl was not visibly hurt, and everyone's attention was on what she held cupped gingerly in her hands. Tears inched down her cheeks as she held the creature out for Peter and her sister to see.

It's a mouse, Gwen thought as she approached. When she saw wings, she assumed it was a dragonfly. Countless speculations flashed through her mind as she neared, but never once did she stop to think it was Bramble, because Bramble was a fairy and fairies glowed, and the little body that Rosemary held was not glowing.

39

GWEN HAD NEVER HEARD A FAIRY CRY. IT WAS A BEAUTIFUL AND heartbreaking noise that Hollyhock made, like the ringing of crystal, the hum of bees… the sound of anything and everything when heard from underwater. For once, Gwen understood the fairy language, not because she could discern the words, but because she could identify the feelings that were trying to be communicated.

Peter had taken Bramble from Rosemary and laid him down on a patch of grass that still held a green color. He sat down cross-legged beside his tiny friend, plucked one of the crisply burned flowers within his reach, and laid it down over Bramble, whispering as he did so, "I do believe in fairies." The brittle, black dandelion sprung to life with these words, and a yellow blossom grew back out of the ash and destruction. The other children did the same, pulling the charred flowers and piling them on Bramble's body, whispering the words that brought the blossoms back to full bloom and color.

A wisp of hope entered Gwen, thinking that this was somehow a process to revive Bramble, but only the flowers sparked back to life. Before Gwen could make peace with the thought that this was merely a goodbye, that *I do believe in fairies* was only whispered in homage, to honor one who had been, Hollyhock arrived. Everyone stepped back to make way for the fairy, tiny in form and large in grief. Only Peter stayed where he was, seated beside Bramble as Hollyhock dug through the flowers, tossing them off him so that she could pull his little body close to hers.

The children bore the loss with quiet pain. Bard stood between Blink and Spurt, holding their hands so that she was the only one of the three who did not have a free hand to wipe away her tears. Jam squatted down, an angry look of betrayal on her face, but tears seeped out of her eyes just the same. Sal and Newt did not cry, but Sal bent over to wrap himself entirely around Newt in a hug. It was impossible to say which boy derived more solace from this embrace. Rosemary only looked confused, slumped down and sitting in the charred grass, her legs spread wide apart, her arms hanging limply at her sides. Gwen went and sat with her, taking her little sister in her arms and kissing her hair. The confusion did not leave Rosemary's face.

Hollyhock's weeping continued, and there was an unspoken understanding that she was the only one allowed to be demonstrative with her grief. Gwen looked around and suddenly realized that the children all understood this exactly as she did, as any adult or human being would. Youth was not a blanket of naivety; it could only shelter them from so much. Somewhere in her growing, Gwen had forgotten to realize how little change had actually occurred. She might have argued that, intellectually, Bramble's death registered with her in a way it didn't for the others, but there was no denying that they all had the same emotional capacity. Age did not—it could not—have any real effect against the nature of a human life.

After a while, Peter could not take it. He stood up and walked away. When he was halfway across the grove, he took off flying. The rage and sadness blurred on his face was the last thing Gwen saw before he turned his back to them. She thought to chase after him, but she was not so egotistical as to think there was anything she could say to help him. Gwen hugged Rosemary tighter, knowing that her little sister was the one who needed her now.

Hollyhock continued to cry, but it was not long after Peter left that Dillweed arrived. He brought with him another fairy that Gwen did not recognize. With somber grace, they landed beside Hollyhock and the body she cradled. It was a painfully long process, separating Hollyhock from Bramble, but once they had done so, Dillweed and the other fairies lifted Bramble up between them and fluttered away with him. Hollyhock trailed behind, quietly sobbing as they disappeared into the jungle.

Peter did not return. The children set to work cleaning the grove. It was a mellow, melancholy sort of play. Long branches from pine trees became brooms to help the girls sweep away the ash and paper that covered the ground. Others pulled pots, pans, buckets, and the laundry basket out of the underground home and raced to the stream to fill them up with fresh water. They came back to sprinkle it over the grass and flowers, watering the scorched land. At the touch of Neverland's water, all the plants seemed to be revitalized. They unfurled back into vibrant green tendrils, leaves, and stems, as if the water promised that all the unpleasantness was over and they could come back now.

Still, Peter did not return. As evening began to set in and the grove grew golden from the glow of the sinking sun, Gwen suggested that they have a nice dinner outside before it got dark. Everyone was in favor of the idea, but it was Blink who articulated the sentiment best, when she announced that they could have all the foods and fruits Bramble had loved best, and put a little aside for him even though he was gone.

Newt and Sal went off, monkeying in the trees and filling up the good wicker basket with all the fruit they could find. Bard took Blink with her when she went to find the Neverland Bird and ask for some milk. Jam was eager to light a fire, but reluctant to stay and actually cook the rice once the campfire was lit. Rosemary kept her company, and together they brewed a rice soup with little grains that were every color of an impossible rainbow. Spurt picked berries because he knew where the best bushes were, and Gwen brought the mismatched dishes and picnic blankets up from the underground home so that she could set everyone's places outside.

No fairies joined them for dinner, and even by the end of it, Peter still had not reappeared. They ate without their usual exuberance, but there was a quiet hum of joy that gradually seeped into their conversation. It was a reverent, cautious joy, but it felt natural. Gwen struggled to recover from the bombing and all its repercussions, wishing she had not forgotten whatever it was that prevented children from dwelling on the misfortunes of life.

CHAPTER 40

WHEN THEY FINISHED DINNER, PLATES AND DISHWARE WERE stacked lazily in the wicker basket that had previously been filled with fruit. Without any vote or discussion, it was unanimously decided that dishes could wait until tomorrow. Everyone moved closer together, clustering in front of Gwen and wrapping themselves up in the picnic blankets. She massaged her arm, both curious and afraid to peel back the bandage and see what the wound looked like now. It still stung under pressure, but Gwen trusted that it would heal well with time… something which would begin moving again once she returned home.

"Are you really leaving tomorrow, Gwenny?" Spurt asked.

Gwen nodded until she found words. "I have to."

"You don't *have* to do anything," Jam muttered, disgruntled that Gwen could still be so tied to the adult world.

"You could stay," Rosemary whispered, but only her sister heard the suggestion, and Gwen would not dignify the possibility by rebuking it.

"Will you tell us a story?" Bard asked. "One more? Before

you go?"

"Yes!" Spurt exclaimed, bouncing on his haunches and pounding the ground in excitement.

"Another story!"

"One with lots of adventure!"

"A princess! Put a Princess Eleanor in it!"

"Tell us a story, Gwendy!"

She was flooded by their desire, and could hardly corral their requests even by consenting to them. "Yes, yes, I will, alright."

The children settled down, their eyes widening as the last drowsy rays of daylight dipped out of the sky. By the glow of an even half-moon, they watched Gwen as she began to tell the story they had mercilessly begged of her.

"Once upon a time, there was a kingdom isolated from all the rest of the world by the largest ocean. A great ring of mountains encircled it. The kingdom was called Fardonia. It was so far away that it was where the very word 'far' comes from. The people lived in the valley at the center, surrounded by the towering mountains. The mountains were so tall and treacherous that no one had ever crossed them to either leave or enter Fardonia.

"The tallest of these was not a mountain, but a volcano. It bubbled with magma lava deep at its core, but it was dormant for the most part. On the rare occasions when it did begin to seep hot lava, the citizens of Fardonia picked up their belongings and headed to the far side of the valley, evacuating their homes and rebuilding after they were sure that the tiny eruption was over. This was a reality of life for them; they could not have left the island if they wanted to, so there was no other option but to evacuate and rebuild each time the volcano erupted. It was never a very big eruption, so the people of Fardonia lived mainly without fear.

"The greatest problem that the eruptions posed was something else entirely. You see, the volcano was home to a great number of dragons. A clan of the monsters lived deep within the lava, swimming through it and breathing in it as easily as fish in water. It was their home, and the powerful monsters resided peacefully within it. The problem was that when the lava bubbled up, it sometimes carried away dragon eggs with it."

Jam gasped and covered her mouth with her hands, a little afraid of dragons even in stories.

"If a dragon egg was taken down into the village, the older dragons and mother dragon would rise up out of the smoking volcano and come down with fury and wrath on the village, looking for the missing egg. Afraid for their little dragon baby, they destroyed anything in their path with their hot fire breath and hideously sharp claws, until they found their egg and carried it back to the warmth and safety of the lava.

"This caused untold damage to all of Fardonia, and risked the lives of its inhabitants, so it was decreed that after any eruption, the affected area would be searched as soon as it was safe. If anyone found a dragon egg, half a dozen of the kingdom's finest soldiers would carry it back up to the volcano and throw it into the crater, where it would splash into the lava far, far below. This was done several times successfully, and the dangerous dragons never came searching for their eggs.

"But weren't the dragon eggs *heavy*?" Spurt demanded.

"That's why it took so many soldiers to carry it!" Newt answered.

This issue clarified, Gwen continued. "It had been several years since anyone had so much as seen a dragon, when the volcano erupted yet again. Everything went according to their emergency plan, and the people were safely evacuated.

Afterward, they searched the lava-soaked village for dragon eggs. However, while they were searching for a dragon egg, they found something much more alarming—the broken shell of a dragon egg.

"Although it had never happened before, it seemed that during this eruption, a dragon egg had been carried down, only to hatch in the valley. A tiny baby dragon was loose somewhere in the village below the volcano."

"Oh no," Bard muttered.

"They followed the scorched footprints and the trail of burnt houses until they found the tiny beast, no bigger than a bobcat, curled up and sleeping in the fireplace of one of the houses. Its crimson body shone with a fiery glimmer, and its golden claws and teeth curled as it slept. As it breathed, little sparks flickered out of its long snout. Very carefully, the kingdom's soldiers trapped it in a net, and then shut it inside of a wine barrel before it even woke up. The king ordered them to deliver it to the top of the mountain as quickly as possible, and the soldiers took off at once in the hope that they would be able to return it to the lava pit deep in the volcano's crater before it awoke."

"How was it sleeping if it was daytime?" Newt demanded.

"Shush!" Sal insisted.

"Babies sleep a lot," Bard answered.

"That they do," Gwen agreed. "So the baby dragon slept while they carried it. The mountainside was treacherous and the cliffs hard to climb, but the soldiers slowly made progress carting the wine barrel with the sleeping dragon inside of it. The top was in sight, the edge of the crater just minutes away, when they felt the dragon tossing in the barrel, restlessly waking itself up. They hurried faster, but the dragon's breath began to burn the wine barrel, and it became obvious they could not contain it. As the barrel caught fire and burned away, the dragon pushed its way through the charred wood and took off running up the hill. The soldiers ran after it, chasing it toward the mouth of the volcano to be sure that it got back home before the elder dragons came looking for it in the villages."

Gwen paused briefly, marveling at the look of rapt attention each of the children gave her. While she took a short moment to gather her thoughts, Jam asked with almost fearful curiosity, "And then what happened?"

"They chased the dragon all the way to the edge of the volcanic crater, and watched it dive back into the pit of molten lava," Gwen continued, "but there was a terrible problem. The lava did not rest down inside the cavernous pit of the volcano; it had bubbled up, almost to the surface. The soldiers realized it was about to explode, destroying not only a few houses or a little land, but covering the entire valley and decimating all of Fardonia. In a mad race, they hurried back down to the valley and went directly to the king to inform him of their discovery.

"There was nothing that could be done, nowhere for the people to go, and just when the people thought that their fate could be no darker, the dragons flew out of the volcano's mouth."

"*They're all going to die!*" Spurt yelled. Bard had to hold him and pet his head before he was calm enough to let Gwen continue.

"Every one of those reptilian monsters launched themselves out of the mountain, soaring into the sky and flinging off the last remnants of the lava on their bodies. As they cooled off in flight, they circled the villages. People began to scream as the dragons descended, but they landed peacefully on the ground. Countless dragons with sparkling red, ruby-like scales lay motionless on the floor of the valley.

"No one knew what to make of this, but before any

conclusions could be reached, the volcano exploded. A flaming mass of magma shot into the air. Ash began to rain down on the valley and smoke billowed down. The sky grew black, and the destruction of Fardonia was imminent.

"With no other option, the people suddenly saw that their one slim chance of survival was to climb atop the dragons, holding to their scales and clinging to the beasts for dear life. As the lava neared, the citizens scrambled to mount the dragons. When all were aboard, the winged monsters took back to the sky, flying away from the smoke, ash, volcano, and valley. The entire island of Fardonia disappeared on the horizon, but the dragons flew on.

"Eventually, they landed on a bright new continent, far away from their original home, but safe and sound. The people dismounted the dragons, shakily climbing down to the field where they had landed. As the people left them, the dragons took to the sky again, to finally return to their home, deep within the volcanic underbelly of Fardonia. The dragons were never seen again, but the people made a new life for themselves. They never forgot the magical beasts that had plagued them for so long, but ultimately saved them all… and that's where dragons come from. They breathe the fire of the Fardonia volcano, and will still ravage any place they believe to have one of their eggs since dragons will defend anything they really love."

Gwen folded her hands in her lap to signify that her story was done. She hadn't been conscious of how dramatically she was gesturing with them until she finished the tale. Her voice had intimated the end of the story, and yet the lost children were compelled to ask questions.

"What happened to the dragons?"

"Where did the people go?"

"Did the baby dragon grow up?"

"Why didn't they just live underground?"

Gwen could hardly keep track of who was asking what. They all talked over each other, with no concern for any question in particular, only the continuation of the story.

She laughed, to see the joy that it had brought them, and batted away the fireflies that seemed to be hovering closer to her and listening as well. The air was alive with warmth, and the night sky still had a trace of purple swirled into its blackness. The half-moon, high in the sky, was tipped like an ear straining to hear the questions and stories of the children below it.

Laughing and taking all of this in, Gwen's eyes lifted, as if they knew better than she did where she should be looking. Leaned against one of the hollow trees—the knotty maple tree—was Peter. He stared at her, and Gwen suspected that he'd been listening from a distance. He said nothing, but he held her eyes. His arms crossed, he bore only a slight, aloof smile on his lips.

CHAPTER 41

GWEN COULD NOT SLEEP THAT NIGHT. FOR HER ENTIRE WEEK IN Neverland, sleep had never come easy for her. Her body clung to the schedule of late nights she had cultured in reality. There was something fundamentally strange about falling asleep without first spending a few hours online. However, the thought that she would be able to return to that pattern tomorrow night left her sleepless altogether.

She buried her face in her pillow, trying not to let Rosemary squeeze her out of the big bed. Every time she thought she was almost asleep, she remembered the burn on her arm and a senseless fear overtook her. Pulling the edge of the covers close around her, Gwen could only lull herself into a groggy sense of tiredness. So, although she did not immediately notice the creeping boy move through the underground home, she was just awake enough to hear him draw in a big breath and vanish up one of the hollow trees.

Sitting up in bed quickly, her eyes were already adjusted to the darkness enough to affirm what she suspected—Peter's hammock was empty.

Unaware of where he was off to, but certain she didn't want to be left behind, Gwen dashed out of bed, leaving Rosemary and Jam plenty of room to sprawl out on their side of the big bed. She didn't even bother with shoes. Gwen skittered across the floor on her bare tiptoes, trying not to wake anyone, even in her hurry. She shot up the hollow oak in her camisole and polka-dotted pants. Once again, she was in her pajamas, following after Peter Pan.

She drew in a breath so big that she felt dizzy as she ascended the dark shaft of the oak's trunk. When it lifted her to the opening, she flung herself out and quietly called, "Peter?"

He was not in earshot, but his motion caught her eye. Diving down after him, Gwen flew as fast as she could in an attempt to catch up as he headed into the woods. Once among the trees, she could see neither hide nor hair of where he had gone, but she could hear that he was again on foot. The air buzzed with fireflies, and moonlight fell in broken puzzle pieces through the jungle's canopy. Gwen hovered lightly above the ground so that her own footsteps would not distract her from the sound of Peter's.

She could not see where she was going; she could only move toward the soft noise of Peter as he paced through the jungle. She marveled at how he could navigate so seamlessly through the darkness, never tripping or running into anything. He did not move quickly, but Gwen had a hard time keeping up even in the air. She held her hands out, braced to run against a slender tree or low-hanging branch she could not see.

In the past week, Gwen had spent a good deal of time exploring the island and running through its woods, but she teemed with the sense that they were going somewhere she had never been before, somewhere magical, even by

Neverland standards.

Sure enough, Peter unknowingly led her to the heart and soul of the island. The vines and ivy grew thick, draping down from the limbs and branches of the trees. Peter pushed the tangled plants aside and disappeared behind a solid wall of foliage. Gwen cautiously followed on foot, brushing aside the voluminous vines to see what hid behind them.

As she stepped, Gwen felt her bare foot squish into a thick mud under a few inches of water. The marsh water was warm, and she watched as the mud began to light up. Each step that Gwen took gave the ground and water directly beneath her foot a faint blue glow.

The marsh was devoid of trees, except for the majestic willow tree in the center of the swampy ground. The entire mire was encircled by the curtain of vines that Gwen had passed through, hidden away in the folds of Neverland's woods.

Hundreds of iridescent lights drifted slowly around the willow tree. The rainbow glow of fairies wove in and out of the canopy created by the willow tree's long, limp branches. Peter had slowed, so Gwen took a moment to roll up the cuffs of her pajama pants before following after him.

Finally, the sound of footsteps through the shallow water behind him alerted Peter to the fact that he had been followed. He turned to see Gwen and paused. She gave a little wave, suddenly feeling out of place. She hadn't known Peter was going to a secret fairy marsh when she started following him. Initially, he looked irritated with her, but rather than be bothered by her presence, he seemed to accept it. As he parted the weeping branches of the willow to walk through, he held them apart for Gwen. She scurried over, splashing the shallow water and leaving glowing blue footprints in the mud. Beside Peter at last, she entered the cocoon of the wide willow tree, the limp branches closing behind the two of them.

Fairies circled the willow tree's trunk, lapping it slowly. Others sat on the knots and protruding roots. There were more fairies than Gwen had ever seen, and she was close enough to distinguish the features of many of them: the metallic hair, the minute noses and mouths, skirts made of lily petals, shirts sewn from ivy leaves, acorn hats, and spider-silk scarves.

At the base of the tree was a little raft, woven out of willow twigs and their slender, green leaves. It was loaded with berries and flowers, all piled beside Bramble's body. Gwen could not find Dillweed in this crowd of fairies, but she did see Hollyhock, lingering beside the little boat, standing waist-deep in the marsh, her long, golden-dark braids trailing behind her and bobbing with the ripples in the water. As if they had been waiting for Peter to come pay his respects, the fairies began pulling leaves off the willow tree. Rolling them up into long tubes, each fairy took their leaf and dragged it quickly across the bark of the tree in an act that was two parts friction and one part magic. The willow leaves instantly began to burn. Three fairies flew down to the raft and pushed it into motion, but the rest of them flew over it, dropping their lighted leaves onto the pyre.

Some of the leaves fell beside it, extinguishing immediately on the water, but enough of the little torches fell on the raft to ignite it. As the pyre boat drifted toward Peter and Gwen, they stepped aside and parted the curtain of willow branches to let it float through.

As the little flame on the water passed by, Gwen whispered reverently, "I do believe in fairies."

The fairies trailed slowly after it, hovering through the opening in the willow curtain that Peter and Gwen held for them. They neither minded nor acknowledged Gwen's presence. They had long since stopped questioning who Peter deemed worthy to witness the intimacies of their world.

As the pyre broke apart into sinking ash and rising smoke, Gwen watched the glow of Bramble's body drift up to the sky. Feathery colors liquidly surged up to the sky like faint trails of smoke. Like a will-o-the-wisp glowing on the surface of the water, Bramble's flames died out, leaving behind a beautiful glow that slipped away to the stars. Vibrant greens and pinks chased after each other in a beautiful aurora of magical energy.

The trail of color drifted away, and what remained of the pyre broke apart and sank away. The fairies were singing.

Gwen had heard Hollyhock sing before, and she adored the bubbly, trilling sound of a fairy's singing voice. That did not prepare her for the enchantment of a fairy chorus. Clinging to branches like rope swings, the fairies swayed back and forth, chanting and singing a beautiful lament.

Peter let go of the branches, and Gwen followed suit, cloistering them all under the willow again. The fairies who were not singing—and there were plenty who weren't—were dancing. Twirling together, fairies held each other and flitted through the air together for comfort and closure. Gwen watched as two winged ladies held each other's hands and bobbed together through the air. Watching a stout fairy dip his partner and spin, unhampered by gravity, she was almost startled to feel a hand take hold of hers.

Looking at Peter, she felt as if she was being pulled away to Neverland for the first time all over again. She shrank within herself as he took her hands, and when they danced, she felt like a child half her age.

She stepped into the positions that he pushed her into, but soon, it did not matter where she sloppily planted her feet because they took to the air. All she had to do was hold to his hands and let herself fly. He gave her direction, he sent her twirling into motion, and when he let go of her, she spun until he caught her again, always flying, always floating.

It is such a simple thing to dance, Gwen thought. She almost laughed at what her conception of dance had been. Sophomore homecoming—one year and a short infinity ago—had been full of stilted motions and untouching movements to abrasive beats and electrically sharp melodies. Her bejeweled dress had been uncomfortable, her palms had been sweaty, she'd held onto a clutch purse awkwardly, and the majority of the evening had been spent giving and receiving shallow compliments.

Now she floated with the grace of childish awe, unafraid to hold Peter's hands as they drifted to the overlapping melodies and harmonies of fairy voices. There was nothing else in the world she would have been doing in that moment; the dance was intrinsic to the nature of life itself. Homecoming, homework… home itself! All of it was a million miles away or more. Gwen didn't even know what metrics measured the distance between Neverland and the rest of the world.

The voices of the fairies charmed her ears, and Peter filled her eyes. His expression, melancholy though it looked, was simple. Gwen was jealous of the way he could be so present in the moment, so free of worry for the future. For him, there was no moment before or after this, and Gwen envied him for that, until she realized he did not have a monopoly on that sense of contentment. Suddenly unconcerned with what would happen in the next ten minutes or the next ten years of her life, schooling, and career, Gwen found herself stranded in the dance, living in the moment in a way only a child could.

42

THE FOLLOWING MORNING MOVED QUICKLY. GWEN DRESSED IN the blue sundress she had worn on her way to Neverland, rolling up her pajama pants and sweater in order to jam them into her satchel. Aside from the headband from Dark Sun and Lasiandra's mermaid scale, both tucked away in her bag, Gwen was leaving with no less or more than she had arrived with.

She would have looked the very same, with not a week's worth of aging to change her, except for the burn she'd endured in yesterday's bombing. The newsprint tattoo was blurred now and hardly legible, but it was not fading quickly. Gwen suspected she would carry the ink on her arm for several more days, and that she'd have to wear long-sleeved shirts for a while in reality to obscure it. She did not know how long it would take the scar from the burn itself to completely fade, or if it ever would. She tried not to let this bother her.

For some reason, they were not leaving from the grove. In a group decision that Gwen had not been part of, it was determined that they would parade out to the weastern shore before Peter and the girls left.

Rosemary volunteered to accompany them back to reality, but only because she was eager to help Peter find the aviator and meet the piper. Gwen had no illusions that she would be able to convince her sister to go home. Rosemary was not so little. She could make a big decision and stand by it, and Gwen had to respect that. The only reason Rosemary wanted to go back at all was to deeper entwine herself with Peter's mission.

Rosemary was happy here, and Gwen knew that there was no way to argue against happiness itself.

Blink had her drum that she pounded contentedly at the head of their parade. Newt and Sal trailed after her, carrying colorful banners of no significance. Everyone marched, skipped, or trotted to the steady beat Blink set. Jam sang a song no one listened to, and Bard collected flowers while Spurt constantly searched the ground for the perfect hiking stick. Peter and Rosemary were the only ones who allowed themselves to actually fly with the fairies. Dillweed and Hollyhock, good to their word, were still resolved to traipse into reality with Peter. Gwen trailed after everyone else, meandering purposefully with the knowledge that this was the last time she would ever walk these woods of youth and dreams.

There was something subtly magical about every tree and plant in Neverland. All fallen logs seemed to be hollow hiding places, every fruit tree was laden with perfectly ripe fruit, the vines that tumbled down from the jungle canopy were always strong enough to swing on, and every tree held its branches out as if inviting her to come climb. The forest was a patchwork of foliage, and the sun flooded down into it through every crack in the canopy.

The children cheered and laughed when they reached

the edge of the jungle, running down the rolling, green hill they immediately found. Newt and Sal waved their flags while screaming a made-up battle cry. Bard and Jam fell instantly into a series of giggles and somersaults. Hollyhock and Dillweed plucked up flowers from Bard's bouquet when she dropped it. Fluttering with those, they chased each other down the hill as well. The contagion of joy infected Gwen, too, and she found herself racing down the hillside just to see how fast she could go without tripping over herself.

Her dress fluttering at her knees, the feeling of the wind against her body took her back to a time when she had known no greater pleasure. She remembered the park her father used to take her to, racing all over the playground with her. There had been a hill there, too, and Gwen had raced down it so many times, wishing the wind would carry her away before she ever reached the bottom of it.

So long after it was abandoned, Gwen's wish came true as she willed herself up toward the sky, flying unburdened by any maturity that had been forced on her in the past ten years. It was a brief validation of everything she had once wanted. She landed peacefully.

Goodbyes were a fitful ordeal. Jam tugged on her hand intermittently, whining, "Don't go, Gwenny! Don't! Stay!" as if her desire alone could persuade Gwen to remain.

"We'll miss you," Bard remarked, giving Gwen an adorable, almost convincing, puppy-dog look.

"Who'll tell us stories?" Spurt was worried, as if this was a pressing problem that had only just come to his attention.

"You can stay," Sal told her. "We don't mind. We like you."

"Right, Peter?" Newt asked.

The children all looked to Peter, mistakenly thinking that his charisma would have more pull over Gwen then their simple pleas. "Of course," Peter said, "but that doesn't mean she will."

The only one who didn't make an effort to convince her was Rosemary. The sisters had called an unspoken truce between themselves, and neither lobbied the other to remain in the world of the other.

"You'll come back, someday, right?" Blink asked timidly, afraid of the answer.

Gwen neither had the will to mislead tiny Blink or the gumption to tell her the truth. Instead, she ruffled the girl's dark hair and told her, "You take care, Blink."

Hollyhock and Dillweed buzzed excitedly, tugging at Gwen and Peter. "We'd better go," Peter announced, standing up from where he was crouched in the uncut grass. He had the deer-hoof rattle Old Willow had given him, firmly clutched in his hand. "The earlier in the night we get there, the better. It will probably take some time to convince the piper to come once we find him."

Gwen wondered briefly about the logistics of time zones in relation to Neverland, but her thoughts were lost in a slew of goodbyes that she and the children threw at each other. The lost children chased after them on foot, running in the little valley and making a vibrant commotion even once Peter Pan, Rosemary, and Gwen were out of earshot. The redskin rattle shook as they flew, reassuringly jingling.

"I'm thinking we'll head up through the cloudgate. What say you, Holly?"

Peter looked to his impish friend, whose miraculous wings carried her just as fast through air. Flinging fairy dust with each quick beat of her wings, she agreed, helping Peter guide the girls up into a bank of bulbous, white clouds.

Passing through the threshold of the cumulus giant felt like diving into water, but not as intense. The cool, damp cloud felt wonderful against Gwen's arm, soothing the burn like a wet cloth. "Peter, where are you?" Gwen called, still flying, but slowing as she lost her sense of direction in the puffy whiteness. She batted away bits of cloud with her hand, pushing through it in a way that she was fairly certain was meteorologically impossible.

"Just keep flying!" he called.

The rattle shook lightly, and she heard Rosemary's laughter. Dillweed weaved ahead of her, drifting in and out of view like a light in a bank of fog. He flew unsteadily, and Gwen questioned whether she should be following him. She was unaware of his tendency to favor the grape, the honeysuckle, the bluebell, and whatever else would leave him in a glowing stupor, but definitely knew that he was unreliable and often confused.

Gwen didn't really worry; she just chased after any familiar sound or glimpse of her comrades. Although she was certain she was going the wrong way, she never lost them. Her wet breaths grew uncomfortable as the cloud began to grow dark. A shiver blew through her body, and she began to wonder when they would emerge on the other side of this endless cloud. As it further darkened, the blackness of her surroundings gave her an unfortunate sense of claustrophobia.

"Is it getting darker for you too?" She didn't care who answered, as long as someone confirmed it.

"We're almost there!" Peter yelled back.

Gwen held to those words and the confidence they gave her. When Peter spoke, every word sounded like a promise.

At last, they broke free of the cloud and into the night air of reality. The moon fought back the darkness, and the city and suburbs glowed beneath them. Peter and Hollyhock were waiting for her, smiling as she burst through the edge of the moist cloud. Gwen shivered again, but she hardly had time to wonder where Rosemary was before the younger girl came tumbling out of the cloud herself.

Peter spun around a little, studying the intricate pattern of suburban lights beneath them. "Your house is that way," he said, pointing. "You shouldn't have any trouble finding it. It's where you live. We've got to get to the airfield."

Gwen followed his finger to the cluster of yellow lights flat against the face of the earth. "I'll go with you first," she offered. "I'm in no hurry."

Peter floated, wearing nothing more than his tattered shorts, a patchwork vest, and his hemp jewelry. Gwen marveled that he did not shiver the way she did in the October night. She was digging her white cardigan out of her satchel for the first time—she hadn't needed it once in summery Neverland—but Peter was utterly immune to the reality of any situation.

He grinned. "Alright, what are we waiting for then?"

Peter led the way, Dillweed and Hollyhock at his side as the Hoffman sisters followed.

His eyes scanned the town, reading it as if he did not know where to begin. Had the trip through the thick cloud cover left him disoriented too? The deer hooves rattled on their bone though, and the sound guided them. They stayed high in the sky, letting themselves float down only as they actually descended onto the airfield. They could not risk being seen by any prying adult eyes. The runway of the private airport was illuminated, but other than that, it remained a long stretch of unlit property, level and dark. Gwen folded her arms in front of her, hugging her warmth to herself. The cardigan didn't do much to ward off the autumn night chill.

They came down like planes, soaring over the length of the runway before touching down. The landing lights guided them to the end of the field, near a large airplane hangar, which Rosemary referred to as the plane garage.

Hollyhock buzzed curiously. She would not have left Neverland today if not for her curiosity, something which compelled her to accompany Peter so that she could get a first look at this ally he had spoken of.

"I don't know..." Peter answered her, panning his gaze across the dark airfield. "He should be here somewhere." He shook the rattle and stepped forward, listening as it got louder little by little.

The planes stood like skeletons, eerily towering over the children in ordered lines. They were motionlessly parked for the night in the deserted field.

"Look there," Gwen said, pointing back down the runway. A tall figure stood just far enough away that she could not tell anything more about him than that he was an adult. She did not think this bode well for their cause. She nervously held her burned arm, stroking it softly and methodically, remembering the danger adults posed to them as she felt the inflamed and inked flesh.

"Good eyes, Dollie-Lyn," Peter replied, and began striding toward him. The man waved, but the gesture was barely visible. Once they began heading toward him, he retreated away from the middle of the runway and back to his plane. The past week had taught Gwen to be skeptical of anyone over twenty, but Peter's confidence in people was never misplaced. She thought of Old Willow and Dark Sun, and decided that there were some adults worth trusting—and maybe even some adults worth growing up to be.

As they approached, Gwen saw that he was smoking a cigarette and wore a pair of old-fashioned aviator goggles on top of his balding head. He couldn't have been younger than forty by Gwen's estimation, but he felt like a relic from some other century. With his cigarette and trench coat distracting her, it took a moment before Gwen even noticed how ancient his plane was. It looked perfectly functional, but the huge propeller and low-resting tail of the plane made it look as anachronistic as he did.

"If it isn't the aviator himself!" Peter declared, marching up to the man.

The man smiled a worn-out smile. "*Bonjour*, Peter. It is good to see you again. I see you've brought friends."

"Are those goggles on your head? Do you wear them when you fly?" Rosemary asked, feeling her questions were a more pressing matter than proper introductions.

The questions put life into the aviator's smile. "You always did keep the best of company, Peter."

Hollyhock had already settled on the top of the propeller, scooting down one end of it like a slide. Dillweed watched and laughed.

While Rosemary ogled his goggles, the aviator turned to Gwen. "And who is the one who doesn't ask questions?"

Gwen felt herself blushing. "I'm Gwen."

The aviator held out his hand, and she shook it. "A pleasure to meet you, Gwen. I'm Antoine de Saint-Exupéry."

Gwen was stunned, but Rosemary was quick to answer. "Hello, Mr. Day Saint Extra-Perry."

He seemed pleased, but he requested, "Call me Antoine."

Gwen found it unlikely that Peter had anything more than a tangential relationship with someone so old, yet she knew who this man was. Two weeks ago, she was reading his book and trying to mesh *The Little Prince* into a speech on fairy tales for her speech and debate class. "You're Peter's ally?"

He seemed to find her question amusing. "Me? I'm just an old pilot."

"Is the piper with you?" Peter asked.

Antoine drew another long breath of smoke and bemoaned the question. "Oh Peter, if you were only more patient, I could have delayed disappointing you. No, he's not with me. I haven't seen the piper since he disappeared six years ago."

CHAPTER 43

GWEN HAD NOT YET HAD THE EXPERIENCE OF SEEING PETER IN A temper. He stomped back and forth flat-footedly, his brow knit and his scowl cemented onto his face. He was not destructive, and the wrath he was desperately trying to convey was still only the make-believe of his peaceful spirit.

"But the mermaids told me you'd know!"

"You should know better than to trust mermaids," Antoine reminded him.

"But they said it! They said it was true. And Old Willow! The redskins—they gave me Deer's hooves so I could find you and get you to tell me where Piper was! You can't not know!" As Peter fumed, Dillweed and Hollyhock sought refuge on the shoulders of Rosemary and Gwen. Pools of fairy dust accumulated on their shoulders as the fairies waited for Peter's temper to pass. He moved from denial to vengeance with admiral swiftness. "You've betrayed our cause. I'll never speak with you again. You're a traitor."

Antoine smiled. "I'm a traitor for not knowing?"

"Exactly!" Peter exclaimed.

"Peter!" Gwen hissed, ashamed of his childish behavior in a way he could never be. "Antoine just flew all the way here to meet us! That's no way to talk to him."

"No, no, no," the aviator answered, sweetly silencing Gwen. "It's quite alright. In these trying times, I completely understand his frustration. But perhaps I have something that can help make it right."

Peter calmed down quickly, and as Antoine reached into his trench coat's inner pocket Rosemary excitedly leapt up into the air. "What is it? What is it?" She tugged on Antoine's trench coat as if to expedite the process of finding out.

Antoine's warm smile persisted as he handed several poorly folded and crinkly papers to Peter. "I do not know where Piper is—but I know how to find him."

"Well, that's the same thing," Peter happily announced, beginning to peruse the papers.

"Perhaps for you. Piper doesn't want to be found though, and he's made it hard for anyone to find him—adult, child, or otherwise. You'll need to do a lot to hunt him down, not the least of which is to find someone who has heard his song. Those are few and far between these days."

"This will be tricky," Peter admitted, yet there was a hint of joy in his voice as he realized the challenge that lay before him.

"He won't be happy to see you," Antoine warned. "After they caught him helping you for that last invasion eight years ago, they threw him in prison. He escaped in a hurry, but you know how he nurses his grudges."

"He'll help," Peter declared. "He'll help Neverland."

Antoine's face was lined with a very grown-up skepticism of Peter's certainty. Rather than argue the point with one so sure of himself, Antoine asked, "How is Neverland?"

"There was a bombing yesterday."

At this remark, Antoine became deeply interested in the conversation. He flicked his cigarette down and ground it out under his shoe. "What sort of bombs are they managing to get past the Neverland boundaries?"

"More Molotov Newsprint. It comes in flaming and coats the place. It can't burn for long, but it does its damage." Peter nodded to Gwen and eyed her arm. When she checked the burn, everyone's eyes turned to it, even the fairies'. Her forearm was still red and tender, and although the newspaper tattoo seared onto her skin was fading, it was still possible to distinguish the words.

Peter crinkled the papers in his hand as his grip tightened, which caught Rosemary's flighty attention. "Peter, what do they say?" She rushed over to see it, leaving Gwen and Antoine to a quiet exchange of their own.

"May I?" Antoine asked, gesturing toward her arm.

"Uh, sure," Gwen replied, pushing up her sweater sleeve farther and holding her arm out. She'd taken the bandage off yesterday. She was finally getting used to the burn on her arm, but it was a novel, new thing for Antoine. He took it in his hands, touching it very gently and turning it over in his hands.

"It was painful, I'm sure."

"Yeah."

He looked at her, his confusion finally manifesting into a tactful question. "You're about Peter's age, aren't you?"

"I'm sixteen," Gwen responded.

"Awfully old for Neverland, aren't you?" Antoine pulled a slender box out of the inner pocket of his trench coat. Gwen didn't realize what it was until he drew a cigarette out of the silver case.

He lit a new cigarette as she told him, with a trace of teenage snark, "I'm on my way home."

"Hmm," he murmured. "That's a shame."

"What about you?" There was accusation in her voice. "Aren't you awfully grown-up to be rendezvousing with flying, ageless children?"

He laughed and took a happy drag off his cigarette. "There's more than one way to fly away and never come back, *ma cheri*. And it's never too late to stop growing up."

Gwen's hostility slunk away. It was replaced by sheer curiosity. Here was someone who confirmed her greatest fear—that growing up really wasn't worth it after all. Antoine was mature and adult in all his mannerisms, and yet he was helping Peter's cause, aiding and abetting him. For whatever reason, the aviator valued this resistance over his own standing in the world of adulthood. Gwen had to know what that reason was. "Why did you fly away?"

"I am a pilot. That's what pilots do." He had a wistful look in his eyes for a second, but more seriously, he explained, "I got tired of fighting grown-up wars. I wanted to lend my skill to forces that would put it to better purpose. I'll fly anywhere for Peter, keep my eyes peeled for Piper. They are fighting for a sort of freedom that reality is afraid to even speak of." He was staring at Peter and Rosemary, but they were unaware that his eyes were on them with admiration, envy, and hope. When he fixed his sights on Gwen again, he asked, "And you? Why are you flying home?"

The reality of home was sinking in, now that Gwen was in the chilly, October dark wearing just a sundress and a sweater. Peter and the fairies seemed to radiate a glow that kept her from freezing, but Gwen was pining for the weight of her purple bedspread, the familiar smell of her room, her father's magic tricks, her mother's cooking, Claire's company, and Jay's smile. There were a million reasons to want to be home, but to articulate simply, Gwen said, "It's where I belong." That seemed to sum up the issue in its entirety.

"Then I hope," he told her, "that you are right."

Gwen didn't want to admit that she hoped so too.

"Hey," she said, interrupting the conversation Peter and Rosemary were having, "I'm getting ready to take off. Nice to actually meet you, Antoine, but I, uh, I should really be going."

"Gwen!" Rosemary whined, drawing the name out with a painful sense of affection. She ran up to her sister and threw her tiny arms around Gwen's waist. Burying her face against her big sister's stomach, she mumbled muffled memories and declarations of love into Gwen. She pulled her face up and looked her squarely in the eye. For a moment, Gwen thought her little sister was about to cry. "This is what Old Willow meant, isn't it? That I was going to see all sorts of people leave my life. That I'm always going to be losing people like you and… and like Bramble."

"Hush," Gwen replied, patting down Rosemary's voluminous hair. "You're not losing me, Rose. I'll be here waiting for you, whenever you decide to come home."

"But you won't wait," Rosemary objected. "You'll get old."

"I'll get old, but I'll still wait. I might be a ninety-year-old lady, but I'll still tell my little sister stories when she comes home." Gwen leaned down to kiss her head. She hugged her close one last time. "Goodbye, Rosemary." she whispered, but as she spoke, she realized she was holding Peter's eyes.

"Fly safe," Antoine cautioned as Gwen let go of her sad little sister and prepared to take off. It was so grown-up of him to tell her to stay safe, so childish of him to believe that she could fly! Gwen only hoped that if she returned home, it would speed up Rosemary's decision to return. After all, Rosemary's first act of business upon arriving in Neverland was to return for her. Maybe luring Rosemary home would be as simple as staying there herself.

Everyone accepted that Gwen was on her own course,

and Peter took little interest in someone who did not share his passionate sense of whimsy. He didn't even bother with goodbye. Antoine, pitying Rosemary, knelt down and showed her his flight goggles. He let her put them on even though they didn't fit, and they had a very nice conversation that took her mind off the beloved sister who was drifting away with the wind as they spoke.

While everyone was thus distracted, Hollyhock had grown bored of the propeller, wheels, and other aspects of the strange old plane. Her curiosity in regard to the airplane had been sated, but she was far from satisfied. As she watched Gwen fly away, a desire bubbled up inside of her to chase after her, to find out where she was going, and what made *home* such a promising prospect for Gwen. Hollyhock could not understand why Gwen was abandoning them. The decision was not hard for her—she knew that she wanted to follow her.

The only one who noticed Hollyhock flutter after the older girl was Dillweed. He objected quietly as Hollyhock took off, but she gave him no heed. Not wanting to involve Peter and get her in trouble, Dillweed chased after her himself, catching up and trying to talk Hollyhock out of stalking Gwen. The tinkling, chiming sound of their argument was too soft to be heard by Gwen though. She had no idea that anyone was trailing her as she glided home. She focused only on preventing the weight of her melancholy from dragging her down. There was just a little farther to go before she was back to her bedroom window, able to climb in and close it for good.

CHAPTER 44

GWEN'S FLYING SLOWED ONCE SHE WAS OUT OF SIGHT OF THE airfield. She stayed only high enough to pass over the rooftops, keeping her eyes peeled for any people. She figured, if nothing else, it was bad etiquette in reality to let people catch you being magical.

She was still unaware of the glittering fairies chasing after her, hanging back and following her home. They were less concerned with being spotted. They knew that adults and others grounded in reality often couldn't help but turn a blind eye to the impossible, even when it manifested in front of them.

However, all these assumptions were predicated on the idea that there were no adults watching for magic. Their usual invisibility did not protect them from the adults who were purposefully watching for magic low in the sky, for careless children who were not wise enough to fly above their radars.

Gwen's mind was occupied with other, less ominous thoughts. She had missed a solid week of school. Gwen figured her best course of action was to just tell people that she'd been sick. She caught an early flu, or acute bronchitis like her mom did last year. Katie and Claire would be going ballistic, probably wondering why Gwen hadn't even been online to chat. It would be easy enough just to say that she'd taken a week to recover from Rosemary's disappearance, which, in many respects, was true.

Gwen looked out at the sprawling suburban neighborhood she flew over. Its square patterns and straight streets intersected and glowed with twinkling, electric light from the power grid. The way it sparkled, Gwen couldn't help but wonder if adults were funneling magic into it too, helping systemically distribute enchanted light to households and passing it off as purely an industrial invention. Soon, she would be home with her family where it didn't matter either way.

God! Going home to her family sans Rosemary—the thought was utterly bizarre. Gwen veered her thoughts to happier subjects. Debate class and parents and friends...she'd missed these things, and at least they would be seamlessly integrated into her life again. She would go home, sneak in through her window, and acclimate herself to her room before going downstairs and finding her parents. They would be so happy to see her again, and surely their peace of mind counted for something, too. Although knowing her mother, Gwen would probably be in trouble for not managing to wrangle Rosemary home with her…

Gwen sped up, committed to going home and ready for the journey to be over. She only wanted some stability now, some knowledge that where she fell asleep tonight would be her bed for the months and years to come. She thought of her poor Facebook account and email, no doubt overflowing with notifications from Claire and emails from prospective colleges.

Her phone would probably be dead, but she would recharge it and call Claire as soon as she got in and let her parents know she was home. Gwen trusted that she would be able to reach Claire. It couldn't have been later than ten o'clock, and what would her friend be up to besides homework and waiting for Michael Kooseman to start a chat conversation with her online? Gwen would check her texts, too, but she doubted there would be too many. The last text she'd gotten had only been Jay sending her his address for the party.

The party.

Gwen came to an abrupt stop in midair. What night was it? What day was it? She had lost track of time in Neverland; the days in paradise all blurred together. She had left on Wednesday night though, and after a few days, Peter had promised to take her back in a week's time… how many days though?

Floating down to a rooftop, Gwen sat against the moderate slope of the black-tiled roof next to someone's brick chimney. She counted the days on her fingers.

The day she arrived and ate a star was memorable, as was the next morning when she met Lasiandra and her fellow mermaids, and Gwen recalled with perfect clarity the day they explored the pirate ship and found the crocodile. There were the easy days, when she had helped Bard with the laundry and chores, a perfect do-nothing day which they had lazed around the grove and climbed trees, and the sword fighting contest had been the next day. There had been the day they went to see Old Willow and the redskins, and then the day after where they had done nothing but played with the gifts. Then there was yesterday, the day of the bombing…

Ten days in all. Ten days she had been gone, and now she returned on Saturday night. Her heart quickened as she considered the reality that at this very moment, Jay's party was happening in a house somewhere below.

Jay had texted her his address. Ten-something on Park Street. She couldn't remember the house number, but it wouldn't be hard to fly over there and find the one house filled with teenagers. She didn't want to miss this party. Her homecoming could wait.

Homecoming! The thought slammed against the walls of her mind. Had Jay asked someone else in her absence? The dance was just a week away now. What if he ended up taking Jenny Malloy? The thought made Gwen feel sick with unpleasant butterflies.

Gwen leapt off the roof and started bolting west, toward Park Street. Hollyhock and Dillweed, looking down on her from the top of the chimney, didn't know what to make of this sudden speed and new direction. They could keep pace with her though, so they did. The fairies did not have any idea where they were headed, although they now suspected Gwen was going somewhere other than home, and Hollyhock would not rest until she knew where.

School could be put on hold, her parents could be kept in suspense, but the world of teenage sociality progressed with or without her. Gwen became very nervous and excited all at once. She had her purse, but her phone was dead and she was missing her wallet. Instead, she had her pajamas and a mermaid scale tucked away inside of a pocket. Her hair was probably a windblown mess. With a little confidence, Gwen knew she could pass it off as voluminous and messy-chic like the sexy models on the covers of magazines she had never picked up.

Gwen pushed up the sleeve of her sweater and checked the newsprint burn. She would have to keep her sweater on so no one else saw it.

As unprepared as she was to head to a Saturday night

party, Gwen felt it would be a far worse mistake to not show up at all. Besides, then she would have a chance to see Jay in person and maybe briefly explain her absence. Flying even lower once she was on Park Street, Gwen remained in the air so that she could zip quickly down the street.

As predicted, Jay's house was easy to find. Cars filled every inch of the driveway and were parked along the street for almost a whole block. The lights were on and music was playing. Not so loud that it would provoke the neighbors to report a disturbance, but loud enough for Gwen to notice the way the heavy techno bass radiated from the house.

She landed at the end of the driveway. With uneasy steps, she reminded her nervous, wiggly legs how to walk. Brushing back her hair with her hand and hoping she looked all right, Gwen left all indecision behind as she marched to the front door and pounded on it so that her knocking would be heard over the clamor and chaos within. She let go of her purse strap, which she realized she was nervously clutching.

Crossing her arms, more awkward than aloof, she waited only for a second before an older boy, tall, dark-haired, and holding a red, plastic cup in his hand, opened the door. Gwen suddenly felt the full chill of the October air hit her.

"Hey, come on in!"

45

GWEN FLICKED HER HAIR OVER HER SHOULDER AND STEPPED inside, immediately confronted with the warmth of dancing bodies. There was a glow of socialization radiating from everyone in the room, and the brightly lit house already smelled of spilled beer and pot.

"Whoa, what's with the dress?" The older boy laughed. Hollyhock zoomed in, Dillweed nervously behind, before the door shut.

"I'm coming from a different party," Gwen told him.

He laughed again, a little tipsy and totally amused. "Well, hey, welcome to the party. I'm Roger Hoek."

He held out his non-beer holding hand, and Gwen shook it. "Oh, so you're Jay's older brother? I'm Gwen."

Roger seemed to be a happy drunk, just intoxicated enough that he felt obligated to laugh before saying anything. "Oh hey, Gwen, so you're that friend of Jimmy's—that girl from his algebra class or whatever."

Gwen didn't even try to restrain her smile. Who was she to Jay that he was telling Roger about her? The possible answers delighted her. The only response she could muster was to chuckle and say, "Jimmy?"

A shrill and elated voice yelled in her ear, "Gwen!" as she felt herself yanked around by the hand that had suddenly grabbed her arm. Just like that, Gwen found herself staring into Claire's smoky eyes. "Oh my *God*, Gwen! You miss a week of school and then you show up *here*?"

"Claire?" Gwen asked, stunned. "What are you doing here?"

"Jay invited me!" she squealed. "He came and found me last week, and wanted to know if I knew where you'd been, or if you were still coming to the party. He invited me and told me he hoped we could make it. Katie's super pissed she didn't get invited and you've been ignoring her."

Every word blew her smoky breath into Gwen's face, and somewhere beyond the sweat-blurred makeup and dark eyeliner, Claire's eyes were red and foggy. "Have you been smoking pot?" Gwen asked, all at once amazed and shocked.

Claire laughed. "Yeah, I finally got a chance to try it. Wesley's here and he brought a—God, I don't even know... fucking metric system... a lot of goddamn pot. That's what he brought."

"You're stoned?" Gwen lowered her voice, as if anyone could hear her over the noise of the music, or as if anyone would possibly care.

Claire didn't hear the question, but she guessed its nature. She had been doing this for the better part of the night with everyone. "I'm not even high right now. But yeah, that's what I've been trying to do for the past half hour. What the hell have you been doing for the past *week*, Gwen? You just disappeared off the face of the earth. I even called your home phone and your parents were all just like, 'So sweet of you to call, but Gwen can't talk right now.'"

"I've been—sick," Gwen told her. "Or just… not feeling normal. I don't know. Everything's been crazy."

"Shit, I guess!" Claire had become a considerably more fluent curser since arriving at the party and comfortably falling to a lower common denominator. It was liberating for her, and Gwen could see the joy that her friend was reaping from throwing the words around with such a strange mix of apathy and intensity. "A whole week of school! You could have at least answered my messages. Fuck it, you're here now. I've got to tell you—Michael asked me to homecoming!"

"Just now?"

"No, hell, like, on Friday. We're kind of a thing, actually. Where is he? I don't know. It's not on Facebook or anything, but I mean, we came here together. Would you believe my dad wouldn't let me go out on a Saturday night? Fucking military dads, right? I had to sneak out. Michael picked me up."

Overhead, unnoticed by any of the partygoers, Hollyhock and Dillweed surveyed the scene from the comfort of the hanging light. They pointed in awe, but they could not hear each other's high hum-and-whirl words over the heavy bass that was shaking their little wings.

"Your parents don't know you're here?" Gwen asked.

"Do yours?"

Gwen was relieved that she wasn't given a chance to answer the question. Michael came up behind Claire and wrapped his hands around her waist. Resting his chin on her shoulder, he then noticed Gwen. "Hey, Gwen."

"Hey," she responded, slightly stunned.

Claire laughed and turned her head to kiss his cheek. "Hey there, Mikey."

Gwen was suddenly conscious of what Claire was wearing. The strapless black dress fit her snuggly and had a wide belt of glittering, black sequins. Looking around, Gwen noticed other girls in yoga pants and low-cut blouses, tiny tops and tight leggings. She could feel her face flushing. She was here in a sundress.

MEANWHILE, HOLLYHOCK HAD FLITTED DOWN OFF THE LIVING ROOM light fixture. Tucked behind the drawn curtains, she overlooked a game of beer pong. When someone aimed wrong and sent the ball flying against the wall, it bounced back and disappeared under the table. Hollyhock fell through the curtains and raced under the table to capture the object.

Clutching the lightweight plastic against her with both her arms, she flew up to the underside of the table so that she was not seen when the drunken contestants bent down to look for their game piece. While they grabbed another ball, Hollyhock ran her hands all over the smooth, boozy surface of the white plastic. In her curiosity regarding the majestic ping-pong ball, she had abandoned Dillweed. His apprehensions had melted into curiosity as well, and he left the safety of the hanging lamp in order to follow Roger into the kitchen, wondering what it was that everyone here was drinking.

"THERE'S A BUNCH OF BEER IN THE KITCHEN," CLAIRE TOLD GWEN. "Apparently, it's cheap and awful, but it's cold, and I'm pretty sure all beer tastes this bad the first time you drink it. Want me to grab you one?"

"Uh, no thanks. I think I'm good."

"Okay, hey, I'll be back in a second then." Claire unwrapped Michael from around her, flinging his arm over her shoulder. "Have you seen Jay yet? I bet he'll be happy to see you. Did you hear? He's homecoming king! He beat out Troy! Can you believe it?"

Gwen was already suffering from sensory overload; now it seemed she was faced with information overload, too.

"Yeah, the man of the hour is around here somewhere," Michael added, happy for his friend, "and, shit, Jenny got elected homecoming queen, right?"

Claire made a horrid face, as if to suggest that Jenny had been struck by a bus or some other tragedy had occurred since then. Before Michael saw her, she resumed a cheerful expression.

Claire's black-and-red eye gave Gwen a wink. She leaned in a little closer, speaking quietly so that Michael would not hear the private remark. "Rumor has it that Jenny had the audacity to ask Jay to homecoming and he turned her down. She's not even here tonight."

Claire smiled at her once more before disappearing off into the kitchen, conjoined at the hip with Michael.

As they entered, neither Claire nor Michael noticed Dillweed. Even if they had seen the little pixie, the sight would not have registered in their reality-conditioned minds. His investigations had revealed that all the beer cans on the tiled kitchen counters were either empty or unopened. After toying with them for a few minutes, Dillweed came to terms with the fact that he didn't know how to open the cans and would not be able to figure out the mechanics of it any time soon. This frustrated him deeply as everyone else progressively got more inebriated with the stuff, and he found himself unable to even taste it.

Disgruntled, he took a seat on top of a blender and surveyed the landscape of Jay's suburban kitchen. That was when the bottle of cherry-flavored vodka caught his attention. The cap had been left off, and all Dillweed knew was that it smelled infinitely better than the rest of what was being drunk. Shot glasses were still out, and Dillweed began the laborious process of tipping the bottle over just enough to pour himself one. Wrapping himself around the neck of the bottle, he flew with all his strength, carefully tipping it and filling the glass to the very brim so that he would be able to drink out of it like a small pond. In that moment, he was a very happy fairy.

CHAPTER 46

GWEN MEANDERED INTO THE LIVING ROOM, PUTTING ALL HER energy into attempting to look less awkward than she felt. Should she be drinking? Everyone else was, even Claire. She didn't know her limits, but surely, a single red cup of beer wouldn't hurt. Gwen knew a drink would make her look more in place, but something told her she would feel even more out of her element if she was drinking.

Someone was already passed out on the couch, which was unfortunate since all she really wanted to do now was sit down. So many of the attendees were seniors; she didn't see anyone that she could start a conversation with. What was there to talk about anyway? What could be said over the throbbing, electronic music? Dancing seemed like her best option, but hopping and bouncing around with the others required getting closer to the massive speakers, and they were deafening enough from this distance.

"Hey, Gwen!"

She felt like a spinning top, turning at the mercy of whoever was calling her name. At the moment, it was Jay calling to her. Leaning against the archway between the living room and TV room, he too had a red cup, but he carried it as if he had forgotten it was in his hand.

The rest of the party melted away. The atmosphere of smoke and anxiety became irrelevant to Gwen. When she saw him, she broke into a smile, unafraid to let her face articulate how happy she was to see him. His playful blue eyes seemed just as glad to see her.

He ambled through the crowd, surrounded by people but never sucked into any given circle. Even at his own party, Jay was orbitally popular, a tangential part of every social circle and welcome in any clique, despite belonging to none.

"Hi, Jay. Nice party." Gwen felt like she was sheepishly whispering, even as she yelled to be heard over the music.

"Thanks. When did you get here?"

"Just a minute ago. Your brother let me in. Nice guy."

"He sure is. Came all the way home from the U just so he could help us get our hands on the beer."

Gwen giggled, awkwardly realizing there was nothing funny about that.

"Hey, so, it's good see you."

She could hardly hear him. "What? I'm sorry, the music—it's loud."

"Yeah. You want to head upstairs or something?"

He gestured over his shoulder at the staircase, so even though Gwen didn't hear the question, she pieced together its meaning. "Yeah, that'd be great." She followed him up the stairs, her heart fluttering as she traipsed up the carpeted steps, one hand on the wooden banister, the other fighting the urge to carry her skirt like a princess' ball gown. Her face no longer felt flushed, but glowing.

The other party guests were absorbed in their own conversations and protective bubbles of sociality, and

Hollyhock was still curiously absorbed in their strange social customs. It was only Dillweed who noticed, and wondered why, Gwen was heading away from the festivities. He pulled himself out of his puddle of alcohol, but was slow on his wings as he followed after Gwen.

"Yeah, I didn't think you were going to come," Jay said, once they were in the upstairs hallway, far enough away from the onslaught of synthesized music that filled the downstairs. "I haven't seen you at school since last week… you okay?"

Gwen knew she didn't look well. Her head was spinning. It was culture shock, not at discovering a foreign culture, but at discovering her own. This was a Saturday night party; this was what kids her age lived for. "I've had a really weird week and—oh my goodness, is this you?"

Captivated by the hanging family portrait, Gwen found it infinitely amusing to see an eleven-year-old Jay posing with his parents and teenage brother. Roger looked so much like Jay did now. Age was a funny thing, and it was strange to see how it turned one person into another.

"Uh, yeah." Jay clumsily laughed. He set his half-empty drink down on the hall table, the red cup an odd counterpart to the potted orchid already there.

"Little Roger and Jimmy," Gwen teased.

Jay rolled his eyes. "Older brothers kind of suck."

Gwen surveyed the hallway. The pale blue walls and family portraits seemed familiar, even if she had never seen them before. This was what houses were like—this was how families lived. This was reality.

Had she turned her attention back to the stairway, she would have seen the sporadic flight of a tipsy fairy who was following her up the stairs.

Still feeling off-kilter, Gwen asked, "Is there somewhere I can sit down? I don't know; I'm just feeling a little out of it." The lightness that had buoyed her all over Neverland was fading. Gwen no longer felt as if she could fly, and that made even standing hard.

"Yeah, sure." Jay went to the nearest door, pulling a key out of his pocket to unlock it. "Everything up here is locked just to, you know, limit the possible places people will throw up in." He laughed, but Gwen didn't see the humor in it.

He held the door open for her and she wandered in, immediately enchanted when she realized where she was.

A small stack of books were piled beside his particle board desk, but a sleek computer and a half-eaten bag of Doritos were on top. His bed by the window was covered in a velvety blue bedspread, and above his TV, he had a bookshelf lined with an impressive selection of video games.

None of this interested Gwen. Her gaze was magnetically drawn to the charcoal drawings pinned up on the walls. She wandered across the room, sitting down on the bed as she stared up at a grey scale drawing of Polk High School, a stunning portrait of a rain forest tree frog, and a landscape with a few knotted, twisted trees. Jay's walls were papered with his art, everything from elaborate doodles torn out of notebooks to masterful scenes on massive art paper.

"Wow," Gwen breathed. "These are really—just beautiful."

Jay smiled. "Thanks."

Gwen surveyed the myriad of drawings, shaking her head in happy amazement. She'd caught sight of a few drawings in his sketchbook, but those were mostly works-in-progress. "When did you develop this passion for art?"

"Umm, in utero?" he answered, laughing. "Really, I got my first charcoal sticks for my twelfth birthday, and that's when I really started getting into it."

Gwen imagined Jay as a twelve-year-old. It wasn't hard after seeing the family portrait in the hallway. She suddenly and deeply regretted that she had not met him sooner, that she had not known him before this awkward, awful age of adolescence. "What did you draw back then, when you were a kid?"

Jay laughed, as if the question was unexpected and had never been asked before. "Honestly, it was mostly monsters and characters for video games I wanted to make."

Gwen looked up at Jay. He leaned against the bookcase as if he couldn't be bothered to stand upright. He was wearing a blue shirt with the name of some band that Gwen had never heard of, but it paled in contrast to the color of his eyes. Gwen had blue eyes, but they were pale, grayish things, not like Jay's bright irises. The sound of the music downstairs seemed a hundred miles away.

Too much time had elapsed for them to continue their previous conversation, but for the life of her, Gwen could not think of anything else to say.

"I'm glad you could come tonight," Jay said.

"I'm glad too."

For a few seconds, they were both quiet.

"Hey, so, I should say congratulations," Gwen announced. "I heard you got elected homecoming king."

"Yeah," Jay admitted.

"How does it feel to beat out the quarterback and the head of drama club?"

Jay paused, thinking and smiling. "Stupid. It's stupid and flattering."

"And Jenny got queen, right?"

Jay nodded, looking bewildered. "She was really excited. That sort of stuff means a lot to her. A lot more than it means to me. I'm… really happy for her." Gwen regretted asking. Jay's expression made everything seem so much more complicated than what Claire's gossip reduced it to. She nervously brushed her hair back behind her ear again before pressing her hands against the bed, as if to help her keep her balance.

"What's that on your wrist?" he asked.

She followed Jay's eyes down to her wrist. She hadn't been actively hiding it, and the sweater sleeve didn't quite cover the entire burn on her arm. Before she could answer, he laughed. "Did you get a tattoo?"

Gwen was trying to come up with an excuse or an explanation, but her mind went blank, her thoughts falling away as soon as Jay sat down beside her on the bed and picked up her hand. He slid her sweater sleeve up, and Gwen didn't even try to stop him. She had no desire to shy away from his touch. She had to say something though; she had an article about childhood obesity sloppily printed on her forearm.

"There was an accident," she announced as Jay stared at her arm, holding it in his hands. "We were playing around with newsprint, except it was freshly printed and the ink was still wet. And then I burned myself."

"Ouch, man," Jay replied, still holding the arm, trying to read the blurred text. Antoine had felt her arm too, but there was something different in the way Jay held it. Something that tickled with longing, as if examining the burn was only an excuse to touch her hand. "It looks like you tried to wash it off, too..."

"Yeah, but with the burn, you know, I couldn't really scrub the ink off without hurting it." She shrugged as if she were too cool to be bothered about what her forearm said. She was all jittery, and she doubted she was fooling anyone by trying to act laid-back.

"Are you doing okay?" Jay seemed moderately amused by how flustered Gwen was. "What's been up with you this week?" He watched her face for some clue as to what was going on. He was no longer holding her arm, but his hand rested on top of hers on the bed.

Gwen laughed at her feet. Looking at Jay, she declared, "You wouldn't believe me if I told you."

Jay considered this. "You're probably right," he admitted. "You go AWOL for a week, just to show up at a party in a long, blue dress… you're pretty unbelievable."

The way he said it, Gwen knew no guy had ever said anything nicer about her. She felt like it shouldn't be a compliment. She was the odd one out, she didn't mesh with the surroundings, and yet the way that Jay spoke, it made her feel like it was the most desirable quality she could hope to possess. She was unbelievable, in all the best ways.

They were both drifting closer to each other, imperceptibly moving as they leaned in. Drawn toward him, Gwen felt pulled by a force she wasn't even fully aware of until it brought her lips to his.

Sitting beside her as they kissed, he put his hand on hers, giving it a squeeze that felt electric to Gwen. When she felt his other hand on her arm, she melted into a girl-shaped blob of joy.

She didn't know if she was doing it right; she didn't know if there was a wrong way to do it. Gwen's first kiss felt exactly as she had known it would, but her imaginings had not done it justice. Excitement and contentment rolled into one and drowned out everything else. She felt Jay's tongue pull out of her mouth, and as the kiss ended, she quickly pecked his lips one more time before opening her eyes.

He was smiling at her, and that sent Gwen into a tiny flurry of bashful giggles. There he was, the boy she had worried so hard about impressing, just sitting there after having kissed her.

"I'm glad you came."

"I'm glad I could."

She ran her hands through her hair again, brushing back what was already securely behind both of her ears. "Could I open the window?" she abruptly asked. "It's been a really weird week for me, Jay, and I just feel like I could use a little fresh air, or something…"

"Sure, go ahead. Do you want me to grab you something to drink?"

She knew he was offering her alcohol, but her mind was elsewhere as she cracked open the window by the bed and brought a small chill of cool air into the room. She didn't look out into the night. The car idling outside of Jay's house had its headlights off.

"No—I don't need anything to drink. I just kind of need to chill."

Jay's eyes smiled with calm affection. "We can chill." He took the single strand of hair that had fallen back into Gwen's face and tucked it sweetly behind her ear. Gwen's heart pounded, and when he wrapped his arm around her, she doubted her heart rate would ever normalize again. "You're cool though, right?" he asked, a little concerned.

"Cool? Yeah, totally." The smile did not come readily to her face, but it was genuine when it did. Gwen was just overwhelmed. On top of all the joy she had experienced in Neverland, this new excitement just left her feeling over-capacity. Her little heart could only take so much.

Jay nodded and revived his smile as well. "Cool."

Gwen leaned into him and happily flooded her senses with his smell. Even all cleaned up for the party, he still smelled a little bit like charcoal. "Can I see more of your art?" she asked.

He kissed her hair. "Alright, but you've got to tell me more about this crazy week of yours."

Gwen giggled, and in order to avoid the conversation,

she kissed him again.

Neither of them heard the car doors slam as two uniformed officers parked and left their patrol car outside.

CHAPTER 47

THE OFFICERS DID NOT KNOCK. THEY ENTERED QUIETLY, RELATIVE to the party. Conversations stopped mid-sentence as dozens of teenagers became bug-eyed in the presence of the police. The techno music continued across the speakers at an irreverent volume.

The high schoolers and poor Roger were not the only ones in peril though. Hollyhock felt her bubbly, warm blood come to a freezing halt in her veins when she recognized the star-atom insignia on the officers' otherwise unmarked uniforms.

Sitting atop the speakers for the delight of feeling them vibrate under her, Hollyhock knew she needed out of this house as fast as was physically possible. All the windows she'd seen so far were securely closed, and she didn't want to take a chance on the others. It was very easy to trap a fairy, and Hollyhock cursed her curiosity for leading her into this house.

The door was her only feasible hope, and in a second, the officers would close it and lock her in. Leaping into the air, she beelined for the door. Dropping as much of her orange fairy-dust on the teenagers as she could, she tried to hold in the rest of it as she sailed over the heads of the two dangerous grown-ups. They slammed the door shut, almost crushing her in the doorframe before she managed to make it out.

Her tiny chest heaved in and out with exhausted panic as she floated in the night air. Dillweed was still inside! Guilt flooded her, but Hollyhock knew she would have been no help to him trapped inside the house. With a deep, courageous breath, she took off, sprinting through the sky in search of help.

Inside, the louder of the two officers barked, "Turn off the music!"

Troy, nearest the stereo, leaned over and killed the power. The house was instantly dead silent, allowing the other officer to announce, "We need everybody lined up against that wall."

"Do you want to search the house, or stay down here with them?" his partner asked.

"I'll do the search," he volunteered, already heading into the kitchen to do a quick check for anyone else.

The partiers were already lining up against the wall. They'd left their drinks on every available surface, as if setting down the incriminating substance could do anything to help them now. Everyone was caught in their own permutation of hell, imagining the consequences that would soon unfold. Wesley Green felt his weed burning a hole in his pocket, Claire Riley imagined what Sergeant Riley would do to her when he found out, and Roger Hoek began considering how much harder college would be if this lost him his scholarship.

"Alright!" the loud policeman yelled. "None of you should be here tonight, but you've probably realized that by now. You all have a chance to make this a lot easier on yourselves though, and help my partner and me." His eyes narrowed as he scanned the line of frightened faces. "We're looking for a child."

Upstairs, Gwen and Jay had not known that anything was wrong until the music went off. Their moment of confusion was resolved when they heard the loud officer's intimidating voice booming orders below. Although they could not hear what he was saying, the situation sent Jay's attention straight away to the window. He saw the cop car was parked alongside the street, confirming his worst fears.

"Shit, shit, SHIT!" he swore. "It's the goddamn cops." He ran his hand over his head and then buried his face in it. "Shit," he muttered once more.

Gwen had gotten used to impossible, dangerous things happening, but this seemed so beyond impossible. A surreal thought occurred to her. It wasn't that long ago that she'd run into a couple of police officers. "What police?" she quietly asked.

"The police!" Jay sat back down on his bed. "The goddamn police."

Gwen went to the window for herself, only to see a black-and-white patrol car that was strangely devoid of any local insignia.

Heavy footsteps came up the stairs. "Anybody up here? Everybody needs to get downstairs now," an authoritative voice called.

Gwen realized her newsprint burn was nakedly exposed on her arm. "My sweater!" she gasped. Her head twisted as she searched her immediate vicinity for it. Where did she drop it when she took it off? "Where's my sweater?"

Jay didn't have an answer—his own concerns were weighing too heavily on his mind to consider Gwen's chaos, and she was too flustered to realize the cardigan had simply slipped off his bed and fallen under.

There was a single, sharp rap immediately before the door began to open. Gwen grabbed a zippered sweatshirt off Jay's chair and threw it on as quickly as she possibly could.

The officer opened the bedroom door to find a high school boy sitting on the bed and a girl hurriedly dressing. He stood in the doorway, hand still on the knob as he held the door open. His skin was only as dark as his light brown eyes, and the crease in his forehead was painfully deep as he angrily knit his brow.

"You two need to go downstairs now. Is there anybody else here?"

"No," Jay answered.

Gwen felt her newsprint burn searing, as if her fear was manifesting into physical pain. The mark was safely hidden in the oversized sleeve of Jay's grey sweatshirt.

"We're looking for a missing child," the officer told them.

Jay's fear was broken briefly by his confusion. "There aren't any kids here."

"We know that there is one. Now get downstairs with the others."

"Yes, sir."

The officer stood over them menacingly as they walked out, and then left down the hall to check the other rooms.

As the two of them passed the family portrait at the top of the stairs, Gwen heard a groggy, muted buzzing. She saw Jay's cup, still on the hall table, and tipsy Dillweed nearly passed out within. "Oh no," she muttered. She stopped and grabbed the cup.

"What's the matter?" Jay then added, "Aside from the obvious."

"I'll be right down," Gwen told him. When he seemed reluctant to leave her, Gwen insisted, "Just go! Before you get in more trouble!"

Gwen knew she had to get Dillweed out of the house

before one of the officers found him. Jay had no inclination of what was going on, and Gwen could not possibly explain it to him, even as he looked at her with those understanding, desiring blue eyes of his. He was in enough trouble as it was, and he did not try to reason with Gwen. "See you down there," he said dismally, knowing she would end up lined up downstairs with the rest of them sooner or later.

"See you," Gwen whispered as he turned his back to her and marched down the stairs.

She pulled Dillweed out of the cup, his body dripping with golden, reeking beer. He was limp in her hand, and his glow was nearly out. Whatever fruity drinks he indulged in at home could not compare to the raw, intoxicating force of hard liquor and beer. She couldn't simply get him to the window: he wouldn't be able to fly in this condition. Gwen didn't have a plan as she rushed back to Jay's room.

Before she could get the door open, she saw the officer's shadow round the bend in the hall. Silently gasping, she froze and waited for him to catch her with a fairy in her palm.

But the officer never came.

The shadow slipped down off the wall and onto the floor. The officer was nowhere in sight. The disembodied shadow approached a locked door, moving of its own volition. Gwen didn't move an inch, and the two-dimensional shadow did not seem to notice her. Flat as a sheet of paper and dark as the night, it seamlessly slipped under the door, exploring the other bedroom without ever unlocking it.

Terrified, Gwen finally opened Jay's bedroom and slipped inside, her mind a hurried mess of thoughts. Everything else preoccupying her, she had forgotten that they had not closed the window, but rather left it open to the starry night and all that flew through it.

In the middle of the room, his dagger drawn, Peter stood with a truculent smile thin on his lips.

CHAPTER 48

"PETER!"

"Gwenny!"

They spoke over each other, their exclamations pure chaos and surprise. Peter's slight smile vanished, and he lowered his dagger. Gwen's heart rose, and a flicker of hope ignited within her. Hollyhock was safe on his shoulder, trilling at the sight of unconscious Dillweed in Gwen's hand.

"Dillweed!" Gwen exclaimed, unable to find words to explain his condition as she held him out for Peter to see.

Peter sheathed his dagger, taking the intoxicated fairy in both his hands. "I do believe in fairies," he announced, his enthusiasm booming in a somber tone. "I do believe in fairies."

"I do believe in fairies," Gwen declared, before announcing it again, perfectly in time with Peter. "I do believe in fairies!"

Dillweed's glow dimly returned. Hollyhock zipped over to take his hands and help pull him up. He got to his wings shakily, and his fellow fairy helped support him as his wings beat irregularly.

"There are police here! They're looking for a lost chi—"

"Hollyhock told me they followed you here," Peter interrupted. "I have to go."

There was cold hurt in his eyes, and Gwen burned with guilt. Hollyhock and Dillweed found this peril by following her to the party. She was the reason that Peter himself was now in this house, magic-hunting officers in the rooms below and beside him. It was all her fault, and she was embarrassed to be found here. What she had abandoned Neverland for was now on display. Peter could see clearly what she was trading him for, and she wanted to scream that it couldn't compare, that she didn't want to be at some drunken party with synthesized music and girls in tiny, sequined dresses. It was just where she belonged. It had nothing to do with… everything. Everything else that she loved and enjoyed and wanted to wrap herself up in, the same way he did.

"Watch out!" Peter yelled, pushing Gwen back and stepping in front of her protectively as someone else entered the room.

But the door had not opened. She gasped and tripped backward, landing on the bed, as the shadow slithered into the room from under the door.

Peter was already in the air. "Fly!" he furiously yelled. "It needs surfaces!"

Once again, Gwen was too panicked to find the happiness she needed to float her up to safety. The shadow saw this and darted liquidly toward her. Gwen yelped and pushed herself back further on the bed, afraid of the thin monster on the floor. The shadow slipped halfway up onto the bed and took hold of her ankle in a tight, opaque hold. She couldn't wrestle herself out of its grip. She couldn't flee a shadow.

Peter pulled his dagger out of its sheath with a courageous quickness. Rather than use it to attack the bodiless monster, Peter threw it up into the air and stepped aside. It twirled up into the air and fell back down, driving its sharp point into the carpet, but not before Peter had snatched its shadow off the wall.

The shady shape of a dagger in his hand, Peter drove it with all his force onto the foot of the shadow, nailing it down to the carpet. The black creature recoiled in pain, letting go of Gwen's foot. Peter grabbed his shadow-less dagger and put it away before sweeping Gwen up into his arms so they could hover safely away from the trapped blackness.

A moment of clarity struck Gwen. All feeling, all fear, left her as she looked into Peter's forest-green eyes. She felt his heart beating through his chest; it pounded as hard as hers.

"Can you fly now?" he asked.

Gwen held Peter's gaze and felt herself growing light. She pushed away from him, but kept holding his hand for support. *Flying was easy*, he'd said. *You just had to think of happy things*. Looking into his eyes, Gwen had no shortage of happy thoughts. She felt that she could fly to the moon and beyond, to the stars and further, if Peter stayed beside her.

No one else gave her this lighthearted joy. Other people could fill her heart with wonderful feelings, maybe even better feelings, but no one else gave this childish joy that Peter did. Was this what she wanted?

The shadow thrashed below. Suddenly, someone pounded at the door. Gwen wasn't sure she even had a choice anymore.

"Are you staying here?" Peter asked. He looked at her, and his eyes held a confusion that boarded on painful.

It was a question, but it demanded more than an answer. It demanded a decision. The conflicted and melancholy organ she called a heart was of no use to her. It was trying to pull her down two radically different paths at the same time. Gwen felt herself coming apart at the seams that she thought defined her. Her wide eyes begged direction from Peter, but as magical as he was, he couldn't give her an answer. Like so much of Neverland, he could only pose a question.

The shadow twisted itself free from the shadow-dagger that had impaled it. Peter jerked his hand out of Gwen's as he watched it vanish. In a flash, the dark silhouette was across the floor and rising up onto the door. With its dark fingers, it twisted the lock, and then slipped back under the crack beneath it. The officer burst in, shadow and all.

The room was empty. All that remained was the shadow of a dagger stuck in the floor. His suspects had already flown off, hand in hand, to hide themselves somewhere beyond horizons. They were happily lost in the magical impossibility of the night.

He went to the window, but all he saw were the stars twinkling with victorious laughter.

Acknowledgements

My gratitude goes to the following fantastic people:

Rosie La Puma, for being the best first reader I could hope to have. Margaret May Hubert, for the use of her most beautiful and adventurous name. My parents, for making sure that if I had to grow up, at least I came out weird. Craig Franklin, for being a phenomenal critique partner. Grant Faulkner and the NaNoWriMo team of 2013, for a wonderful month and first draft. Andrew Todhunter and the Stanford Creative Writing Society, for all the advice and encouragement. Mr. Rockwood, for turning me into a lean, mean, dream-chasing machine. And Alison Leonard, for fifteen years of friendship and first lending me her copy of Peter Pan.

About the Author

Audrey Greathouse is a lost child in a perpetual and footloose quest for her own post-adolescent Neverland. Originally from Seattle, she earned her English B.A. from Southern New Hampshire University's online program while backpacking around the west coast and pretending to be a student at Stanford. A pianist, circus artist, fire-eater, street mime, swing dancer, and novelist, Audrey wears many hats wherever she is. She has grand hopes for the future which include publishing more books and owning a crockpot. You can find her at audreygreathouse.com